THE DEAD HUSBAND

GILLIAN JACKSON

First published in 2024 by Bloodhound Books.

www.bloodhoundbooks.com

Print ISBN: 978-1-916978-21-8

PROLOGUE

THURSDAY 8TH DECEMBER

It snowed heavily overnight and while some enjoyed the scenery and dreamed of a white Christmas, others struggled to get to work. New Middridge Primary School, built on a hill with the surrounding roads and pavements treacherous, had closed its doors. Doubtless, there'd be frustrated parents, excited children and smiling teachers. Gritting lorries had cleared the town's main roads but most side streets were untouched, picturesque yet problematic for those trying to travel.

Four miles south of town in a hamlet of three cottages, one family enjoyed the wintry weather. With school closed, Harriet Smith had rung into work to book the day off. It was one less she'd have over the coming Christmas holidays but that was another day's problem. Harriet's two children were hyper and for the last hour had pestered her relentlessly to go out in the snow to play.

'Give me ten minutes and then we'll take Barnie out for a walk over the field.'

'Great! Can we build a snowman?'

'Why not?' Harriet winked at her children and started to

stack the breakfast pots in the dishwasher. 'Find your wellies and wrap up warmly.'

The Smiths' cottage was set back from the B-road, which saw very little traffic, exactly how Harriet liked it. The neighbouring cottages were second homes for city dwellers and were rarely occupied at this time of year. With the children running ahead of their mother, whooping excitedly as they kicked up the snow, Harriet kept Barnie on his lead until they'd crossed the road. The spaniel pulled to catch up with the children and once in the field Harriet released him and smiled as he bounded across the as-yet-untouched white carpet, tail wagging furiously.

It was a perfect morning. The fresh snow was untrampled and the air crisp with a quietness only such a deep covering can bring. Harriet watched her six-year-old twins, Isla and Josh, cheeks and noses red with cold but laughing as they gathered snow into a pile for a snowman. Barnie scooted around, tail wagging madly and nose sniffing the white mounds around him. They didn't often have as much snow; it was a rare treat for the dog and the children.

'I need some twigs for the snowman's arms, Mum!' Josh shouted. Isla stood, hands on hips and glared at her brother. 'Why does it have to be a snow *man* and not a snow *lady*?'

'Go over to the trees; there'll be some branches there, but mind the ditch.' Harriet followed the twins as they ran towards the edge of the field. Barnie appeared to have found something in the ditch to interest him and was barking excitedly. While the children gathered twigs, Harriet caught up with her dog and called at him to stop digging in the snow. As usual, he ignored the command, so Harriet leaned down to pull him out of the hole he was working on. What she saw next stunned and shocked her.

Barnie had uncovered what was undoubtedly a man's head.

The battered profile of his face horrified Harriet, who stifled the scream rising in her throat so as not to attract the children's attention. Barnie remained busily shifting the snow from the body, enjoying his game until Harriet grabbed his collar and dragged him out of the shallow ditch, clipping on his lead. Feeling weak and shaky she hobbled towards the children. 'Isla, Josh, take Barnie and go back to the house! The back door's open. Wait for me inside.' Harriet felt decidedly sick yet tried not to vomit in front of the children.

'What, on our own? You never let us stay in the house alone.'

'Why, Mum? We haven't finished our snowman yet.'

'Please, just do as I say – I'll be with you in a few minutes.' She scrambled for her phone as the children took a reluctant Barnie and tramped back across the field, muttering as their playtime was cut short. Harriet offered up a silent prayer of gratitude that they hadn't seen the disturbing sight of a dead man so close to their home.

It wasn't ideal to send the children home alone but Harriet didn't want them to hear the call she needed to make or see Barnie's discovery. The man in the ditch was clearly dead. His face was turned to the side but what was visible showed his skin to be bluish-purple, almost like wine stains, with eyes open, staring, yet unseeing. The hand Barnie had also uncovered was similarly discoloured, and blood encrusted the man's face and hair.

Harriet tapped in 999 with unsteady fingers and asked for the police and an ambulance, although the latter was far too late for the poor man in the ditch.

The call-handler asked Harriet to stay with the body until the police arrived, but after explaining how her children were at home and alone, she gave the address for the police to come to her, then without a backward glance, headed for the warmth and safety of her home.

After shrugging off her wet coat, Harriet followed the sound of chatter, found the twins in the lounge and hugged them both tightly. Josh was the first to wriggle free. 'What's wrong, Mum?'

'Nothing, Josh, it was just too cold to stay outside.'

'Can we watch telly?'

Harriet, grateful the children were ignorant of Barnie's discovery, agreed. 'Yes, but only for an hour. Who wants hot chocolate?'

'Me!' they shouted in unison and jumped on the sofa, tussling for the remote control. Harriet sighed – maybe something stronger than hot chocolate would be more appropriate for herself.

Just as Harriet placed the hot chocolate in her children's eager hands, she heard sirens and dashed to the door before the police could ring the bell. Two uniformed officers hurried towards her, holding out their ID cards which she barely glanced at. The young man spoke first.

'Mrs Smith? I'm PC Mark Davies.' He held his warrant card for her inspection and smiled as Harriet nodded solemnly. 'Can you take us to where you found the body?'

Harriet chewed on her bottom lip; with no desire to return to the horrific scene her dog had discovered she felt sick at the thought. 'I don't want to leave the children alone again.'

As the first officer attending, it was Mark Davies' responsibility to secure the scene until back-up arrived. 'Perhaps my colleague could stay with them? You don't have to see the body again, only take me to where you discovered it and point me in the right direction.' Harriet thought he must have read her mind.

'Okay, just let me tell the kids what's happening.'

Afterwards, as they headed to the field, two other police

vehicles arrived. PC Davies beckoned to his colleagues to follow him and then gently asked Harriet, 'Did you disturb the scene at all, Mrs Smith?'

'I'm afraid my dog did and I had to drag him away. You can see where my foot slid down as I tried to grab him.' Harriet stood well back and pointed to the skid marks on the side of the ditch.

'And the children, did they go near at all?'

'No, they were over by the trees and didn't see anything. I'd rather they didn't know what's happened.'

'Of course. You can go back to your children now and we'll secure the area. Someone will take a more formal statement later. Do you want an officer to accompany you?'

'No, thanks, I'll be fine.'

Mark's initial assessment was that a detective and CSI would be needed – at the least, this appeared to be a hit-and-run – the road was near enough for a car to have hit the man, knocking him into the shallow ditch. At worst the body had been dumped. Further investigation was appropriate.

He returned to his car which was parked adjacent to the field. Pulling on protective boots first, he then grabbed the tape and pegs needed to secure the area, rummaged in his car boot to find a clipboard, then trudged back to the crime scene. Mark asked one of the other officers to ring in the details and ask for CSI support while his colleague helped with the scene preservation. Having informally established the basic details from Harriet Smith, when the taping was complete, he rang his partner at the Smiths' house to ask her to take a more formal witness statement.

All he could do now as first response officer was wait for

CSI and begin a scene log. With time to pause, Mark looked again at the grisly sight of the body in the ditch, so incongruous with the peaceful area. The blanket of snow presented a serene impression which was about to be destroyed by the ruthless machine of investigation. A detective would take charge of the case and forensics would soon be swarming all over the field, processing the scene, recording and collecting physical evidence.

Mark was relieved it was the dog that had found the body and not the children. The poor mother looked traumatised enough – what effect would the grisly sight have had on the two bairns?

PART 1

ONE
A WEEK EARLIER

Amy Cooper crossed and uncrossed her legs several times while fiddling with the cuff of her sleeve. The consultant's waiting room was too hot, but she didn't want to remove her coat – keeping it on might miraculously shorten her time in the hospital. Three other patients shared the small stuffy room and another two had already been called into the consultant's inner sanctum. Amy was jittery, hoping to be next in line.

Today's appointment was to hear the results of various tests and scans which would tell her if a brain tumour had been causing her recent symptoms as the consultant suspected – and if it was, to discuss available treatment options. Over the last four weeks the hospital had become a familiar place – the lengthy journey to and from, a habitual routine with which Amy was wholly fed up.

A nurse appeared and called a name – not Amy's but an older lady, a woman the age her mother would be if she'd still been alive. A book was nestled in the bottom of Amy's bag yet she was disinclined to read, knowing concentration would fail her. Instead, she settled down to study her two remaining companions, a man and a woman, clearly together and as antsy as Amy. The woman wore dangling earrings which sparkled each time she moved her head. She wondered which one was the patient and whether they were also anticipating bad news.

Only six short weeks ago Amy would have claimed to be reasonably healthy for a woman in her early forties with no reason to think otherwise until the headaches began, headaches like none other she'd experienced, a gripping pain which took her by surprise.

Mornings were the worst, when Amy woke up to a pounding head and a dreadful nauseous feeling. Then there was the dizziness – but what finally sent her scurrying to her GP was finding herself coming around on the floor with no recollection of what had occurred or for how long she'd lain unconscious. The doctor's actions were remarkably swift and an appointment to see a consultant arrived within two weeks, giving Amy a clue that her GP thought there was something seriously amiss.

After the initial appointment with Mr Matthews, CT and MRI scans were booked and Amy was in the system, progressing from one department to another as if on a conveyer belt. Finally, the consultant broke the news that they suspected a brain tumour, and today was results day. The waiting was driving Amy crazy. In her darker moments she anticipated the prospect of an operation. Curiosity sent her to the internet, which presented more questions than answers and nothing by way of comfort. Now, those questions were stored in her brain – her defective brain – ready to ask. Amy dreaded the answers and feared the worst. The thought of having her hair shaved and her skull drilled open made her shudder. Having always feared a check-up at the dentist, this was unthinkable.

'Amy Cooper!' the nurse called loudly.

'Yes.' Jolted back to reality she followed the young woman

into the consultation room. Mr Matthews looked up from his desk and smiled.

'Good morning, Amy. Please take a seat.' His head dropped to a folder on his desk and then jerked up to his computer, where he studied the screen, frowning. The silence in the room was stifling, the consultant's expression inscrutable. Eventually the man looked at her. 'Have you come alone today, Amy?'

It must be bad news – the worst?

'Yes.'

'Ahh.' Mr Matthews nodded. He was a kindly man, early fifties perhaps, although generally she was rubbish at guessing ages. His silver-grey hair was receding and rather too long at the back, curling over his collar. She wondered if he had a wife to remind him it was time to get a trim. Slowly he removed his wire-rimmed glasses and gave his patient his full attention.

'Amy, I'm afraid the news is not good. As we suspected you have a brain tumour – the CT and MRI scans are self-explanatory.'

Here we go – surgery, then probably chemo and radiation therapy – months of feeling rotten and bye-bye hair!

'I'm so sorry, Amy. If we'd found it earlier we may have been able to offer a craniotomy, but I'm afraid the tumour's progressed too far to operate.' Mr Matthews paused, searching her face, a frown on his own. 'Do you understand what I'm saying?'

Amy nodded, feeling strangely detached from the scenario playing around her – it was surely someone else's life, a soap opera she was watching on TV perhaps. The room started to spin and the nurse standing in the corner was suddenly beside her, steadying Amy on the chair.

'I'm going to be sick...' Amy leaned forward and the nurse grabbed a receptacle just in time. Closing her eyes, Amy waited for the dizziness to pass, to wake up from this nightmare and find herself in bed at home, but it didn't happen. Mr Matthews offered her a glass of water which the nurse held while Amy drank.

'Why don't you take your coat off – it's rather warm in here.'

Amy nodded, fumbling with the buttons. The simple task had a grounding effect, pulling her back to reality, a reality she didn't want to face.

'Feeling better now?' the consultant asked, and Amy nodded. 'You must have questions, Amy. Can you talk today, or would you like another appointment? Perhaps your husband could attend with you?'

'No – tell me today. What happens next? Will I have chemotherapy?'

The frown appeared on Mr Matthew's brow again, and he drew in a deep breath. 'The category of tumour you have is called a glioblastoma, a grade four aggressive tumour. I'm afraid chemotherapy would have little effect other than to make you feel very ill, affecting the quality of life you have left.'

I'm going to die!

'How long do I have?'

Is that me asking; it doesn't sound like my voice.

'It's always difficult to put a timescale on this sort of tumour. Glioblastoma sufferers can expect twelve to eighteen months, but we re-evaluate the prognosis regularly. We can monitor the tumour to map the growth rate although everyone is different – it could be a few months or perhaps even a year or two.' The nurse held her hand, and Amy was aware of squeezing it tightly. The woman must be in pain – the room still swam...

'Amy.' Mr Matthew's voice echoed in her mind, startling her. 'We'll arrange for one of our Macmillan nurses to visit you soon. She'll be able to answer any other questions you might have and outline what help and support we can offer. I'm very sorry, and naturally I'll be happy to see you again if you wish to discuss your condition further.'

Somehow, Amy was out in the corridor with the nurse asking how she'd come to the hospital.

'On the bus.'

'Well, you can't go home on the bus, sweetheart. Come and sit in here while I arrange for one of our volunteer drivers to take you, and I'll get your prescription filled for you too.' With no strength to argue, Amy allowed herself to be led into a quiet room where she waited for a few minutes, which could have been hours, for her driver to appear.

A kindly man treated Amy as if she was a Ming vase. His polite manner and soothing words were almost too much, and she struggled to hold back the deluge of tears which threatened to overwhelm her. Fortunately, he lapsed into silence when the car started to move and Amy turned towards the window watching New Middridge, her hometown, race past her. It was raining, the sky heavy, the forecast was for snow over the next few days. It was dusk and through the steamy car window the houses blinked with coloured lights. The first day of December – it would soon be Christmas – Amy swallowed at the thought it could be her last. She and Callum never bothered with outside lights, perhaps because they'd never had children. Would a family have made any difference? Would they have been parents who indulged their children with gaudy lights, flashing reindeer and tacky inflatable Santas? She would never know.

Amy was dying. She was actually dying.

TWO
WEDNESDAY 7TH DECEMBER

DI Samantha Freeman dropped her bag beside her desk and slumped into the seat. Running her fingers through her short hair, she rested her elbows on the desk and sighed. The morning had started badly with a row with Ravi, her partner – a stupid argument over some irrelevancy which she now regretted. To make matters worse, Ravi would be working late again and she'd have to wait until late evening to apologise for being so ratty and to make it up to him.

Ravi was also a DI, working in Fraud at Aykley Heads in Durham, which gave him a longer daily commute than Sam. The pressures of policing occasionally triggered friction between the couple but generally, they worked hard at their relationship, aware of the pitfalls. Perhaps they were simply tired and needed a holiday. Sam couldn't remember the last time they'd shared as much as a full weekend together. Some R&R would be welcome – she'd suggest it to Ravi later.

The empty office-cum-incident room was beginning to warm through and Sam was grateful for a few minutes alone in her little corner chamber to collect her thoughts before her colleagues arrived. At five foot two with an elfin face, usually devoid of make-up, Sam was known among her colleagues in New Middridge police station as a force to be reckoned with, a terrier in the best possible way. Her reputation was one of being firm but fair. Sam was mostly well-liked, mainly because she was a DI who led by example, putting in more hours than she expected from others on her team.

Next to arrive was Jenny Newcombe, Sam's DS. Stray flakes of snow fell to the floor as she shrugged off her coat and shivered. Sam appeared in the main office and Jen studied her DI closely. 'Not had time to comb your hair, boss, or was it a rough night?'

'Rough morning more like. Ravi and I had a few words – choice words – from me anyway, and we parted on bad terms. Hell, I need a holiday.' Samantha finger-combed her hair to flatten the unruly spikes.

'You'll make it up, you always do. The gorgeous Ravi will arrive home with flowers and chocolates and whisk you off to dinner.'

'I doubt it. He's working late, it'll be bedtime before he's home.'

'Ah, well...' Jenny chuckled and moved to her desk. The DS was four inches taller than Samantha and carried more weight but it was mostly muscle and suited her frame. Her blonde hair was swept up into a knot on top of her head. 'Talking of romance, here comes Layla and Paul.'

Paul Roper yawned as he placed his coffee cup on the desk. 'Morning, all,' he breezed. Layla Gupta followed him closely, wrapped up sensibly against the winter chill. She nodded at her boss and Jenny before switching on her computer. The others followed her example.

'What's the priority today, boss?' Jenny swivelled her chair to face Sam. 'Are we having another crack at those kids who set fire to the warehouse?'

'Yes, I want them brought in. It's time to get serious with this – it's just one big joke to them but someone could have been killed.'

'Shall I get uniform to pick them up?'

'Please, and I suppose Baxter's mouthy mother will want to be in on the interview. Tell uniform to try to get the kid alone and we'll find an appropriate adult from social services or the Youth Offending Team to sit in, and then ring the fire officer to see if they've anything new to work with – preferably something resembling evidence.'

'Okay.' Jenny swivelled back on her chair and picked up her phone.

An hour later, two uniformed officers arrived at reception with the three youths in question. Ethan Baxter was seventeen and his friends, Tim Dennison and Tyler Green both sixteen. DI Freeman was at the desk talking to the duty sergeant and rolled her eyes when she heard Sylvie Baxter's grating voice shouting at the officers, telling them what they could and couldn't do to her son. Sam winced at the woman's colourful language and left reception to prepare for what would undoubtedly be a frustrating interview.

Jenny glanced up as Sam returned to the office. 'The accelerant was petrol, as expected, and the investigators have collected evidence of alcohol and drug use. They've sent the items off for fingerprinting and DNA, but the soot could be problematic. There's also evidence of the warehouse being used by rough sleepers; there could be dozens of prints. Still, we could have been looking at manslaughter had the fire been started later in the day.'

'Damned idiots. They think it's cool to be in trouble and a

charge will give them a bit of kudos – bragging rights with their mates. Anyway, we'll be interviewing them in half an hour, Jen. I'll let you kick things off.'

Jenny rubbed her hands together to warm them up. 'Great. Thanks, boss.'

THREE
WEDNESDAY 7TH DECEMBER

'Bloody woman! Honestly, I could swing for her.' The interview with Ethan Baxter had been every bit as frustrating as Sam Freeman expected, mainly due to the boy's mother, Sylvie. 'The slimy little toad actually had the cheek to wink at me when I entered the room!'

Jen smiled. Ethan Baxter had chewed gum throughout the whole interview and answered every question with *no comment* while grinning like a hyena. His mother said more than the boy, telling the detectives they should be ashamed of themselves for picking on innocent children when they should be out catching real villains. Sam wondered if Sylvie believed her son was innocent or if it was just a line she'd picked up from television.

Dennison and Green were a little different and not as arrogant. Clearly, the three had a pact of silence and after short interviews, Sam and Jen realised they'd need concrete evidence or a confession before they could charge them. They'd briefly hoped Tim Dennison would crack. He seemed a more decent sort than the others, with none of the cheek or arrogance of Baxter and what appeared to be remorse, or perhaps shame, in his eyes. He was a young-looking sixteen, skinny with a bad case of acne which made him more of a sympathetic character than his mates. It was hoped being brought in for an interview would somehow shake the boys into the realisation of the seriousness of the incident, but it proved a vain hope.

As they left the interview rooms, Jenny agreed with Sam's sentiments. 'Perhaps forensics will give us something solid to charge them with. All three deny setting the fire, but I'm convinced they did; you could see it on Baxter's smug face. He was silently gloating.'

'Makes you wonder what kind of *citizens* they'll grow into. Arson today, and I'm sure I could smell cannabis on him, then who knows what tomorrow? Makes you fear for the future of the planet.'

'There are some good kids too.'

'Yeah, I know. We just see things from the bottom of the pit in this job and it's hard to remember there are decent families out there too. Must be lunchtime, Jen. Let's go to the pub, my treat!'

'You've twisted my arm, boss.'

The pub in question was a block away from the station and a favourite haunt of many police officers. Not a particularly salubrious establishment but they served good old-fashioned pub grub. The pair dashed through the snow, which was falling more heavily, and found a table in the corner where they could chat without being overheard.

Jenny studied the laminated menu she knew by heart and asked as casually as possible, 'This row with Ravi isn't serious, is it?'

'No, but I don't like confrontation.'

'You?' Jen blinked hard. 'You're the most confrontational person I know.'

'Maybe at work, but never at home. I like to keep my personal life as peaceful as possible to counterbalance the job, and usually Ravi's the same. It'll blow over – I'll apologise tonight, and the making-up will be fun!'

Jenny chuckled. 'Please, don't make me blush!'

Sam decided to change the subject. 'How's your rape case progressing? Have you heard back from the CPS?'

'Yes. There was an email today – they agree there's enough to make a case. The poor woman is terrified of going to court so if it gets that far, I'll request a video link or at least a screen. Hopefully, he'll confess before the trial to get a more lenient sentence – if he has any sense, which is debatable.'

'Good. DCI Kent will be pleased to get another case cleared.'

'It'll be a result if we get anything on this warehouse arson too. I hope those kids get into some kind of intervention programme; they need a short, sharp shock to make them change their ways before they end up as hardened criminals.'

Samantha smiled. 'You'd have made a good social worker, Jenny.'

The DS rolled her eyes. 'Not me, I'd be too hard, not enough sympathy.'

'Anything else interesting on the books?'

'I've got a couple of interviews to complete from the betting shop raid and you're in court this afternoon, aren't you?'

'Yeah, that misogynist who poured a pan of hot oil over his girlfriend. I was trying to forget. Order me a cheese sarnie and a lemonade, will you, Jen? We'd better get a wriggle on.'

After eating at an indigestion-inducing rate, they hurried back to the station amid another fall of snow, carefully navigating the slippery paths as the world continued to be bathed in a blanket of white.

FOUR
WEDNESDAY 7TH DECEMBER

The heavy doors to New Middridge police station opened, blowing a swirling gust of icy wind into the lobby and entrance area, where a forty-something woman paused and looked nervously around at the chaotic scene. Amy Cooper had never been inside a police station before and this was an awful time for such a first – it had been less than a week since her brain tumour diagnosis – and now she had this to contend with. Her head was pounding and her legs shook as Amy forced herself to step forward.

A reception desk was to the right of the doors, probably where she needed to go, but there was an argument in progress between the desk officer and a rather loud woman, while three youths stood to the side looking bored to tears.

Amy moved quietly to a seat to wait for the commotion to die down. It was cold outside, yet not much warmer in the draughty corridor. She'd left home in a hurry and should have put on a warmer coat rather than the first one which came to hand, but Amy wasn't thinking straight – this morning everything felt surreal – she could have been existing in some alternative universe as her heart pounded beneath her ribs and her mouth was dry. Was she really here?

Two police constables took the youths away from the desk and through another set of doors while the woman continued to rant at the desk sergeant, obscenities spitting from her mouth as the poor sergeant waited patiently for her to run out of steam. When the woman finally hurried after the youths, Amy stood on unsteady legs and moved towards the desk.

Attracting the officer's attention, she cleared her throat and forced herself to speak. 'I'd like to report a missing person.' A reassuring nod encouraged her to continue. 'It's my husband, Callum. He... he didn't come home last night.' The words dried up and she swallowed hard, unable to think of anything more to say although Amy knew they'd need details.

'Would you like to take a seat and I'll find someone to come and talk to you?' The man's voice was soothing and kind as Amy nodded obediently and returned to the line of chairs.

Before long a detective constable, who introduced herself as Layla Gupta, came to take her to an interview room. The pretty young detective offered coffee which Amy declined, sure she'd be sick if she drank or ate anything. Nerves always affected her stomach.

Layla turned to a clean page on a pad and smiled reassuringly. 'Can you tell me your full name first and then we'll take some details about your husband.'

'Amy Susan Cooper.'

'And your date of birth and address, Amy.'

'Sixth of June 1980, and I live at 43 Cypress Close, New Middridge.'

'And your husband's name.'

'Callum Cooper, no middle name.' Amy felt her throat constricting and knew she was close to tears. Taking out a tissue she blew her nose and took a deep breath. 'His date of birth is twelfth March 1978 and the address is the same.'

'That's great, thanks. I know this must be difficult for you but can you tell me why you think Callum's missing?'

'He didn't come home last night – which is unheard of. Cal's never done anything like this before.' Amy's eyes were wide and shiny as she tore tiny pieces off the tissue in her hand. Even to herself she sounded like a woman in a bad film. 'Something must have happened to him.'

'And when did you last see him?'

'When he left for work yesterday morning.'

Layla smiled and spoke softly. 'I need to ask a few questions which may seem a bit personal, Amy, but I'm sorry, it's procedure. Is there any reason you can think of why he didn't come home? Any problems in your marriage, recent arguments perhaps?'

'No, nothing! We had breakfast together as usual and I made his sandwiches, cheese and ham, then he left in good time... and I haven't seen him since.'

'Where does Callum work?'

'At Blacketts, the kitchen manufacturers. He's been there for the last ten years.'

'Have you rung Blacketts?'

'Yes, I rang before I came out. Cal wasn't there and they said he'd left as usual yesterday, which would be 5pm. He's a creature of habit, very punctual.'

'Okay, and have you rung any friends or family to see if he's with them?'

'There's only my sister and her husband. I rang them last night but they hadn't seen him.'

'What about friends, Amy, any mates or colleagues he might have gone for a drink with?'

'Cal doesn't have many friends. I tried some of his pals from the pub but no one's heard from him. He's not great at socialising and would never go off without letting me know. Callum's a quiet home-loving man.'

'No family?'

'We don't have children. His dad's dead and his mother lives in a care home, she has dementia. He has a brother who lives in New Zealand but they've sort of lost contact, Cal wouldn't go there.'

'All the same, we may need to contact him to see if your husband's been in touch recently. Perhaps you could let us have his details?'

Amy sniffed and nodded.

Layla scribbled hurriedly as Amy spoke, then sat back to look at the anxious lady before her. 'It's possible your husband will turn up very soon. In most cases like this the missing person has just gone off somewhere for a while – maybe a case of things getting on top of him or problems at work which he hasn't shared with you.'

'But Callum wouldn't, he'd not want to worry me like this. Are you not going to do anything?'

'That's not what I'm saying. Have you brought a photograph of Callum?'

Amy reached into her bag and pulled one out. 'This was taken last summer, it's the most recent I have.' After staring at the image for a few seconds she handed it to Layla. 'What will happen now?'

'We'll circulate this photo and check with the local hospitals. If you give me your husband's telephone number we'll try to track his location from his phone or get a list of any calls he's made recently from his service provider.'

'I've been ringing him all night – it must be switched off.' A tear slipped down Amy's cheek. 'Do you think something's happened to him?'

'It's too early to be speculating. Most missing persons come home within a day or two. The best thing you can do is go home and wait. If Callum does turn up, please ring us immediately, and also if you think of anything else which might help us locate him. I'll put these details into the computer and we'll start searching for him. I know it's hard but please try not to worry.'

Amy allowed the young detective to see her to the door. As soon as Layla left her, she pulled out her phone and found her sister's number.

'Beth? I'm just leaving the police station and heading home.'

'What did they say?'

'You'd better come round. We'll talk then but give me half an hour to get home.' Amy was trembling from her ordeal. She needed to see her sister in the flesh rather than speak to a disembodied voice on the phone.

'Put the kettle on. I'll be there.'

FIVE
WEDNESDAY 7TH DECEMBER

'It was hellish,' Amy moaned as she opened the door to her sister, 'and this is only the beginning!' Beth Moorhouse lived on the other side of New Middridge from the Coopers', a ten-minute drive, and true to her word Beth arrived on her sister's doorstep within half an hour of receiving her call, shivering in the cold wind, her husband's ancient little van not having the luxury of a working heating system. Stepping inside, she opened her arms and hugged a jittery Amy whose skin was grey and eyes sunken and red. They made their way to the kitchen where Beth wasted no time in asking for details while Amy put the kettle on.

'Tell me exactly what happened.'

Amy took a deep breath. 'I saw a detective constable who wrote down Callum's details and asked how long he'd been missing. She didn't seem to think it unusual and suggested that Cal might have left of his own accord. There were the expected questions, you know – if we'd argued at all lately. I suppose they have to ask, but why are they always so suspicious? I took a photograph as you suggested. The detective said missing persons usually turn up within a few days, yet they would start looking for him.'

'Yeah, but how thoroughly do they look? I mean, will they get search parties out to physically search for him?'

'They'll put Callum's details into their computer and check local hospitals. I can't see them having the resources to send officers out searching; they'll probably think it's too soon. Maybe they'll rethink their actions if they don't find him within a couple of days. Oh, Beth, I hope it won't drag on. I just want them to find him – for all of this to be over.'

'On the telly, the police always quiz the family and friends when someone's missing and if they suspect foul play.'

'I don't think they automatically suspect foul play, do they? The detective asked me to try to think of anywhere he might go. I said I'd rung you and some of his mates last night when he didn't come home.' Amy had been absently making tea as she spoke and now handed a mug to her sister, and they moved into the lounge. 'I feel bloody awful, which isn't surprising as I didn't sleep a wink last night.' She flopped onto the sofa and Beth sat beside her.

'It's not going to be easy, but we're in this together, and you're one of the strongest people I know.'

This last remark wasn't the comfort Beth intended it to be and it angered Amy. *Why the hell do I always have to be the strong one, the sensible one? Why can't someone else sort out the family problems?* Instead of snapping at her sister, Amy sighed and said, 'I don't feel particularly strong. I only hope they find him quickly. I can't bear for this to be a long, drawn-out thing.'

'I'm sure they'll find him soon and then life can return to normal.'

'Whatever normal is.' For a moment, Amy wanted to blurt out that she was dying – to tell her sister and accept comfort, but she couldn't – the timing was all wrong. Beth was right, Amy had to be the strong one.

'Do you want to come back to mine? Maybe you'll feel better with some company?'

'No, the police might visit. I wouldn't want to miss them.'

'Didn't you give them your mobile number?'

'Yeah, but I think I should stay here. Maybe I'll do something to take my mind off things, perhaps clean out the kitchen cupboards.' Amy chewed on a fingernail, frowning.

'You'd be better off resting – you look bloody awful. Take a couple of paracetamols, they should help.'

'Oh, Beth, I can't rest. All sorts of horrible scenarios are buzzing through my brain. I can't imagine what will happen, it's like living in a nightmare.'

Beth moved closer to her sister and put a comforting arm around her. 'I know, and I'm so sorry. But try not to worry. We've been through some tough times together and always coped, we'll see this one through, too.'

Alone again, Amy mooched into the kitchen, restless. The view from the window was depressing; dirty packed-down snow, icicles hanging from the guttering and a freezing draught blowing under the ill-fitting kitchen door. Turning up the thermostat – to hell with the expense – Amy returned to the lounge and her place on the sofa, tucking her feet beneath her. With closed eyes, Amy's thoughts drifted back to her childhood – and Beth.

Beth knew how to wind up their father, even at six years old. His anger didn't deter her – she goaded him even more and took the beatings with her chin held high, or ran away, staying hidden in the garden until his wrath abated, sometimes hours later. Amy would sneak out with food or a blanket if it was cold, hoping not to be seen by their parents, and tell Beth when it was safe to return to the house, often only when their father was out. At almost two years older than her sister, Amy felt guilt at not protecting her, yet their father scared her. Their mother was no help either; perhaps she was even more afraid of him than her daughters were. Amy witnessed several beatings which her mother took like a cowed dog – it was impossible to help or stop her father when he was in one of his moods. To her shame, Amy would rather keep out of his way and be the good girl, even though it meant many hours alone in her room. If only she were brave enough to stand up to him, to protect Beth – but even then, Amy knew herself to be a coward.

SIX
WEDNESDAY 7TH DECEMBER

Amy was brought back to the present when the doorbell rang. *Damn it,* she thought. She'd forgotten the Macmillan nurse was calling. Jumping up from the sofa and steadying herself, she went to open the door.

'Hi, Amy, I'm Fran Jenkinson. We spoke on the phone?' The woman was short and plump with straight grey hair cut into a bob with a full fringe. Her smile was warm and genuine and Amy instantly liked this motherly woman.

'Yes, I remember. Please come in.' Fran followed Amy into the lounge. 'Would you like coffee?' she asked.

'That would be wonderful, but can I use your loo first? I'm onto my sixth cup today,' she said with a grin. Amy pointed her toward the downstairs toilet and went to make the drinks. Carrying the mugs into the lounge, Fran was back and sitting waiting, so Amy handed her the drink and sat opposite the nurse. Taking a sip from her mug – the hot liquid soothed some of the restlessness in her mind and body.

Fran got down to business. 'Now, I believe you saw Mr Matthews last Thursday which means you'll have had time to reflect on your diagnosis?' Thursday seemed a lifetime ago. *If only she knew*. When Amy didn't answer, Fran continued. 'I'm hoping we can get to know each other, Amy. My role is to support you through this difficult time, answer any questions, and help with any practical things you may need. If you want a family member or a friend to be at our meetings, it's fine by me – whatever makes you comfortable. How have you been since Thursday – it must have been quite a shock?'

Amy wanted to run upstairs and crawl under the duvet but decided that she must be strong and that she did need to talk to someone. Fran was eager to help but deserved to be put in the picture. 'Yes, the diagnosis was a shock, but since then my husband's gone missing. I've been to the police this morning and they're looking for him.'

'Oh, you poor thing, how awful for you!' Fran put her mug on the coffee table and shuffled her ample rear to the edge of the seat. 'How long's he been missing?'

'He didn't come home last night, which isn't like him. The police say it's early days yet and he may turn up, but I don't know what to think.'

'I'm not surprised – what a horrible position to find yourself in, especially when you're unwell. Look, if you don't feel like talking now, I can always come back another day.'

'No, please stay. I have some questions to ask and thinking about the tumour will take my mind off other things.' This thing was growing in her body and Amy needed to know what to expect, to get the measure of what she was up against. 'I want to know what's going to happen.'

'Okay, I'll try to explain. I've seen your notes and understand some of the symptoms you're experiencing already – nausea and vomiting, fatigue, drowsiness and even seizures – is that right?'

'Yeah, all that and more. The symptoms started so suddenly; is that usual?'

'Tumours grow at different rates and sadly yours seems particularly aggressive. It could be that you didn't notice some of the symptoms in the early days, the headaches and fatigue we often put down to being a bit under the weather.'

'Huh! I thought I was a bit depressed and kept taking paracetamol.' A tear escaped and ran down Amy's cheek. Fran pulled a wad of tissues from her bag and waved them in front of her face, like a magician presenting her with paper flowers.

'Unfortunately, the symptoms won't improve, but we can offer medication to control them, even the seizures. The medication will be monitored and the dosage altered as necessary, and I'll be available to listen to any concerns you have and try to help. The fatigue will probably affect you more as time moves on, and rest is important. You may experience sleep problems and possibly memory problems, but being aware of these possibilities will help you cope, and never be afraid to ask for help. It's why we're here.' Fran smiled and Amy relaxed slightly. 'Do you have anyone who can be with you during this time – I don't just mean the illness – anyone you can talk to and confide in about your husband?'

'Yes, my sister, Beth. She lives in New Middridge and we're quite close. She was here earlier today.'

'Good. Sometimes life seems to kick us in the teeth at the worst possible times but don't be afraid to ask for help. I can signpost the relevant organisations for counselling, financial help, or almost anything. You only have to ask.'

'You sound like my fairy godmother!' Amy surprised herself by smiling.

'Do they make fairies in my size?' Fran bobbed her head from side to side and laughed.

An hour and two cups of coffee later, the nurse left, giving Amy two telephone numbers to contact her – anytime – she stressed. Propping them up on the mantelpiece, Amy sighed. She should eat something, but could only manage another coffee.

SEVEN
THURSDAY 8TH DECEMBER

Samantha's face told Jenny all she needed to know on her arrival at the station on Thursday morning. Blowing her hands to warm them through and regain some feeling, she asked, 'How did the trial go?'

'Dismissed. The girlfriend withdrew her complaint – said she'd been confused at the time and wasn't sure he was even in the house when the *accident* happened.' Sam made air quotation marks with her forefingers. 'Damn it! Why do they do it – let these men walk all over them – the number of times we see it happen, it's so frustrating.'

'Not to mention the cost to the taxpayer and all those wasted hours. Let's hope he doesn't take it out on her now he's back home.' The conversation was interrupted by Sam's phone. Answering it, the DI picked up a pen and scribbled something on her notepad. 'On my way.' She ended the call and turned to Jenny. 'A body's been found in a ditch on the south side of town. Grab your coat!'

For once Samantha chose to take a pool car. Generally preferring to drive her little Mini, the current weather conditions called for something larger with four-wheel drive, so she booked out a Toyota RAV4 and climbed into the driver's seat. Jenny took the passenger seat and began fiddling with the knobs on the dashboard. 'I hope the heater works. It's bloody freezing today.'

'We're off into the sticks so don't get too cosy.' Sam pulled away and headed south out of New Middridge. The main roads had been gritted overnight but once away from the built-up area, snow was packed down on the roads making driving hazardous. Sam adjusted her speed accordingly. Hurrying wouldn't help their victim – it was far too late for that.

In any other circumstance the vista before them would have been admired. After days of steadily falling snow, the trees were heavy and branches bowed down to form an arch over the road on which they travelled. It was fresh and white, like a passage to Santa's grotto.

The scene of the accident was clear to spot as the detectives approached. Three vehicles were already in situ, having driven through a large gap in the hedge and parked in a field at a reasonable distance from where the body had been discovered. About sixty yards away, Sam could see a tent being erected as cover for the CSIs to work beneath. Snow wasn't falling but could begin again anytime and until they knew what they were dealing with it was imperative to preserve the scene.

As the women approached the fluttering tape, Samantha recognised PC Mark Davies who stood with a clipboard taking names of all those on site.

'Morning, Mark. Were you first on the scene?'

'Yes, ma'am. The lady who found the body lives just over the road from where you parked your car. Harriet Smith, she's called – gave me a verbal statement and now she's back at the house with PC Walker. She has a couple of bairns but fortunately they didn't see anything.'

Sam ducked under the tape which Mark held up for her.

'Good work, Mark. Not the best of days to be hanging around in a frozen field.' The constable smiled solemnly and as they headed towards the ditch, made a note of their names on his log.

Samantha squatted beside the shallow ditch and nodded at Rick, the pathologist, who was beside the body, carefully scraping snow off his clothing. 'Anything useful yet?'

'This bloody weather doesn't help. It could have been a car accident, although he has a nasty gash on the side of his head – maybe from striking a rock as he fell – we're searching the immediate area, looking for possibilities. Time of death's screwed as well. The freezing temperature will make accuracy difficult; I'll have to check the last few night's temperatures and do the calculations.'

'So, he could have been here a couple of nights?'

'Possible, no more I shouldn't think.'

'Any ID?'

'When I've cleared the snow and photographed the body, I'll have a look.'

Samantha and Jenny walked the area, already becoming a quagmire with the trampling of heavy boots. 'Should we go talk to the woman who found him?' Jenny asked.

'And hope she's got the kettle on?' Sam turned and headed back to the car.

Harriet Smith opened the door as the detectives were stamping their feet on the mat in the porch. 'Oh, don't bother about that, it's a slate floor and I've got two children and a dog – there's nothing to spoil here. As they followed her into the kitchen where PC Rachel Walker was entertaining a boy and a girl, Harriet offered them tea which they gratefully accepted. While the PC was successfully making the children chuckle, their mother was still ashen. They took their drinks through to the lounge away from little ears while the children happily remained with Rachel.

Sam thanked the woman for her hospitality and apologised for interrupting her day. 'It's a very isolated spot, Mrs Smith. Who lives in the other two properties?'

'They're both second homes, so no one at the moment. The Carter family who own the nearest house may come for Christmas, they live in London and visit as often as they can manage. The other cottage is owned by a single man who lets it for holidays and only comes himself a couple of times a year. I have emergency numbers for them both if you'd like?'

'Yes, that would be great, thank you.'

Harriet left the lounge and returned a few minutes later with the numbers which she passed to Jenny. Samantha asked her to go over the events of the morning again and Harriet began to do so, until tears filled her eyes and she faltered.

'Mrs Smith, is there anyone we can call for you so you won't be alone with the children today?' Jenny feared the woman was suffering from shock. Harriet blew her nose and thanked Jenny.

'My husband will be able to come home, but I'll ring him, he'll only worry if he gets a call from a police officer.'

After a few more questions Sam gave Harriet a card with her contact numbers. 'We'll leave you in peace now but PC Walker will stay until your husband arrives. I'm sorry for what's happened and if you remember anything which might help, please ring.'

Samantha decided they should go back over the field to see if there was anything new to report before returning to the station. It was pointless having too many personnel standing around freezing.

'Anything yet?' she asked Rick, the pathologist they'd spoken to earlier. Rick shook his head. 'The body's literally frozen stiff and I haven't turned it yet to get into his pockets. I'll let you know if we find anything, and take some photos to send over.'

'Great, thanks, Rick.'

The women trudged back to the car.

'Gosh, is it still morning? Feels like I've done a full day's work already and my feet are like blocks of ice.' Jenny sighed and reached for the heater again, turning it to its highest setting. 'Lovely house the Smiths have.'

'I suppose so if you like dead bodies in the vicinity.'

'You're a cynic, boss. I dream of a kitchen like that – those slate floors and granite worktops. Do you think the beams are original?'

'Yeah, I noticed genuine woodworm too.'

'No. seriously! I know I'll never be able to afford a place like it, but I can dream, can't I? Harriet Smith has good taste, too. All her lovely blue-and-white china on the dresser and those sweet little teapots. It had such an authentic feel, the Belfast sink, the Aga...'

'Oh, Jen. Why waste time pining for things you'll never have? Anyway, I thought you were the modern type, don't you like your flat?'

'Yes, but it's so – square. Square rooms, square windows, you know – no character. It reminds me of the song my mum used to sing to me. D'you know it – *Little Boxes?*'

'If you're going to sing you can walk back to the station.'

'No, I'll not sing, promise, but I often feel like I live in one of those boxes...'

'Pleaseee!' Sam groaned.

'Okay, we'll talk about dead bodies instead, shall we?'

EIGHT
THURSDAY 8TH DECEMBER

DI Freeman entered the office and went straight to her DC's desk. 'Layla, was the misper you took yesterday a forty-something male?'

'Yes, why? Is it a man's body you've found?'

'Afraid so. Did she bring a photograph?'

Layla pulled her phone from her pocket. 'Here it is, what do you think?' The DC passed it to Sam who studied it carefully.

'It could be him, although I only saw his profile and the blood and mud didn't help.' Just then her phone pinged with a message from Rick, the pathologist at the crime scene, who'd sent the promised photograph in an attachment. Opening the image Sam placed it beside the one on Layla's phone. 'Not conclusive but it looks very much like the same man to me.'

Layla nodded and Jenny joined them to offer her opinion. 'Yes, boss, I'd say this is Callum Cooper. How long had he been missing, Layla?'

'His wife last saw him on Tuesday morning when he left for work. He works at Blacketts and they've confirmed he was there until 5pm but no one can account for him since. The poor woman.'

Samantha sighed. 'That would fit in with CSI's initial thoughts. The freezing temperatures will play havoc with predicting time of death but I think we should proceed on the assumption of our body being Callum Cooper. Layla, I think it's best if you come with me to see his wife, a familiar face might help. Jen, can you start full disclosure on our victim, Paul can help.'

Layla grabbed her coat and hurried after her DI, and within fifteen minutes the two detectives were pulling up in front of number 43 Cypress Close. It was in a pleasant enough suburb, a terrace of Edwardian houses with small forecourts to the front. Number 43 was well maintained with a low wall enclosing a double-fronted bay-windowed house. Snow covered the path but Sam assumed clearing snow would be the last thing on Amy Cooper's mind. 'I hate this part of the job,' she half whispered and Layla nodded her agreement.

A nervous-looking woman, somewhere in her early- to mid-forties, Sam guessed, opened the door and looked anxiously from one detective to the other. As recognition dawned on her, Amy's eyes widened and she asked Layla, 'Have you found him?'

Steering the woman inside, Sam asked her to take a seat while she and Layla took the sofa opposite. 'I'm so sorry, Mrs Cooper but we've found a man's body and have reason to believe it could be your husband.'

'Nooo...!' Amy Cooper wrapped her arms around her body and rocked backwards and forwards in the chair as huge sobs racked her body. A quick glance from Sam had Layla rushing to the kitchen to make tea while the DI crouched in front of Amy and spoke softly.

'We need a formal identification before we know for sure.' Sam grabbed a packet of tissues from her bag and gave them to Amy who suddenly jumped up and ran into the downstairs toilet. Retching could be heard from inside and as Layla entered with a tray of tea, she looked at Sam and grimaced.

'Poor thing, it must be such a shock.'

Amy returned to the lounge and accepted the mug of tea Layla offered. Seemingly more composed, Amy almost whispered her questions. 'How did he die? Where was he?'

'We won't be certain until the autopsy but it's possible he was hit by a car. His body was found in a ditch about four miles south of New Middridge. Do you know of any reason he would have been in that area?'

Amy's face was pained. 'No. He should have come straight home – I don't understand – had he been there since Tuesday?'

'Again, we can't be sure at this time.' Sam couldn't give her definitive answers.

Amy began furiously scratching at her arm. 'If he was hit by a car why didn't the driver stop and call an ambulance?'

'It appears to be a hit-and-run, Mrs Cooper. It's a quiet country road with no CCTV cameras – we'll be seeking witnesses and investigating the circumstances.' Sam knew her words were inadequate and any investigation would be difficult. It was unlikely anyone witnessed the incident in the quiet location and such appalling weather conditions. 'Can we call someone to come and be with you? Layla said you have a sister in town.'

Amy nodded and passed her phone to Layla. 'Her number's in there, under *Beth*.' Layla took the phone into the kitchen to make the call and break the news to Amy's sister that they suspected her brother-in-law was dead.

While they waited for Beth Moorhouse to arrive, Sam turned to Amy. 'I know how much of a shock this must be but I have to ask a few more questions so we can establish what happened to your husband. Did Callum drive to work?'

'No, he preferred to walk – it was only about a twenty-minute walk. He enjoyed the exercise and it left the car free for me to use if I needed it.'

'And do you work, Mrs Cooper?'

'Not any longer. I was made redundant during the Covid lockdown. Will I have to identify... the... Callum?'

'If you feel up to it, yes, but we'll let you know later. Do you have any children, Amy?' Sam switched to using her Christian name, attempting to put the woman at ease and develop a rapport with her; she would be seeing a lot of Callum's widow in the days to come. Amy took a sip of tea before answering. 'No, we couldn't have children, there's just the two of us.' The sensitive subject brought more tears and Sam waited for her to recover before asking her next question.

'I know I asked before, but can you think of any reason why your husband would be on that stretch of road?'

'No, I can't understand it...' The doorbell ended the conversation and Beth dashed inside and ran straight to her sister. After a few moments and a repeat of the few facts the detectives knew, Sam and Layla left the sisters, promising to be in touch later concerning the identification of the body.

NINE
THURSDAY 8TH DECEMBER

It was late afternoon when Sam and Layla returned to the police station. Jenny turned from her computer to give them an update. 'The body's at the morgue but Rick can't perform the autopsy until tomorrow afternoon at the earliest. He said something about it needing to defrost.'

Sam wrinkled her nose at the thought – she knew this was quick and Rick would try his best. It was usual to wait three or four days for an autopsy. 'Can you give him a ring and see if he can prepare for an ID this evening or early tomorrow? We need a positive ID as soon as possible.'

Jenny swung her chair back to her desk and took out her phone. Paul gave an update on his search into Callum Cooper. 'Nothing out of the ordinary, boss – no police record. I assumed you'd want to wait for a positive ID before I dig any deeper.'

'Yes, thanks, Paul. Can you get Tom and Kim to search for CCTV from near Blacketts? He was last seen leaving there at 5pm and I want to know how he ended up in a ditch at the other side of town.' Tom Wilson and Kim Thatcher were new to Sam's team and she was committed to giving them both as much experience as possible, recognising the potential in both of these young DCs. Tom possessed excellent computer skills and could be an asset to Paul's side of the enquiry. Kim was keen to be at the forefront of the investigation and her people skills could prove useful. Sam turned back to Jenny who was ending her call.

'Rick says if you give him an hour, he can have the body ready for viewing.'

'Great. Layla, will you ring Mrs Cooper and pick her up to bring her to the morgue? Perhaps her sister would accompany her, and I'll meet you there in an hour.'

The morgue wasn't Sam's favourite place, she could never understand why anyone would choose a career in forensic medicine. Yet attending autopsies was unfortunately a necessary part of her job when death was deemed suspicious, which this case appeared to be. She arrived only a minute before Layla brought the two sisters in, and the four women sat in the corridor until Rick appeared to tell them he was ready. In preparation for the ordeal, Layla had explained that the viewing would be through glass as contact with the body would be inappropriate and may cause contamination. She told them to take their time to make sure their identification was correct.

As the sheet was removed from the victim's face both women gasped, staring for only a few moments at the body before Amy sobbed and almost collapsed into her sister's arms. Beth helped her back to her seat and Layla offered her a bottle of water.

'Amy.' After allowing her a minute to compose herself Samantha asked softly, 'Can you tell me if this is Callum?'

'Yes... it's Callum.' Amy turned her head onto her sister's shoulder. Beth nodded in agreement and the detectives moved away to give them time and space.

'If she's up to it, Layla, perhaps you could prepare her for what will happen over the next few days.' Layla nodded and when Beth stood, she moved back to the women to take them home.

Amy Cooper sat in the back of the car and cried softly all the way home with her sister comforting her as best as she could. Several times Amy thought she'd be sick and asked Layla to open the window – the biting cold helped and the nausea passed. Beth too was glad of the fresh air, the sight of the body appeared to have affected her almost as much as her sister.

The house in Cypress Close felt cold and empty when they entered with Layla following them, hoping for a chance to discuss the days ahead and the investigation that the positive ID had set in motion. Beth made tea and Amy blew her nose and tried to compose herself.

'I'm sorry but it was such a shock... to see him... I've never seen a dead body before... he looked so cold and grey.'

'You did really well, Amy. It's a difficult ordeal for anyone but it's over now and we can try to find out what happened to Callum.'

'Was it a hit-and-run?'

'We won't know for certain until later, it's going to be tomorrow afternoon before the pathologist is able to perform the autopsy, and even then we may have to wait for tests to confirm how Callum died.'

Amy's eyes widened as she looked at Layla with such a sad expression. 'What kind of tests?'

'The pathologist will primarily be looking for cause of death, in this case it could be a hit-and-run but it may be that your husband had an underlying illness or condition which caused his death, an unknown heart condition for example. Toxicology tests are routinely done too, and as these things all take time it may be a few days before we can reach any conclusions.'

Beth entered the room with a tray of tea. Having clearly heard the conversation from the kitchen she asked Layla, 'So will nothing happen until you know the cause of death?'

'No, the investigation's already underway. The crime-scene investigators have been gathering physical evidence where your husband was found and if there's anything you can tell us about Callum it will help. For example, if you know the route he usually walked home from work it will give us a starting point and help build up a picture of Callum's routine. We can check any CCTV cameras near his place of work and try to get a sighting of him. We'll also be visiting Blacketts to interview his colleagues and see if anyone saw him leave – walked with him part of the way, perhaps.'

Amy turned to her sister as if wanting her to answer. Beth sipped her tea thoughtfully. 'We can put a route together quite easily; do you want to do it now?'

'If you're up to it.'

Amy nodded and Layla took out her phone and brought up Google Maps. She found Blacketts and asked Amy to point out the way her husband would take on his journey home.

When Layla left the Coopers' house twenty minutes later, it was with a route, somewhere to start. She rang the office to update her boss and then went home. Tomorrow would be an early start and a long day.

After taking Layla's call Samantha chased most of her team off home to rest. The investigation would begin in earnest when they had the autopsy report and the coming days could be long ones. Taking her own advice, she too left for home where a delicious aroma of curry greeted Samantha as she stepped into the lobby, a welcome clue to Ravi being home first. She smiled, the memory of *making up* for their argument the previous night still fresh in her mind. It was almost worth the aggravation of the row.

'Hi.' Ravi appeared in the kitchen doorway, her tiny yellow apron stretched around his waist and a wooden spoon held in his hand, dripping with curry sauce.

'Hi, yourself,' Sam replied. A warm contented feeling flooded her body on seeing this handsome man who had chosen to spend his life with her. This is what home should feel like, she thought – relaxed and carefree. There were bound to be the occasional arguments, especially when both partners had stressful jobs, but the sight of Ravi's smile and the gentle way he looked at her made Samantha feel vital, cherished. She stood on tiptoes to kiss him before hurrying upstairs to change.

'Curry in twenty minutes!' He waved the spoon after her.

'So, how was your day?' Ravi asked later as they sat side by side on the sofa, content after a delicious curry and fruit to follow.

'Cold and miserable. I attended the scene of a suspicious death, a man in a ditch, either hit by a car or dumped there – I'll start fitting the pieces together when the autopsy gives us a few pointers.'

'Do you know who it is?'

'Yeah, Layla had taken a misper case yesterday and it turns out to be the same man. His wife was able to give us a positive ID. I'll be attending the autopsy tomorrow afternoon.'

Ravi rolled his eyes. 'I'm so glad you don't bring work home with you!'

TEN
FRIDAY 9TH DECEMBER

The autopsy was scheduled for 2.30pm. DI Samantha Freeman would attend with her usual reluctance, as would her DS, Jenny Newcombe.

The team spent Friday morning in the office, collating what little information they had. The case was still officially a suspicious death, at best manslaughter, at worst, murder, yet either scenario would require a full investigation. Sam was keen to set the wheels in motion even without cause and time of death. She made a couple of phone calls then turned to her DC.

'Paul, can you contact the owners of the two cottages near Harriet Smith's? There's a slim chance one of them might have been in the area and seen something, or even been responsible for running the man down.' She knew it was a long shot but it was something they could be doing while they waited for the autopsy. 'Layla, would you ring Mrs Cooper to see how things are with her this morning – ask if she's thought of anything which may help us. Jen and I are going to visit Beth and Dave Moorhouse.'

Jen looked up from her computer. 'Okay, boss.' She was

already struggling into her coat. 'Yes, I've rung and they're both at home, get a wriggle on will you.'

Taking the same pool car they'd used the day before, Sam drove while Jen entered the address into the satnav. 'What are we hoping for from Mr and Mrs Moorhouse?'

'Some background on her sister's marriage and a general feel for them, particularly Beth. When she accompanied her sister to identify the body, I noticed traces of a nasty bruise on the side of her face. It looked to be a couple of days old but I'm always curious about these things.'

Beth and Dave Moorhouse lived in a small house, which estate agents would probably describe as semi-detached yet there was hardly any space between the neighbouring property. It looked like a seventies' or eighties' build and was identical to the surrounding houses. The doorbell played a Christmas carol, a bit early, Sam thought, and hardly appropriate when her brother-in-law had just been found dead.

Beth showed them into a room where a sofa and two armchairs filled the space at the front and at the rear stood a dining table where a man sat with a mug and a newspaper, glancing up only briefly.

'Sorry about the mess, we're starting decorating when we get the paint.' The walls looked in need of a lick of paint and the carpet had been taken up in readiness. 'This is my husband, Dave. Would you like tea or coffee?'

Samantha and Jenny accepted, welcoming the thought of something hot. 'Perhaps we can have a chat with your husband first?' Sam watched the man reluctantly stand and move towards them, stumbling slightly as he placed his mug on the dresser. When they were all seated she asked Dave Moorhouse what his relationship with his brother-in-law had been like.

'We got on okay I suppose – never best mates or anything

but our wives are close, so the four of us got together occasionally.'

'And when did you last see him?'

Dave frowned. 'Must be three or four weeks ago, I can't rightly remember. How are asking these questions going to find out what happened to Cal?'

'Presently we're gathering information, trying to build up a picture of Mr Cooper which will hopefully help us discover what exactly happened. Do you know why he would have been on that particular stretch of road?'

'Haven't a clue, but as I said we weren't exactly close.'

Beth returned with a tray of tea which she passed around then sat beside her husband. Jenny thanked her before asking, 'Have you spoken to your sister today, Mrs Moorhouse? How's she holding up?'

'I rang this morning. She's not good as I'm sure you can imagine. I asked if she'd like to come and stay here for a few days for the company, but she declined – Amy's always been the independent sort – said she'd be okay on her own.'

'That's a nasty bruise on your face, Beth. How did it happen?' Sam's question took Beth by surprise and she glanced briefly at her husband before replying.

'Oh, I walked into the bookcase when I came downstairs the other night. I should have put the light on – stupid of me.' She gave a self-deprecating smile before sipping her tea, then turned her eyes away from the detectives.

Sam asked a few more questions and received little information of value, while Jenny made notes. Finally, she stood to leave. 'Thank you for your co-operation and the tea. The autopsy is this afternoon and I'll contact your sister if we learn anything more about what happened to Callum.'

Back in the car Jenny shivered and turned the heating full on. 'She didn't like your question about the bruising, did she?'

'No. I'm not sure I buy her explanation either. Dave Moorhouse seemed rather quiet on the subject, too.'

ELEVEN
FRIDAY 9TH DECEMBER

Samantha and Jenny returned to the station with coffees and a bag of doughnuts from the deli across the road. Sam was unsure she wanted one, it may not stay in her stomach during the autopsy but the others tucked in enthusiastically. The only news to report was from Paul who'd spoken to both owners of the nearby cottages and neither had been in the area in the last few weeks. It was too early in the investigation to assemble alibis, as they hadn't yet a time frame, so Paul thanked them for their help.

'How was Amy Cooper yesterday, Layla?' Layla swallowed a mouthful of doughnut then swivelled her chair to face Sam.

'Holding up I suppose – she asked about the autopsy and appeared quite interested in the procedure and what information we'd glean from it. I thought maybe she would be one of those people who don't want their loved one's body touched which always causes problems, but she accepted what I said without comment. I told her someone would be in touch to let her know the outcome.'

'Yes, I thought I'd go there straight afterwards.'

At 2.30pm, Samantha pushed open the heavy double doors, entered the morgue and took in the scene. Rick was suited up and ready to begin, his tools arranged neatly on the table beside him. Callum Cooper's body was covered with a sheet and as Sam and Jenny approached the workstation Rick pulled his mask over his face and nodded at his colleagues. His assistant switched on a tape recorder and pulled the sheet from the cadaver.

'The subject is male, early forties with...' As Rick's voice described what he saw, Samantha stepped back. She hated this moment and wished the forensic pathologist would speed things up, although she appreciated Rick for being thorough and methodical. No matter how many autopsies she attended, it was still an ordeal and Sam tried to concentrate on the facts rather than the sight of the body and the smell of death. Eventually she was distracted from the inevitable nausea she felt by the details that interested her.

'Cause of death is a blow to the head – either of two blows although the deeper one is probably the last and fatal wound, inflicted by a heavy and smooth rounded instrument. The other injuries, sustained when he was mowed down by the car, were all post mortem, several hours after death I should think.' Rick lifted his eyes to ensure he had everyone's attention and continued to answer questions before the detectives could ask them. 'The pattern of livor mortis is apparent about an hour after death and well formed after three or four. In this case, livor mortis was fixed before our victim was moved which indicates he died at another location where he remained for six to eight hours and only then was taken to the ditch where he was found. The timing can be variable but the fixation of lividity certainly occurred before he was moved.'

Jenny was studying the cadaver closely and asked, 'So the

blows to the head couldn't have been a result of being hit by a car?'

'No. As I said whatever he was struck with was smooth and rounded, which rules out hitting his head on a rock as he tumbled into the ditch. I would have expected to find particles in the wound if that were the case but he was definitely dead by then anyway.' Jenny scribbled down a few notes although she knew Rick's report would be detailed.

'When do you think our victim died?' Samantha asked the all-important question.

'I think we're looking at Tuesday or early Wednesday of this week. I've considered the weather conditions – frozen snow isn't a pathologist's best friend – but I don't think I'm far out.'

'And what about toxicology? Was he drugged or drunk at all?'

'No obvious signs, Samantha, but you know I can't tell you much more until the reports come back from the lab which will be sometime next week. I've also requested medical records from his GP but again they'll take time and the weekend always slows things down.'

Samantha turned away from the table as the pathologist began to make the Y-incision, unable to watch the removal of organs. Finally, Rick neared the end of his examination. 'Our victim wasn't in the best of health. Hardening of the arteries around the heart suggests he was a candidate for a heart attack, and his lungs are badly damaged from years of heavy smoking. However, neither of these conditions appear to have contributed to his death and I'm satisfied the sole cause was the blow to the head. Thank you for attending and I'll have my preliminary report on your desk as soon as possible.' Rick stepped away from the table leaving his assistant to replace the organs and sew up the cadaver.

Samantha was first out the door and headed for the exit,

grateful for the blast of cold fresh air. Jenny followed close behind trying to catch her boss's words. 'Well, it looks like we can rule manslaughter out. It wasn't a hit-and-run but someone went to the trouble to make it appear to be. Ring Paul and tell him we're now investigating a murder, then you and I will go to see Amy Cooper.'

TWELVE
FRIDAY 9TH DECEMBER

It was dusk as Sam and Jenny set off to visit Amy Cooper and the first day without fresh snow, but the roads were still packed with ice and the gritting lorries already rumbled through the town.

Amy opened the door and stood aside to allow them in. Sam noticed her pale skin and the dark circles beneath her eyes. Declining coffee, she waited until they were all seated before sharing the autopsy results with Callum's widow.

'I'm sorry to have to tell you but the pathologist's examination has revealed that your husband wasn't the victim of a hit-and-run – he was killed by a blow to his head and was already dead when he was left in the ditch.'

Amy's hand flew to her mouth and tears welled in her eyes. After a moment's hesitation she asked, 'How can you know all this?'

'Forensic science is very exact these days. The pathologist is confident your husband was killed in another location where he lay for several hours before being moved. Patterns of lividity can tell us much and the other injuries, from the car, were all inflicted post mortem.'

'But he was struck by a car?'

'Yes, presumably to make his death appear to be an accident. I'm afraid this is now a murder enquiry. I'm sorry, Amy, I know it must be a shock and over the next few days we'll be digging into Callum's life – interviewing friends and relations to try to find out who did this. The investigation may seem intrusive at times and I apologise in advance but it is necessary. Jenny here will be your family liaison officer and she'll keep in touch daily and spend time here with you.' Sam was unsure if Amy was taking anything in – she appeared stunned, her eyes almost glazed. 'Would you like me to ring your sister for you? Maybe you'd feel better with someone here.'

'Er, yes, maybe... sorry, I just don't know what to say.'

'Can I make you some tea?' Jenny asked.

'Please.'

While Jen went to make tea, Sam phoned Beth who agreed to drive straight over. She asked about the autopsy findings and Sam said they'd discuss it when she arrived.

Fifteen minutes later a breathless Beth rang the doorbell then entered her sister's home. 'So what's happened?' Her question was addressed to the detectives.

'We attended the autopsy this afternoon and it appears Callum was killed several hours before his body was left in the ditch. The investigation is now a murder enquiry and I've been explaining to Amy what will happen next.' Beth wrinkled her brow and sniffed and Sam decided not to distress Amy further by going over the details again. Assuming the women would need some time alone, she made an excuse about the time being late and said they'd be in touch the following morning. Amy could fill her sister in on whatever she wanted her to know.

Back in the car, Jenny turned to her boss. 'I checked out the bruising on Beth's face. It's still there but she appears to have covered it with more make-up since we saw her earlier.'

'Yes, I noticed. I wonder if Dave's a bit too handy with his fists or if she really did walk into a bookcase. Anyway, it's hardly relevant to our murder case. You okay for a bit of overtime tomorrow?'

Jenny nodded her agreement. 'Yes, now we know what we're up against we need to get moving. Do you want me at Amy's house first thing or at the station?'

'We'll meet at the station and go to Amy's together. I have a feeling she won't like what we need to do.'

'Can't say I blame her – it's an intrusion at the worst possible time for a family, but it's best to get it over with, see what we find.'

They drove back to the station to pick up their own cars and leave for the day. It was 6pm and they would return at 8am the following morning.

THIRTEEN
SATURDAY 10TH DECEMBER

Ravi Patel lay in bed with his arms behind his head, watching Sam dress. 'I thought you said we'd have the weekend off together. It's ages since our rest days have coincided.'

'I know, sorry, but you know how important the first few days of a murder investigation are. We lost time waiting for the autopsy before we knew exactly what we were dealing with, so I want to crack on today. I'll make it up to you, promise.' Sam climbed onto the bed and kissed Ravi lingeringly on the lips.

'I hope you have more than a kiss in mind.' He grinned as they parted. 'I'm not even sure if there's football on the telly – with this weather half the matches are postponed.'

'You can't blame me for the weather and if you're bored you can always do that pile of ironing.'

Ravi pulled the covers over his head as Sam shouted goodbye.

By 8am Samantha and Jenny were once again knocking on the door of Amy Cooper's home. A very pale, weary-looking Amy answered and invited the detectives inside out of the cold. Still in her dressing gown, it appeared she'd had very little sleep.

Sam noticed the lines on her face, more prominent than ever. Amy's mouth turned down at the corners with deep grooves running down her chin, rather like a ventriloquist's dummy.

'Would you like a coffee?'

'That would be very welcome, thank you.'

'Come through to the kitchen.' Amy led the way and began the mechanics of coffee making. Sam and Jenny sat at the kitchen table but as Amy appeared to be in a trance and almost dropped the jar of coffee, Jen offered to take over. 'Perhaps you'd like to get dressed while I see to the coffee?'

Amy turned silently and left the kitchen. Jenny shook her head. 'She looks terrible, poor thing. I suppose it's a shock to lose your husband but then to find out he was murdered is something else.'

'Let's hope we find something today to give us a lead.'

Amy returned within five minutes, dressed but still rather dishevelled, and accepted the coffee Jenny handed her. Sitting at the table she asked, 'So what happens next?' almost flinching in anticipation of the answer.

'We're still at the evidence-gathering stage. Because it's now a murder enquiry we'll have more resources and more officers to assist. One of the reasons we're here today is to ask if you'll allow us to search Callum's things – his papers, laptop and mobile phone.'

'But why? Shouldn't you be out there looking for who did this?'

Samantha encountered this attitude often; it could be difficult to understand why the investigation commenced with the victim. 'If we find a motive, it may help us discover who killed Callum. Can you think of anyone who held a grudge or perhaps was angry with Callum for some reason?'

'No, he was well-liked by everyone. Surely it was just a random attack?'

'We won't know until we learn more, such as where Callum was killed. The route he took home from work will be key to this, so you've already been a big help, and we have colleagues checking CCTV for sightings of Callum on Tuesday after he left work.'

'I still don't see how searching the house will help.' Amy sniffed and wiped her eyes with her sleeve.

'It's routine, Amy. We start with Callum and the people he knew. His phone and laptop will help, and any bank statements. Had he borrowed any money recently?'

'No! We have a mortgage but we don't buy stuff on HP. We live quite simply, especially since I lost my job. Look, you'd better just get on with it. I haven't got his phone; Cal would have had it with him but his laptop's in the little back bedroom he used as a study. Bank statements, bills and everything should be there too.' Amy blew her nose and stood. 'I'm going to ring Beth now, okay?'

'Of course, we'll try not to disturb anything and be as quick as we can.' Sam and Jenny climbed upstairs and entered the study, a small boxy room furnished simply with an MDF desk, a tall shelving unit holding box files and a few paperback novels. Callum's laptop was on the desk.

'Bag that, Jen, and then start with the shelves – I'll take the desk. There wasn't a mobile with the body but the bank statements should give us the provider so we can still get a record of calls.'

Jenny lifted down a pile of box files and began sifting through them. It appeared Callum Cooper was very organised in running the couple's finances – utility bills were in one box, old bank statements in another, nothing out of the ordinary. The third file was more interesting. Jen found a life insurance policy for Callum and one for Amy. Her eyes widened and would probably have popped out of her head if the policies had been taken out recently, but no. They were both dated 2009, standard policies which many couples would have. She would bag them with the bank statements to examine more closely back at the station.

Samantha closed the drawer in the desk. 'Not much to go on – the most recent bank statement shows a balance of less than £100 and credit card receipts which are paid off as soon as they arrive – very commendable. Amy was right, they don't seem the type to get into debt although they're almost living on the breadline.'

A little over an hour later, Samantha and Jenny left the Coopers' home to take their finds back to the station, promising to keep Amy up to date with any developments. They would sift through the paperwork and Jen would visit again later in the day.

FOURTEEN
MONDAY 12TH DECEMBER

Weekends were always difficult in a murder investigation, slowing down toxicology reports, having to wait for GP's notes to be sent over and many other things Sam would like to set in motion, like visiting Callum Cooper's place of work to interview his colleagues. The DI had spent the remainder of Saturday and Sunday at the station keen to progress the case, and satisfied herself by going over the paperwork they'd taken from the Coopers' home, trying to build a picture of the couple's life. But there was nothing of real interest, no leads to give an insight into who the murderer could be.

Further scrutiny of the life insurance policies proved them to be pretty standard. Suspicion might have rested on Amy Cooper if the policies were recent, but it was unlikely she'd wait over ten years to bump off her husband simply for the insurance money. The payout was in the region of £7,000, hardly sufficient to take the risk.

'Amy doesn't seem like a murderer to me, I think she's genuine,' Jenny mused as they'd shared a coffee break on Sunday. Sam agreed. 'She'd have needed help to kill him, transport him to the countryside, run him over with a car and then push him into the ditch.' It was a scenario to consider but an unlikely one.

When Monday arrived, Sam could do what she loved best, getting out and about digging for evidence. Her first stop, with Jenny at her side was to Blacketts kitchen manufacturers where the manager met them.

'It's so sad, unbelievable. And you think Callum was murdered? Bloody hell, I can't believe it.' The smell of sawn timber and putty surrounded them as they trailed behind the manager to his office.

'Yes, I'm afraid so. We'd like to ask a few questions regarding Callum's employment here.'

'Anything to be of help, pet. Fire away.' Mr Formby's office was a small untidy windowless room. Piles of paper looked in danger of toppling over if they were as much as breathed upon and the desk was scattered with a selection of dirty coffee mugs surrounding a dated computer. Formby motioned for the detectives to sit down and Jenny took out her notebook.

'How long did Callum work here?'

'Must be ten years or more now. A good bloke, got on well with everyone, well-liked he was.' He'd answered Sam's second question too.

'Have you ever had any trouble regarding his employment, any disagreement with a colleague perhaps?'

'Never! If all my men were like Callum Cooper my life would be much easier. As I said, everyone's buddy.'

'Anyone in particular – a friend I mean – someone he went to the pub with perhaps?'

'He wasn't a big drinker mind, a quiet sort, but I think he was pally with George King. They worked together on the shop floor; he'll be able to tell you a bit more about the man. Mind you, now I come to think on it, they had a bit of a barney a couple of weeks ago although I think they made it up.'

'Is Mr King in today?'

'Aye, shall I ask him to come and see you?'

'Yes please.'

Mr Formby picked up a telephone and they heard his voice booming over the PA system, asking George King to come to his office. George arrived in only a couple of minutes, enough time for the manager to enquire after Callum's wife and ask Sam to offer his condolences. He said he'd be in touch with Amy officially in the next few days.

George King was a small, rotund man somewhere in his fifties with a wide mouth and a balding head. He expressed sadness at the shocking news and was happy to talk about Callum. 'I don't know who the hell would want to kill him, he was harmless, an inoffensive bloke if ever there was one. I can't think of anyone he rubbed up the wrong way – ask anyone here – Cal was a good sort. Never spoke much about his home life, but then I don't either – come here to get away from the wife! We shared a love of football and had the occasional drink after work on a Friday, but Cal always stopped at one then he was off home for the weekend.'

'We heard you had an altercation with Callum quite recently. Can you tell us what it was about?'

King glanced at Mr Formby who was pretending not to listen. 'Ah, that was somat and nowt. We have a bit of a syndicate for lottery tickets and Cal thought I hadn't paid up for a few weeks. I'd actually given the money to Ed to pass on but he'd forgotten. It was soon sorted.'

'Thank you, Mr King. Could you give your contact details to Sergeant Newcombe please, we may want to speak to you again.'

Samantha thanked Mr Formby and asked if he would ring her if he thought of anything else which might be helpful.

'Same old, same old.' Jenny sighed as they left the factory. 'It appears our victim had no enemies, which makes our job rather difficult.'

Samantha frowned. 'Yes, he seems almost too good to be true, a rather bland figure and an unlikely target of such a violent death. It looks like we'll be struggling to find a motive, let alone a killer.'

At the police station Paul and Layla had completed background checks on Callum and Amy Cooper and also Beth and Dave Moorhouse. 'Nothing much has flagged up, boss.' Layla sounded almost apologetic as she updated them on what little they'd discovered. 'Bank statements show the Coopers are solvent, certainly not well off and they've struggled lately but appear to have adjusted accordingly. They're not extravagant, nor ones to have debts, even on credit cards, and their mortgage is only small. The Moorhouses have even less, he's on benefits and she doesn't appear to work. None of the four are on our system with the exception of Dave Moorhouse who had a fine and points on his licence for speeding two years ago.'

Samantha stood, hands on hips, staring at the sparse whiteboard. 'It looks like we're going to have to work hard on this one – no motive, no debt, clean living – what's going on here? Who would murder such an inoffensive bloke, and why? Layla, can you add a man called George King to your search list, Jen has his contact details. So far, he's the only friend of Cooper's we have, and as yet I don't want to have to dig into all his colleagues. I'm going to visit Amy again, then hopefully we'll have some more names to look at. The teams on door-to-door today will be reporting back soon, so if you can log any new info into the system as well.' Sam stared at the board again and sighed. 'What are we missing here? There must be someone who had a motive to kill Callum Cooper. Also, whoever left him in the ditch took his wallet and phone, maybe a fingertip search of the wider area will turn something up. Cooper wouldn't have been carrying much money, I think the wallet and phone were taken more to hamper identification than for their value, so we still need a motive.'

'I'm on it, boss.' Layla turned back to her computer while Samantha headed off to call on Amy once again, to see if she'd thought of anything else which might be relevant and update her on the investigation.

FIFTEEN
TUESDAY 13TH DECEMBER

The call came in early morning, before Samantha had removed her coat or poured her first cup of coffee. All plans were put on hold when she received the message to attend the scene of a fire at a former nightclub, less than a mile from the station. The fire was under control with firefighters and uniformed police in attendance, but a body had been discovered and detectives were required to attend the scene.

Samantha arrived within minutes and nodded to a couple of uniformed constables she recognised. 'What's the story?'

'The place has been closed down for a month or more and the building was supposedly secure, but clearly not enough. We haven't been allowed in yet but I was told there's evidence it's been used as a doss house, and there's a body in the room they think is the seat of the fire. It could be a rough sleeper.'

'Do they suspect an accident or is it malicious?'

'Too early to say. Maybe he was lighting a fire to keep warm and it got out of control, but that's speculation at the moment. The fire investigator's been in there a while and they won't let anyone else in until they're sure the building's safe.'

Stomping around to keep warm, Sam took a good look at the

building. The shell seemed secure; the fire apparently localised on the ground floor with damage less than might have been expected. A member of the public had called it in, in the early stages but sadly not soon enough to save a life.

Twenty minutes later the fire investigator appeared from inside the building and Sam approached him, introducing herself, although they'd met before she was unsure he'd remember her.

'I know it's early but is there anything you can tell me?'

'One dead body; looks like his clothes caught fire which would be why he didn't get out. It's going to be difficult to ID the man – if it is a man. I'll get a team in for further investigation this morning and maybe liaise with your guys when they know a little more.'

'Thanks. Any signs of arson?' Samantha pushed for more information.

'Too early to say, but nothing apparent. Could be a tragic accident – the place looks as if it's been a base for a few homeless folk, old sleeping bags, cardboard boxes and the like – not surprising in the weather we've been having.'

Samantha thanked the investigator and made her way back to the station. Jenny greeted her and wrinkled her nose. 'No need to ask where you've been, or have you taken up smoking?'

'Funny. We now have another body to identify and so close to Christmas, it always seems worse at this time of year. Expect a call from the fire investigators later today. When they give us the okay, we'll get the body to Rick and begin to identify him, or her.'

'That bad, huh?'

Sam wrinkled her nose. 'Yes, the seat of the fire could have been his clothes from what they've seen so far. That's one autopsy I really don't want to attend. Right, back to the Cooper case. Anything new come in overnight?'

Jenny sighed. 'I wish. We badly need a break with this one, maybe today?'

'Don't hold your breath, Jen.'

Settling down at her computer, the phone rang before Sam switched it on. She listened to the desk sergeant for a few minutes before finishing the call and turning to Jenny. 'We have a visitor. Tim Dennison and his mother are in reception. Apparently, he's quite distressed.'

'Tim who? Oh, one of the yobs who torched the warehouse?'

'The very same. Come on, let's see what he wants.'

It was impossible to decide who was the most distressed, Tim or Mrs Dennison. They sat close together in the interview room and looked up as Sam and Jenny entered.

An agitated Eileen Dennison spoke before the detectives could take a seat. 'We've come here of our own accord! My Tim's a good lad, it's that crowd he's gotten in with who lead him astray.'

Sam smiled and sat opposite the woman. 'Mrs Dennison, please calm down and tell me what's happened to bring you here. Can I get you both a coffee?' The woman seemed taken aback. 'Oh, yes please, thanks.'

Jen left the room and found someone to bring in coffee. Returning, she found the woman noisily blowing her nose and Tim with his arms on the table, head resting on them. She reached for a box of tissues and placed it on the table as she sat. Samantha nudged the box towards Mrs Dennison. 'What's prompted this visit?' she asked.

'Tim was hanging around with those two lads last night – you know, Ethan and Tyler. He didn't come home until early this morning, stinking of smoke.' She nudged her son who sat up, his face streaked with tears. Samantha thought he looked much younger than his sixteen years, all bravado drained from him. 'Tell them what you told me, Tim.' The boy sniffed and stared at the table while he spoke.

'Me an' Ethan an' Tyler went to that empty nightclub last night. It wasn't my idea, it was Ethan – he wanted to do weed and stuff – it's a good place to get out of the cold.' He looked up, glancing at his mother who nudged him sharply to continue. 'On the way, Ethan nicked a bottle of vodka from the offy; he got me and Tyler to pretend to have a fight at the back of the shop and when the old guy came out from behind the till, Ethan ran off with the bottle. When we got to the nightclub, a couple of homeless guys were in one of the rooms bedding down for the night and Ethan started in on them – name calling at first but then he began kicking them. The guys ran off. Ethan searched their stuff but only found a few dog-ends, so we opened the vodka and Ethan smoked some weed.' He paused and sniffed loudly.

'Carry on, Tim, you're doing fine.'

'I suppose Ethan was a bit off his head when he decided to light a fire; he was going to burn the homeless guys' sleeping bags to keep warm. He started larking about and stuff, swigging the vodka – and he spilt some over himself but just laughed. Ethan was sitting on some old newspapers and a flattened cardboard box, and as he tried to light the sleeping bag the paper flared up under him and his clothes caught fire.' Tears were falling down Tim's cheeks as he continued. 'It was awful – he screamed and screamed.'

'And what did you and Tyler do?' Samantha asked.

'We tried to throw the sleeping bag over him to put it out but it caught fire too an' we had to leg it before we got burned an' all. Tyler called the fire service and we hid and watched until they came. Honest, miss, there was nothing else we could do!' Tears streaked the boy's face and he rubbed his runny nose with his sleeve.

A knock on the door halted the dialogue as a constable entered with coffee for Tim and his mum. They accepted it gratefully, sipping the hot liquid in the solemn silence of the room. Samantha spoke quietly.

'You've done the right thing by coming in to report this, Tim, thank you, and you too, Mrs Dennison – I know this isn't easy for either of you. I've been to the fire scene this morning and I'm sorry to have to tell you that a body was found inside the building. From what you tell me it seems likely to be Ethan, although we'll not know for certain until later today.'

Tim chewed his thumbnail, his eyes wide pools in a pale face. 'Will... I be in trouble?'

'It's too early to say but coming here is in your favour. It will help us identify him quickly which will be better for his family. I think you should finish your coffee and then go home. We'll speak to you later. Please don't contact Ethan's family, we'll be visiting them soon.'

SIXTEEN
TUESDAY 13TH DECEMBER

'What a sorry mess!' Samantha ran her fingers through her hair. 'I know he was a nasty piece of work but he was just a kid, and to die in such a horrendous way is unthinkable. We'd better get to his parents before they hear from someone else, it'll be all around the town by now.'

It felt as if Samantha had done a full day's work yet it was only 10am as she and Jenny set off to visit the Baxter family. The council estate was an area the police were familiar with and even though it was still early, there were groups of youngsters hanging around the streets, rising curls of breath and smoke mingling in the cold air. Sam was back to using her Mini again which wasn't as conspicuous as a pool car might have been, and consequently, no one paid them any attention.

The snow had almost melted. A night of heavy rain had cleared all but the shovelled piles at the side of the roads and soon they'd be gone too. Sam frowned as they pulled up in front of the Baxters' semi, noticing the weedy line of fairy lights strung across the doorway. A scrawny artificial tree stood in the bay window, baubles and tinsel which had seen better days adorning its half-bare branches.

'Sod it, this is going to ruin the family's Christmas for sure. I hate notifying a death at this time of year.'

Jenny sighed in agreement and pressed the doorbell which burst into a rendition of 'Ding Dong Merrily on High'. The detectives exchanged a pained look as they waited for the door to be opened.

Sylvie Baxter glowered at the women. Wearing a dressing gown, a cigarette between her fingers, she leaned against the door-jamb and folded her arms. 'He ain't in – whatever you're after fitting him up for will have to wait, so sling yer hook!' Sylvie made to close the door but Jenny stepped forward.

'Mrs Baxter, it's you we've come to see. May we come in for a minute?' Something in Jen's tone appeared to surprise Sylvie and she stepped aside allowing them entry. They were immediately in a lounge where the television blared and a bulky man sat eating a bacon sandwich. He paid no attention to their visitors, his eyes glued to the screen.

'Is this Mr Baxter?' Sam asked. Sylvie nodded and addressed the man as Kev. He finally seemed aware of their presence. Kev Baxter was heavyset with flabby jowls and broad shoulders. 'Could you switch the television off and sit down please?' The woman nodded to her husband who switched it off and then she sat down. Sylvie looked worried but was still on the defensive.

'We haven't seen our Ethan since last night, he was staying at a mate's house.'

'Mrs Baxter. We've just spoken to one of Ethan's friends who was with him and another boy in town last night, inside an abandoned nightclub. There was a fire in the early hours of this morning and sadly we've found a body on the premises which we believe to be Ethan.'

'Nooo...' Sylvie Baxter's eyes rolled back in her head as a noise like a wounded animal escaped her lips – her husband gasped and dropped his plate on the floor. A scrawny dog appeared from under the chair and greedily grabbed the sandwich.

'I'm so sorry. As I say, we'll need to formally identify the body before we can be certain but from the information we've received, there's a strong possibility it's Ethan.'

'I want to see him!' Sylvie struggled to her feet and pushed past Jen to make for the door. Her husband, light on his feet for such a big man, caught her shoulder and pulled her into his arms. 'No, love. We need to take it in – it may not be him, let's wait and see, eh?'

Samantha was surprised at the man's clear thinking and addressed him. 'Could we take something of Ethan's for a DNA sample; a toothbrush or hairbrush perhaps?'

'Yes, I'll get it.' Mr Baxter steered his sobbing wife back to the sofa and went upstairs, returning a few moments later to hand over a toothbrush. Jenny held out a plastic evidence bag for him to drop the item in, then sealed it and put it in her bag. Mr Baxter sat beside his wife and drew her into his side.

'Can we call anyone for you before we go?' Samantha asked.

'No, we'll be fine. When... will you know... for sure?'

'Later today, Mr Baxter. We'll prioritise it, naturally, and be in touch as soon as we know.' The man nodded, his eyes brimming with tears. The detectives left the couple and saw themselves out.

'They seem an oddly matched couple, he's a much more reasonable sort than Sylvie,' Jen remarked. Sam unlocked the car and climbed inside. 'Yes, let's hope he remains so as the investigation progresses. You'd better drop that toothbrush off at the morgue, Jen. I'll update the team.'

The team were still concentrating on Callum Cooper's murder when she arrived but as no one was excitedly waiting to see her, Sam correctly assumed there was nothing new to report.

Calling them together she told them the outcome of her morning's activities.

'Poor kid! He might have been a pain but no one would wish this on him.' Paul shook his head.

'And just before Christmas – it's always worse for the family – Christmas will never be the same again,' Layla added.

'Yes, well if you two can go and visit Tyler Green to get a statement, Jen and I will interview Tim Dennison again more formally. It'll give you a break from the Cooper case and we'll get back to it with fresh eyes tomorrow.'

SEVENTEEN
WEDNESDAY 14TH DECEMBER

'It would be good to have Callum Cooper's murder wrapped up for Christmas.' Jenny Newcombe winced at her inadvertent pun.

'Don't think it's going to happen unless something gives – this is one of the most frustrating cases yet. We'll have to widen the net to find so much as a motive, never mind the killer. So far it appears that everyone liked the man and Paul hasn't ferreted out anything unusual in his finances or online activities.'

'What about Cooper's elderly mother? She can hardly be a suspect but perhaps we could interview her, see if she can throw up anything from his past which may be relevant.'

'Yeah, why not, we'll have to dig deeper on this one. Ask Layla to go, she's good at getting people to open up and might succeed, and then make your daily visit to Amy Cooper. Is she any more forthcoming?'

'Not really. I don't think my presence is appreciated. She makes it clear I'm not welcome for more than a brief visit but I understand, and her sister's around most of the time. When I'm there they say very little. I don't think they distrust me, it's just a surreal situation, they don't know what's expected of them so clam up and drink too much coffee. Layla...' Jenny moved off to Layla Gupta's desk and Samantha sighed, exasperated at the continued lack of progress.

'Boss?' Paul approached her desk. 'I've been digging into Cooper's friend, George King, and he has a history with us. It's way back, 2010, but he was charged and convicted of affray. As a first offence he got off with a fine and community service, so not entirely an upstanding citizen and perhaps even violent.'

'Good work, Paul, can you and Layla pay him another visit at Blacketts and go over his story again? Maybe a shove or two to stir him up – oh and ask a bit more about the argument with Cooper and see if you can confirm it with his colleagues.'

Paul waited for his DI to leave before going over to Layla's desk. 'Fancy a trip out? We could grab a coffee to go?'

'Thought I was going to visit Cooper's mother?' Layla rubbed her hands together, still cold from her journey to work.

Paul risked giving her a quick hug. 'You can do that later. We have a suspect to visit which takes priority.'

In the car, Paul filled Layla in on the details. 'George King is a mate of Cooper's and he's on our system. A charge of affray in 2010, of which he was convicted, fined and given community service. Apparently, he also had a bit of a bust-up with Cooper not too long ago which the boss wants us to confirm, and discover what it was all about.'

The factory floor was cold and noisy. Both detectives were glad to be invited into Mr Formby's office where they asked to speak again to George King.

'He's not in today, rang in sick I'm afraid and I don't know when he'll be back.'

Paul Roper raised his eyebrows. 'Did he say what was wrong? Nothing too serious I hope.'

'I didn't take the call and my secretary didn't think to ask.'

'Thank you, Mr Formby. We'll visit him at home and hope he's up to seeing us.' Paul and Layla stood to leave.

'George isn't in any trouble, is he?'

'Nothing to worry about, just routine questions but please don't ring him to let him know we're on our way.' The pair left and hurried back to the car. Layla turned the heating up high. 'It'll be all around the factory that George King is a suspect in Cooper's murder – I'd say in under the hour.' She smiled at the thought and they set off to visit the man at home.

George looked somewhat rough when he answered the door and was rather surprised to see the detectives. He invited them in and they sat in his tiny lounge on a threadbare sofa – the room appeared to be stuck in the 1980s.

'Just confirming the details you gave the DI when she spoke to you, Mr King. We won't keep you long and I'm sorry to intrude when you're under the weather.' Paul offered his best smile to get the man onside.

'I haven't thought of anything else since then, have you not caught the blighter?'

'Enquiries are still ongoing. Can you tell me the last time you saw Callum?'

'It would be the Tuesday when he left work. The sixth, wasn't it?'

'And how did he appear, anything unusual, out of character?'

'He shouted goodbye, seemed keen to get off home but the weather was bloody awful, we all wanted to get away.'

'And when did you have the falling out you told the DI about?'

'Aye, I wondered when you'd get around to that. I told your

boss it was a misunderstanding and was soon sorted. Ask Ed if you don't believe me – he caused it by forgetting to pass my money on to Callum.'

'What's Ed's surname?' Layla was taking notes.

'Smith, Edward Smith, he works on the shop floor with me and Cal, or rather he did work with Cal...'

'Did the argument turn aggressive, Mr King? You do have a history of violence.'

'Damn it, I wondered when you'd throw that one back in my face. It was years ago, a drunken brawl for which I paid my dues! Look, I really don't feel up to answering any more questions. I understand you're looking for suspects but I didn't do it, why the hell would I? If you're after a motive, isn't it usually money? Perhaps you should talk to his wife – she'll be worth a pretty penny now he's dead, what with the insurance and everything.'

'What insurance, Mr King?'

'Work's money. Part of the package for those who started with Blacketts years ago is a life insurance policy. They don't offer it now of course, things are much tighter, but they have to honour our contracts and there are about half a dozen of us who still have the insurance package, Callum was one of them.'

'Do you know how much the policy is worth?' Layla had stopped writing and stared at George King.

'Yes, a nice fat one hundred grand! Now that would be motive enough for anyone. My old lady often says it would be worth the risk of doing me in.'

Paul and Layla thanked George King and hurried back to the car. 'Wow!' Layla sank into the car seat and closed the door quickly. 'Now there's a nice motive for murder.'

'Absolutely. Ring Blacketts will you and ask to speak to Edward Smith. If he can back King up about the argument, I think we can cross him off our list of suspects – and move Amy Cooper to the top.' Paul's voice was laced with excitement as he switched on the engine and steered towards New Middridge police station.

EIGHTEEN
WEDNESDAY 14TH DECEMBER

DC Paul Roper almost ran into Samantha's office, face beaming and clearly bursting with news – good news she hoped.

'I don't think George King had anything to do with Cooper's death but he did suggest a motive. Apparently Amy Cooper is due a payout from Blacketts of £100,000, a cracking motive, eh, boss? An insurance policy was part of her husband's contract; if he dies while still employed there, she gets the money!'

Samantha could have kissed her DC but refrained from doing so, although her smile matched his. 'Did you check the altercation between King and Cooper?' She wasn't one for chicken counting.

'Yes, boss. It proved to be nothing but a misunderstanding over a syndicate payment, we spoke to another employee at Blacketts and he confirmed it.'

'Right. Get the team together and we'll decide where to go from here.'

DI Freeman stood in front of the whiteboard as her team squeezed into the small office. She rubbed George King's name from the top, rewrote it at the bottom, then moved Amy Cooper into poll position. 'DC Roper, would you like to tell us about your discovery?' Listening to him describing the interview with George King, Sam thought he looked so young and enthusiastic and was maybe bigging up his role a little. Layla looked puzzled at one or two things he said and flipped her notebook from page to page. She wouldn't say anything to embarrass him, Layla was in love with her colleague – and as Sam was pleased with the outcome she didn't interrupt or ask for clarification.

After ten minutes, which could have been five, Paul sat down and Sam asked for any questions or comments.

'Have we enough to interview Amy Cooper under caution?' Tom Wilson asked.

'Probably, but there's certainly enough for a search warrant for the Coopers' home. If we can get the CSI team in today to search for any blood, then we may find our locus. Amy's not going anywhere and I'll be interested to see her reaction to the search. Okay, folks – Layla, can you arrange the CSI, Paul the warrant? Even if it takes until tonight I want to get it done today – this feels like our first breakthrough and hell do we need one!'

The team dispersed to move the investigation on, more upbeat than they'd been in days but it took four frustrating hours to get everything in place. Sam was just delighted they would get the job done that day and she and Jenny set off with the warrant to Amy Cooper's house.

Cypress Close was quiet. Curtains were closed against the cold dark evening and flickering lights cast shadows from television sets. For a moment, Sam wished she was at home with Ravi, curled up on the sofa with one of his delicious meals on her knee. Yet the excitement was building inside her – adrenaline giving her energy a much-needed boost – if they could find traces of blood they would have their crime scene and the case would be on its way to being cut and dried.

The CSI team were a few minutes behind the detectives but Sam didn't want to wait, she'd go in with the warrant and prepare Amy for what was to come.

Amy blinked rapidly when she opened the door, peering into the damp gloomy evening as if she couldn't see the women on her doorstep. Sam thought maybe she'd been asleep but she stood back to allow the detectives inside and closed the door quickly to keep out the cold.

'Amy, we have a warrant to search your home.' Jenny passed her the document. 'A CSI team will be here shortly and we'd appreciate it if you could remain in the lounge while they complete their task.'

Amy made no move to read the warrant. 'Do I need a solicitor or someone?'

'Yes, that's your right and we'll be happy to wait if you wish to call one.' Sam spoke quietly and smiled – *innocent until proven guilty,* she thought. Amy appeared to think better about a solicitor and asked if she could call Beth instead.

'Certainly. It's a good idea to have someone here with you.'

Amy made the call at the same time the CSI team arrived. Once suited and booted they started in the kitchen. Amy went into the lounge with Jenny and Sam.

'What are they going to do? You've already searched Cal's things.' Amy spoke softly, groggily. Sam wondered if she was taking medication and was unsure of the wisdom in telling Amy they suspected her home could be the crime scene.

'This is a more detailed search. They're looking for things which might not be seen with the naked eye.'

'You mean blood? Tell me the truth, please.'

'Yes. I'm sorry, Amy, but if you had nothing to do with Callum's death then there's nothing to worry about.'

'They won't find anything.'

'Good, let's hope they don't.'

Beth came thundering through the door and went straight to her sister. 'Are you okay, Amy?'

'Yes, I just needed some company.'

'Is this really necessary?' A red-faced Beth swivelled to face Sam who found it hard to tell if the woman was angry or nervous.

'I'm afraid so. Your sister tells me we'll find nothing incriminating and if that's the case we'll leave you in peace. We have to do this, it's all part of the elimination process.'

Beth sat beside her sister, arms folded, face grim.

It's going to be a long evening, Sam thought.

NINETEEN
THURSDAY 15TH DECEMBER

The search of Amy Cooper's house lasted almost three hours and revealed no traces of blood or a possible murder weapon. Beth almost crowed at them with a lengthy tirade about wasting police time and harassing the innocent when they should be out looking for Callum's killer, and Sam and Jenny left for home feeling weary and frustrated.

Arriving home that evening, Sam was beyond hungry. Ravi made hot chocolate and they nibbled on shortbread before going to bed. With a brain refusing to shut down, Sam wondered where to go next. Eventually, Ravi pulled her to him and ensured she was tired enough to sleep.

At 7am Samantha was woken by her telephone ringing and the pathologist's name lit up her screen.

'Hi, Rick, you're an early bird. I hope you've caught a nice juicy worm to cheer me up.' Sam heard a muffled chuckle as he answered:

'I'm not sure, but I have something which will certainly surprise you. Come over to the morgue, I want to see your face when you hear this.'

'On my way.' Samantha's curiosity was aroused, she dressed

hurriedly and then rang Jenny, asking her to meet her at the morgue.

'I feel used!' Ravi complained as she grabbed a slice of toast and headed for the door. Samantha winked at him and left.

Jenny was waiting outside for her, and Sam shuddered as they entered the morgue. There was little time for speculation between the detectives and they'd come up with no reason why Rick should wish to see them so early, but they were about to find out.

The pathologist was waiting for them with an enigmatic expression which puzzled Samantha even more. Callum Cooper's body lay in the middle of the room, Rick stood beside it holding a clipboard. His grin was mischievous as he hesitated, increasing Sam's impatience. 'Well, what is it?'

'Cooper's medical records arrived from his GP this morning.' He paused and looked at the two detectives.

'And...' Sam asked.

'It appears his doctor wasn't treating him for any of the conditions he suffered from. There's no regular prescription for the medication I'd expect to be present in the body, so I chased up the toxicology report.' Rick paused for effect, his eyes darting from Sam to Jen. 'As I anticipated, theophylline was in evidence – a bronchodilator to ease breathing, and bisoprolol – a beta blocker for hardening of the arteries. Yet Cooper's medical records show neither had been prescribed.' Another well-timed pause allowed Sam and Jenny to process the information.

'Perhaps he changed his GP lately?' Samantha offered.

Rick smiled. 'My initial thought too, but the records are otherwise up to date – he received his Covid vaccinations from this surgery. But there is something else.'

'Come on, Rick, less of the am-drams, just spit it out!'

'The medical records show Callum Cooper to be five foot

ten inches tall. Our cadaver here is five foot six, seven at a stretch.'

'So, what are you saying?' Jenny too appeared impatient. Rick smiled again. 'That this man is most certainly *not* Callum Cooper.'

Samantha had reached the same conclusion moments before Rick verbalised it, but it seemed too incredible to be true. 'Are you absolutely sure? We had a positive ID from his wife and even I thought it was the same man from the picture she gave us, despite the swelling and facial injuries.'

'I'm certain. Either Mrs Cooper was confused with the stress and grief of the occasion and only *thought* this was her husband, or she's lying to you. Fortunately, it's your job to decide which, not mine.' With a flourish, Rick covered the now unidentified body with the sheet, folded his arms and tilted his head to one side.

'You're enjoying this, aren't you?' Sam chided.

'Only a little.'

Jenny sighed. 'So, we're back to square one – we again have an unidentified murder victim and no leads. We'd better go and inform Amy Cooper.'

'Yes, and I'm curious to know what she'll say. Thanks, Rick. As this man's been dead over a week now and we've no idea who he is, it looks like it could be down to dental records. Can I leave it with you?'

'Send me a list of possibles and I'll do my best – have a good day, detectives!'

TWENTY
THURSDAY 15TH DECEMBER

'You've got to be kidding!' Paul Roper slapped his hand on the desk. Samantha glared at him, her face answering his question. Layla's mouth dropped open as they all tried to process this new information. 'So I can cancel my visit to Cooper's mother?'

Sam nodded. 'Rick's convinced it's not Callum Cooper, so it appears we're back where we started – who is our murder victim? Jenny will fill you in on the details and you can get back to playing on HOLMES – change all the details already logged and start again. Sorry, Paul!'

DC Kim Thatcher listened to the conversation and watched Samantha with sympathy as she left the room to update the DCI about their latest setback. Sam's usual light steps were decidedly slower and heavier than usual.

Like Paul, a self-confessed computer geek, Kim was in awe of the HOLMES system and had been fascinated to learn about it at Hendon. It was a true invention of necessity and she marvelled at how it came about in 1985 due to mistakes made in the case of Peter Sutcliffe, the Yorkshire Ripper. It was incredible to think how everything had been recorded manually then, and records of interviews with over 250,000 people were handwritten on index cards. Kim remembered sniggering when learning how the volume of paperwork resulted in the floor of the incident room at Millgarth Nick in Leeds needing reinforcement due to the weight. But she was horrified to learn that Sutcliffe was interviewed nine times before finally being arrested. Thousands of man-hours were spent gathering evidence, but indications of Sutcliffe's guilt were still missed.

'However did they manage without HOLMES?' Kim asked Paul.

'*Home Office Large Major Enquiry System* is probably the best invention in policing history,' Paul replied. 'Every detail entered is cross-referenced by the computer in a fraction of the time the manual system took and it's more reliable too. Peter Sutcliffe killed thirteen women in five years. If we'd had this system in operation then, many of the victims would still be alive today, so you can see why I have such respect for it. Today we use HOLMES 2, the original's big brother, and presumably, advances will update it even more.'

'It is brilliant.'

Paul checked his watch and grimaced. 'I wonder how the boss is getting on with the DCI?'

DCI Aiden Kent called for his visitor to enter. He removed his glasses and sat back in his chair. 'Samantha. What can I do for you?'

'Our murder case, sir...'

'Ah, yes, Callum Cooper. Have you got a result?'

'Sadly no. I've just been to the morgue and it appears the body we thought to be Cooper isn't. The pathologist received Cooper's medical records this morning and they strongly suggest it's not him.' Kent's eyebrows shot up, almost meeting his hairline.

'What? Is he certain – didn't you get a positive ID from the wife?'

'Yes on both counts, sir. But Rick is confident the body can't possibly be Cooper and Amy Cooper must have been mistaken – she was very emotional – it's a confusing time for anyone. The body did have severe head injuries and had been in the ditch for a couple of days at least.'

DCI Kent drew in a deep breath, his nostrils flaring. 'So, you've wasted a whole week investigating the wrong victim? Bloody hell, Samantha, surely the woman would know her own husband?'

'Yes, sir, I thought so too. I'm going to see Mrs Cooper now. She needs to know the body isn't her husband and I need to know why she said it was.'

TWENTY-ONE
THURSDAY 15TH DECEMBER

DI Sam Freeman was fully motivated – it was turning into a busy week, and she now had three major investigations on the go. The fire and subsequent death of Ethan Baxter would prove to be the less complicated case for sure. Rick's news that their body wasn't Callum Cooper presented them with an unidentified cadaver in the morgue and Callum Cooper was still missing.

Before visiting Amy, Sam briefly returned to her office to task Layla and Paul with searching the Police National Computer for any misper who might fit the description of their victim. Her request had been anticipated and while Paul was updating HOLMES, Layla and Kim searched for possible matches to their cadaver.

Sam thanked them all. 'We know there are no local matches so spread the search area nationwide. We're looking for a forty-something man, five foot six, who suffers from heart problems and breathing difficulties. Ring me if a match turns up, and get any possible names to Rick so he can match dental records if they're available.'

Jenny was waiting for Sam, both of them eager to find

answers. 'Do you really think Amy thought the body was her husband?' she asked as they climbed into the car.

'I don't know. I keep thinking if it were Ravi, I'd recognise him, but the body was disfigured and had been frozen in a ditch for a couple of days – and viewing was through glass. It could be a case of seeing what you expect to see and I admit I thought it was Cooper from the photo she gave us.'

Pulling up outside the Coopers' home, Beth's little white van was again parked at the front. Sam wondered if she'd stayed the night with her sister. 'This is a first for me – telling someone the body they'd identified isn't their husband. I'll be interested to see her reaction; relief maybe?'

'We'll soon find out.' Jenny pressed the doorbell.

Once inside and with the atmosphere decidedly chilly, Sam broke the news they'd come to impart, there was no way to dress it up. 'We're now in possession of Callum's medical records and the toxicology report, and in light of this information, the pathologist is convinced the body you identified as your husband isn't him.'

'What! Of course it's him – we both saw him!' Beth was the first to react, Amy appeared to shrink back in the chair, wide-eyed and pale. Beth was fired up. 'You saw the photo – you thought it was Callum too. Why the hell would we say it was him if we didn't think it was?'

'I know, and sadly the man did look strikingly like Callum. I'm sorry, Amy, but this at least gives us hope that Callum is still alive.'

'Yes, it does, doesn't it?' Amy's expression was difficult to read, relief perhaps but Sam thought there was an element of anxiety too. 'So will you still keep looking for him?' she asked.

'Yes, the case will continue but clearly no longer as a murder investigation.'

Beth took over again. 'What do *you* think's happened to Callum if he isn't dead?'

'We'll be re-evaluating our evidence and returning to a missing person case. I don't want to speculate but if anything new has occurred to either of you which may help, please don't hold back.' Sam paused to allow the sisters time to think but as neither spoke she continued. 'We still have the CCTV from near Blacketts which gives us a last known sighting and our focus will return to trying to trace subsequent sightings. Unfortunately, we also have an unidentified body, so my team's time will be divided between cases.'

'Oh yeah! You put us through that ridiculous search last night and now because he's only missing and not dead, Callum's not important anymore!' Beth snapped.

Sam's reply was immediate and firm. 'Not at all. There's a good chance Callum's still alive – the man in the morgue has a family somewhere who'll be missing him, and yesterday we also discovered the body of a seventeen-year-old boy whose parents will probably never view Christmas as a celebration again!'

Beth looked suitably rebuked and as the detectives stood to leave, she at least had the grace to whisper 'Sorry' before opening the door for them.

Sam's parting words were addressed to her sister. 'We'll keep in touch, Amy.'

Jenny fastened her seat belt. 'Not what I was expecting.' She waited for her boss's comments which came after a moment's deliberation.

'Even though I didn't have expectations, I know what you mean. If it had been me, I'd have been delighted at the possibility that my husband could still be alive, but Amy barely raised a smile.'

'Could be shock. She's just got used to her husband being

dead and now he's back to missing, it's still a traumatic situation.'

'Hmm, but there's something *off* with Amy. She's a bundle of nerves and seems unsure how to react, what questions to ask, you know? Almost as if she's trying to get it right – say the right things. And Beth's a bit *full in your face* for my liking.' Sam was silent for a moment, mentally rerunning the sisters' reactions. 'The alternative is that Amy lied to us and knew it wasn't her husband – which opens up a whole new area of possibilities – why the hell would she lie?'

'The search for a lead will be even harder now we don't have a body. Perhaps Callum just left of his own accord or he's gone off on a bender. Let's hope he turns up soon, safe and well – that would be a good outcome for Christmas, eh, boss?'

'Don't remind me about Christmas! I haven't started any shopping. Ravi keeps hinting he's looking forward to a traditional Christmas lunch, which will have to be in the evening as I'm working, but the thought terrifies me. As a kid, I remember Mum getting stressed trying to make everything perfect. She even counted the sprouts – six per person – no one dared to take more. I vowed never to be put under such pressure. What are you planning, Jen?'

'I'm off Christmas Eve and Christmas Day – it'll be the whole family thing with my brother and his wife and kids all cooped up at Mum and Dad's. I'm dreading the hints that it's time I settle down and provide more grandchildren for them to spoil. I was thinking of offering to work on Christmas Day.'

'Oh no you don't! I'll be in on Christmas Day; you can cover from Boxing Day through to New Year when I'll be away. Ravi's been moaning about us never having time off together and as I worked last year, I'm due the holiday. Whatever happens, we'll have a better time than the Coopers or the Baxters.' Jen and Samantha lapsed into silence for the rest of the journey.

TWENTY-TWO
THURSDAY 15TH DECEMBER

Tim Dennison and his mother arrived at the station after lunch to make a formal statement which Samantha and Layla took, while Jenny and Paul interviewed a more reluctant Tyler Green, accompanied by his rather solemn mother.

Layla switched on the tape recorder and recited the names of all those present. Mrs Dennison had been advised to secure the service of a solicitor but had declined, confident Tim wouldn't be charged with any offence.

'Tim, I know you told us about the fire on Tuesday, but we need to go over the details again now you've had time to think about the incident and get over the shock. Have you spoken to Tyler since the fire?'

'No. Mum said I wasn't to, but I don't want to see him anyway.' The boy hung his head. Sam hoped his regret was genuine and this incident would change the course of his life – that he might become a more responsible adult rather than throwing his life away for a few passing thrills.

'I think that's very sensible of you. Now, we need you to go over exactly what happened on Tuesday – this is being taped so we'll have a record of everything you say.'

'Am I going to be in trouble?'

'I can't say for certain until we've finished our investigations. It's likely we'll refer your case to the Youth Offending Team and if some form of punishment is deemed necessary, it will be up to them to decide what it will be. They're not police officers and offer what we call early intervention to try and prevent youngsters moving on into criminal activities. Now back to Tuesday.' Samantha smiled encouragingly at the boy who started the sorry tale of exactly what had happened – his account much the same as the one he'd given after the event.

When Tim finished, he looked exhausted and Layla asked, 'Do you want a break now, Tim? I could get you and your mum a drink if you like?' The boy nodded so Layla switched off the recorder and left the room to arrange the drinks. Samantha followed, giving the two time to consider their situation – there were more difficult questions to come.

Twenty minutes later, Sam and Layla returned to the interview room. Tim and his mother pushed their empty coffee cups away and shuffled to get comfortable. When the recorder was running again, Sam continued.

'Tim, you've been really helpful so far and I can see how upsetting this is for you but I want to take you back to Wednesday 7th December. It's just over a week ago when we spoke to you, Tyler and Ethan about the fire at the warehouse, remember?'

Tim whispered, 'Yes,' and dropped his gaze to study the scratches on the table.

'You refused to answer questions then, which was your right, but I'd like to ask you about the incident again. Did you, Tyler and Ethan start the fire?'

Tim's mother gave him a nudge. Perhaps she'd been expecting the question and even discussed it beforehand with her son. Tim sat up. 'I was there with Ethan and Tyler but it was Ethan who started the fire, honest – I'm not just saying it was him 'cause he's dead and can't defend himself – both me and Tyler tried to stop him but he wouldn't listen. When we ran away, he said not to grass as we were as guilty as him.' The boy's eyes brimmed with tears and Sam nodded.

'Thank you, Tim. We'll be talking to Tyler about this incident too and I appreciate you telling me what happened.'

Mrs Dennison spoke up for her son. 'I'm not one to speak ill of the dead but Ethan was a bad influence on Tim and Tyler...'

'Thank you, but as I said we'll speak to Tyler for his account. You've done the right thing by admitting to being there, Tim; it can only help.'

After a few more questions, Samantha allowed Tim and his mother to go home, knowing Tyler Green was in the station so the boys would be unable to speak and decide on their stories. When Jenny and Paul finished their interview, they reported that the boy's account of Ethan's death matched Tim's. He admitted harassing the rough sleepers but denied physically attacking them and claimed only Ethan kicked them. They were satisfied he was telling the truth.

Sam and Layla entered the room to confront Tyler. If anything, Tyler Green looked even more nervous than Tim Dennison had. Having known he was to be formally interviewed about the nightclub fire in which Ethan Baxter had died, Sam hoped he didn't expect her to ask about the previous fire.

'Last week, Tyler, we interviewed you and your friends about a fire at a warehouse. I assume you remember?'

Tyler nodded then said, 'Yes,' when Layla pointed to the microphone.

'You refused to answer our questions on that occasion but I'd like to ask you again if you were there and had any part in starting the fire.' Sam's gaze remained on Tyler's face. The boy reddened. 'I was there but it was Ethan who started the fire. Tim and I told him not to, but he was stoned – thought it would be a laugh. Afterwards he told us to say *no comment* to any questions so you wouldn't know we were there. I'm sorry but I didn't want to be a grass, Ethan was my friend...' Tyler tried to blink back the tears which filled his eyes. Samantha thought he suddenly looked very young.

Before leaving for the day, Samantha gathered her team for a briefing, first addressing Kim and Tom, the two newest DCs on her team. 'Any luck with a match for our body?'

'Only two possibles and neither are local.' DC Kim Thatcher spoke up. 'One is from Dorset, the other Bristol but both are in the general age range and the time frame could fit.'

'Good work, Kim. Can you call the families and ask for more details – and if there's the slightest chance ask if we can have something with their DNA on to test or the name of a dentist to check their records? Then request local officers to collect it ASAP.'

Kim nodded eagerly; her eyes wide. It was a responsibility Sam felt she could handle with the necessary sensitivity. After going over a few more points, they dispersed to finish their tasks for the day. Although it was getting late, Kim offered to make the calls before she left in the hope they'd have new leads to chase up the following day.

TWENTY-THREE
THURSDAY 15TH DECEMBER

Ravi was preparing dinner when Sam arrived home. Frequently, she thanked her lucky stars for having a partner who enjoyed cooking – a task she hated and never found the time nor the inclination to attempt.

'Tandoori chicken, okay?' Ravi bent down to kiss the top of Sam's head, pepper mill in his hand.

'Mmm, smells delicious.' Sam realised just how hungry she was.

Ten minutes later the couple were seated in their lounge, eating Ravi's amazing tandoori chicken. With his mouth full, Ravi asked, 'So did you arrest the *black widow* today then?'

'Ah, no. The plot twists yet again. Rick informed me that the body in the morgue is *not* Callum Cooper.'

Ravi swallowed and wiped his lips. 'But you got a positive ID from the wife, didn't you?'

'We did and even I thought it was him after comparing the body to the photograph, but unless he'd shrunk a few inches and developed several health problems, it isn't our man.' Sam stuffed another forkful of tandoori into her mouth. 'This is really good!'

'So, you now have a misper and an unidentified body – two families who'll have a bloody rotten Christmas.'

'More than two if you count the Baxters and his mates. We interviewed them today and it's looking almost certain that Ethan Baxter was the ringleader. I think the others were afraid of him but didn't want to lose face. Peer pressure's a pig.'

'So, any ideas who your cadaver is?'

'Nope – not one. I left Kim making phone calls to a couple of families who've reported missing men of a similar age. Wretched job, having to tell them we have a body which may or may not be their loved one – *and by the way, can you let me have his toothbrush or a comb*?'

'Yeah, if it is their relative it'll be devastating, if not then they go through the agony of waiting to see if he's dead or still missing.'

'Both mispers are from a distance, making it unlikely to be our man. Who would be travelling to New Middridge in this awful weather?'

'I can't say I envy you all these bodies. Let's hope you find out who your John Doe is before Christmas so we can have some time together. You have booked New Year off, haven't you?' Ravi squinted at Sam, clearly not trusting her.

'I can't see anything stopping me from taking it. Surely there won't be any more major incidents before Christmas.'

'Good, so how would you feel about a few days at my parents' house?'

Sam dropped her fork. 'What? Are you serious?'

'Absolutely. It's time you got to know them a little better and they've invited us – my brother and his family will be there too. It's a good chance to meet the clan.'

Sam retrieved her fork, yet her appetite was suddenly absent. 'But I thought you didn't want your parents dropping hints about weddings and babies and stuff. If your brother's there and his children, they're bound to have another go at you.'

'Would that be so bad, Sam?' Ravi's voice was low, his head tilted to one side, and Sam thought he looked almost nervous, yet devastatingly attractive.

'Ravi! I can't believe we're having this conversation. You're the one who gets irritated when they drop hints, saying they should mind their own business. What's this all about, a change of heart?'

'I've been thinking lately, maybe we should put our relationship on more solid ground – think of the future, you know?'

'No. I don't know. Are you sounding me out about marriage and a family?'

'Almost.' Ravi's dark eyes sparkled, crinkling at the corners as he smiled. 'I'm asking you to marry me.'

'But...' Sam was speechless. They'd decided long ago that they didn't need marriage – they were committed to each other and happy as they were. Could Ravi really have changed his mind? And had she? As the thoughts swam around her mind, Ravi was suddenly kneeling before her.

'Samantha Freeman, will you do me the honour of becoming my wife?'

'Yes, yes, yes!' Sam threw her arms around his neck. The realisation that this was what she wanted too, almost made her light-headed. 'Whatever's prompted your change of mind?'

'Why ask such difficult questions, Sam? I can't honestly answer. I love you and I know we've always said we're happy as we are, but I want more – I want you and a family – a boy and a girl who'll look just like you...' Ravi grinned.

'Hey, slow down. Let me get used to the marriage bit before we get around to children! So where's the ring?' She pretended to look hurt.

'I wouldn't dare make such a choice without you. I'd only get it wrong. The next day off we have together we're going ring shopping, my Christmas present to you!'

Samantha threw her arms around him and squeezed as tightly as she could. He was right about the ring, she wanted to choose it herself. 'Well, this is certainly a surprise – not only because you asked me, but that I've said yes – I do love you, Ravi Patel!'

PART 2

THIRTEEN DAYS EARLIER

TWENTY-FOUR
FRIDAY 2ND DECEMBER

Callum Cooper turned up his collar and dragged his woollen hat over his ears against the biting wind. The rain was blowing almost horizontally but at least it kept away the forecasted snow. Cal was in a reflective mood, probably prompted by what he needed to do when he arrived home. His life path bore little resemblance to the one he'd anticipated in his youth. At forty-five he felt in danger of becoming a middle-aged bore without a single achievement of which to be proud. He'd often asked himself if it was his own fault – if his life choices had been made without enough forethought, his aspirations too low, and he knew the answer was a resounding yes.

Callum's biggest mistake by far was marrying Amy. They'd both been young, stifled at home by parents who wanted to dictate their lives, and their unrealistic concept of marriage seemed the ideal solution, a way to escape life's drudgery. True, sex had played a part in their desire to marry, lust mistaken for love. Amy was slim, attractive and willing. Callum was hormone led, and the thought of having Amy whenever he liked without having to use the back seat of his dad's car was a great temptation.

Both sets of parents objected to them seeing so much of each other which only made the young couple more determined. Realising they'd never get their parents' blessing to marry, Callum came up with a plan to get their families onside.

'Tell your mum and dad you're pregnant!'

'What? Dad'll kill me and then you, a dozen times over!'

'He can only kill me once, stupid. But listen – if they think you're pregnant they'll *want* us to get married. We'll be a disgrace to our families and they'll go out of their way to get us to the altar.' Callum snorted. 'Huh, they'll even pay for it all, it'll be fantastic!'

'But what happens when they discover I'm not having a baby?'

'It'll be too late then, won't it? Don't you want us to get married, Amy?' He ran his hand along her thigh and under her skirt. Amy giggled and pushed him away. 'Yeah, I want us to get married, we'll make a lovely little home for ourselves and – heavenly – we'll finally escape from our parents!'

Callum's plans were running away with him. 'Hell, maybe if everyone thinks you're pregnant we'll get a council house.' Swinging her down from the wall where they sat, he pulled her along by the hand. 'Come on; there's no time like the present!'

'What! We can't do it now. We should think about it some more, make plans...' But Callum was on a roll and before Amy could protest further, he'd dragged her home where the lie took root. As Amy predicted, her dad was furious, but with the younger, stronger Callum to contend with he wasn't going to lash out at his daughter, even though he probably wanted to beat her black and blue. A verbal lashing sufficed for the time being – it was one thing to bully your daughter but not a prospective son-in-law.

In many ways, the invention of a baby proved effective. There was shouting and recriminations from both sets of parents but eventually, it was agreed that the best way to avoid the inevitable shame and gossip was for the young couple to marry as soon as possible. Even the council fell into line and offered a small two-bedroomed terraced house. No one doubted Amy's pregnancy, and the problems they'd anticipated, like her mother wanting to take her to the doctor, didn't materialise. Amy's disappointed mother told her harshly that if she was old enough to get herself into such a predicament, she could damn well deal with it herself.

For Callum the only disquieting part of his plan was when Amy begged for her younger sister, Beth, to move in with them. Her continual nagging annoyed him, but Callum stood his ground. Beth was a couple of years younger than Amy and okay, but he wanted Amy to himself and couldn't understand her stupid idea. But Amy persisted.

'You don't know what it's like at home. I need to look out for Beth – she'll struggle without me.'

'Don't be daft, she's got your mum to look after her – this is our time, I don't want your kid sister hanging around, it won't be any fun.' He squeezed her bottom and grinned. Cal could be as stubborn as Amy, more so, and eventually she stopped asking. And so, at nineteen years old, the couple were married and moved into their first home together.

Callum's thoughts drifted back to those days. The wedded bliss didn't last long. Initially, he'd thought their combined wages would give them enough disposable income to enjoy life – he was an apprentice joiner and she worked as an office junior in an accountancy firm, but he hadn't factored in the bills they'd have to pay and how expensive it was to feed and clothe themselves. Amy didn't help by going all sensible on him and insisting they save for a deposit on their own house. It was as if she'd suddenly turned into his mother – even the sex was different – he missed the excitement of their illicit fumbles and Amy seemed more drawn to watching telly than satisfying his needs.

Soon after the wedding, they told their families Amy had miscarried the baby, and it wasn't long before Callum regretted his *clever* idea – and his marriage. He experienced the awful sensation of having exchanged one prison for another. As if to taunt them, they discovered in time that they couldn't have children, which was rather a slap in the face, particularly for Amy. Maybe life would have been different...

But it was twenty-six years later and until recently Callum thought things would never change. The marriage was dead and if he didn't get out soon, he felt he'd be dead too – maybe even by his own hand. Perhaps, he thought, Amy would also be glad to see the end of their union. Surely, she couldn't be happy in the daily grind they endured either, there must be more to life than simply existing day to day. Life shouldn't be so predictable; cold cuts and fry-up on Monday, sausage and mash on Tuesday, chicken and chips...

Fairy lights twinkled in the windows of the houses he passed, an iridescent haze through the piercing rain. A scattering of Christmas trees lit up windows – displayed earlier each year as people yearned for something to celebrate, an excuse to party and forget the drudgery of their little lives.

Callum purposely changed the downward focus of his reflections and a smile spread across his face. Yes, he did have *options* – a delightful thought which made him shudder with possibility – perhaps there could still be some excitement left for him to enjoy before it was too late. Emotions he thought he'd never experience again now seared his body – desires Callum had pushed to the back of his mind, like covering an old broken vehicle with a dirty tarpaulin. But the cover was off and new life was in sight – with a new, unexpected love which had taken him completely by surprise. The excitement of clandestine meetings gave Callum a new purpose and he wanted to grab the opportunity for happiness before it was too late.

Callum had secured a rental flat, a love nest, which would be available from Tuesday and he could hardly wait. He'd made bold promises – one of which was to tell Amy he was leaving her – and he would tell her tonight.

TWENTY-FIVE
FRIDAY 2ND DECEMBER

Amy heard Callum close the front door and drop his keys onto the console table. The same routine every night. *Pointless* was halfway through on the telly, she'd pause it to dish up tea then they'd sit, meals on lap trays, and watch the end together.

The first full day of Amy's newly curbed life had passed in a blur of tears and feeling sorry for herself. But she intentionally kept the news of her diagnosis from Callum, unsure why she didn't want him to know. It wasn't some unselfish desire to protect him but more because it was her secret and hers alone. She'd tell him if and when she was ready. The same went for Beth, yet keeping the awful news from her sister was perhaps to protect Beth's feelings. Amy had much to process and decisions couldn't be rushed into in a blur of jumbled emotions. By mid-afternoon Amy'd had enough of self-pity, pulled herself together and started the evening meal. *Que sera, sera.*

'Hi.' Callum glanced in her direction before climbing the stairs to wash and change. It would take him four minutes to return, while Amy served their meal. Her actions were robotic, if suddenly struck blind, she'd still perform the chores which had become so familiar over the last twenty-six years. Checking the air fryer (which she'd asked Callum to buy her for their silver wedding anniversary), everything was perfectly cooked. Putting the plates to warm, Amy poured two glasses of water and served the food – it was Friday – fish and chips. By the time she'd carried it through to the lounge, Callum was coming down the stairs.

They watched her favourite quiz show in silence. With nothing inspiring to talk about, neither made the effort at conversation. Callum's work at Blacketts didn't interest Amy and as the most exciting part of her day had been changing the bedding, they remained silent, Alexander Armstrong and Richard Osman providing the only background noise.

After their meal and the news headlines, Callum coughed to get her attention. Pulling his shoulders back and taking a deep breath, he said, 'We need to talk.'

'Talk?' Amy raised an eyebrow as if she'd never heard the word. 'What about?'

Callum's right eye twitched, a sign Amy knew meant he was nervous. 'Us. Things can't go on like this much longer. I've had enough.' His following mute stare made it clear he was waiting for a response but Amy wasn't going to oblige and simply nodded. Callum continued. 'I've decided to leave. I'll sort my things out this weekend and be gone by Sunday evening.'

'Where will you go?' Amy felt surprisingly calm and was shocked to identify a tiny sprig of excitement blossoming in her stomach. *Was something finally going to happen in her life? But why now, after all these wasted years, when it's too late for me?*

'I'll move into a rented flat until we can sort something out, it's available from Tuesday.'

'Oh, so you've been planning this? Cal, why's it taken so long to realise you don't want me anymore?' Amy was remarkably cool and held her husband's gaze steadily while his eye twitched more noticeably.

'Does it matter?' he stuttered.

'I suppose not.'

'You don't seem surprised.'

'Because I'm not. One of us should have left years ago. We've wasted our lives together but isn't it too late to make changes now?' Amy peered into her husband's face and watched the colour rise from his neck. She didn't think she had the energy for this conversation. 'Have you found someone else?'

'That's irrelevant. Our marriage is over so we can discuss it like adults or go the expensive route through solicitors, it's up to you.'

'Oh, Cal! Did you think I'd fight you on this? I'm quite relieved one of us is finally putting an end to this mockery of a marriage – and I'm glad it's you – I don't think I have the strength.'

'That's the trouble, you have no life in you at all. We never go out, there's no romance, no spontaneity in our relationship.'

Amy stifled a laugh.

'Damn you, Amy. Are you laughing at me?'

'Sorry, but *romance,* Cal? There's never been romance in our marriage, not since we were teenagers. And if you're trying to provoke an argument, don't, I can't be bothered. I'll give you a divorce if you're sure it's what you want and let's be grown up about it, eh? If there is someone else it's okay by me, I passed the jealous stage years ago and you can stay here until your flat's ready. I don't want to play the blame game – it is what it is.'

Callum appeared deflated. He stood still for a full minute, staring at Amy as if he'd never seen her before. 'Fine,' he eventually said. 'I'll move my things into the spare room.' He walked quietly up the stairs. Amy listened until she heard their bedroom door close, sighed heavily and then switched the telly back on to see if *The One Show* had started.

He doesn't need to know. No one needs to know. It's for the best.

A silent tear trickled down her cheek.

TWENTY-SIX
SATURDAY 3RD DECEMBER

Callum Cooper was awake early on Saturday morning. The lumpy spare bed and the previous evening's conversation with his wife conspired to keep him awake most of the night. After escaping from the uneasy discussion, the next hour was spent moving his things from the bedroom he'd shared with Amy into the little back room. Most of his clothes he folded into suitcases, hanging up only the ones he would need over the weekend.

Amy's suggestion of him staying in their home until the flat was ready completely threw him. Now he'd finally scraped up the courage to tell her he wanted a divorce, he'd expected to leave and not see her again, contact through solicitors only. He'd been prepared to sleep in the car over the weekend or maybe ask a mate to put him up until Tuesday, expecting Amy to throw him out. Staying made life easier although it seemed almost too civilised, as did Amy's reaction.

Callum had anticipated a blazing row with recriminations and insults from them both – a right ding-dong – isn't that how marriages ended? Amy's cool acceptance of the end of their union was astounding, could she really welcome it as much as he did?

After moving into the spare bedroom, Callum had made a phone call to say he'd fulfilled his promise. The new love of his life wasn't too happy when he explained he was staying in the marital home, she'd assumed he'd be somewhere they could meet up and be together.

'We'll have to take things slowly and see what happens,' he cautioned, and could almost hear her pouting on the other end of the phone. Callum spoke in whispers, although he was sure Amy wouldn't be eavesdropping at the other side of the door – she was plainly disinterested in his future plans, which left him with a bizarre feeling of being a step removed from reality. Callum assumed he was taking charge of the situation but now he was unsure.

How would Amy be this morning, he wondered as he heard her in the kitchen downstairs. Would she make his breakfast as usual, or would he now be expected to fend for himself? This was not what Callum had anticipated at all.

Amy hadn't slept well either, which wasn't unusual for her. The dark hours were spent tossing and turning and now she was up, feeling no malice, simply a sense of calm relief and a curiosity to learn what the day would hold.

After Callum had said his piece the previous night and went to bed, she'd rung her sister to tell her of the evening's events. Beth offered to come round but Amy didn't need comforting, she was unsure what she needed or wanted.

'Come tomorrow. I don't know what Callum will be doing but I don't think he'll hang around here all day.'

Tentatively, Beth asked, 'Is there someone else?'

'Oh undoubtedly.'

'Hell, Amy! How can you be so calm? Did he say who she is?' Beth was almost whispering and Amy wondered if Dave was within hearing distance.

'No and I'm not particularly interested.'

'But you must be curious?'

'Strangely, no.'

Their brief conversation would continue when Beth came in person. She'd want to know every detail and then offer her opinion whether it was asked for or not.

Callum appeared in the kitchen. Amy looked up, her face betraying nothing. 'There's a fresh pot of tea, I'll leave you to get whatever you want to eat.'

Amy watched as Callum ran his fingers through his hair and drew in a deep breath. He put two slices of bread in the toaster and poured a mug of tea. When the toast popped up, he slathered it with butter and took his breakfast back upstairs without a word. Amy turned and carried her tea and toast into the lounge where she settled down on the sofa and switched on breakfast television.

TWENTY-SEVEN
SATURDAY 3RD DECEMBER

As Amy cleared the breakfast pots, Callum reappeared downstairs holding his mug and a plate, clearly unsure what to do with them.

'I'll take them,' Amy said, not knowing whether to smile or scowl as Callum allowed her to take the items.

'Thank you. I'm off out now.' He didn't say where he was going or when he'd be back, and Amy didn't ask – their relationship was no longer one of man and wife – they owed each other nothing.

Ten minutes later Beth rang the doorbell and walked in, her eyes scanning the room. 'Are you alone?' she asked. Amy dried her hands and hugged her sister.

'Yes, it's okay, he's not here.' She made tea which she didn't want and they sat together on the sofa in the lounge. Beth pulled a throw around their knees and looked into Amy's pale face. 'Tell me again what happened?'

'There's not much to tell. Callum arrived home from work and said he'd had enough and he was leaving. I think he expected a row or for me to beg and plead for him to stay – he seemed a tad disappointed.'

Beth chewed on her lip, eyes wide as she listened. 'Weren't you surprised, had you seen this coming?'

Amy shrugged. 'I think I've been expecting it for years; the only surprise is that he's taken so long to make the decision.'

'And, umm... the other woman, what did he say about her?'

'He didn't actually admit there was another woman but he didn't deny it either. To be honest, all I feel is a huge sense of relief. I've probably wanted out of this marriage as much as Callum but you know me, I couldn't make the effort to do it myself.'

'So has he left for good?'

'Oh, no. He's renting a flat which will be ready on Tuesday, so I told him he could stay until then. He's moved into the spare room.'

'Bloody hell, Amy, you're a daft sod! You're being far too nice about it, you should kick him out – not be so soft – if he's got someone else he should go to her! You always were the sensible one, the peacemaker. Have you no fire in your belly?'

'Huh, you always had enough fire for both of us. I'm tired, Beth, tired of this life, such as it is. Callum and I have nothing solid enough to hold us together, you should know how that feels.' For a moment Amy considered telling her sister about the brain tumour but decided against it, wanting to be sure it was the right thing to do. Beth nodded. 'How did we both end up with dysfunctional marriages? When we were kids, we dreamed about escaping and I suppose marriage seemed the only way out for girls like us. Maybe Dad was right when he said we didn't have a brain cell between us.'

Amy turned sharply on her sister. 'Don't say that, it's not true! You could have gone places if you'd been allowed to stay on at school, and we hardly had a great role model, did we?' Her eyes welled with tears as she reached for Beth's hand and Amy was suddenly back in her childhood home, in her bedroom which had been both her refuge and her prison.

Amy squeezed her eyes shut and pressed her hands over her ears, but the sound of shouting and her mother's screaming couldn't be blocked out. An awful fear gripped her, restricting her breathing and reminding her what a coward she was. Then she heard Beth shriek and Amy could almost feel her sister's pain. Dad must have hit her again. Why couldn't Beth keep quiet like Amy did? Why did she always have to antagonise their father? She knew it wouldn't end well, for herself or their mother.

Amy sniffed back the tears, her body trembling when she heard footsteps on the stairs, too fast for anyone other than her sister, and then Beth was banging on her bedroom door. Quickly, Amy let her in and closed the door as their dad's shadow turned on the landing in lumbering pursuit. Together the girls dragged a chest of drawers behind the door just as the handle turned.

Dad was shouting obscenities and banging on the door. 'I'll bloody kill you when I get hold of you!'

Amy thought the door was going to splinter, Dad was shouldering it forcefully, but the girls pushed against the drawers with all the strength they could summon, praying they'd manage to keep him out. They could hear Mum pleading for him to stop, to leave them alone but the pounding continued.

'I... I think he really will kill me this time. Can I stay in your room tonight?' Beth's ten-year-old body trembled. Amy enfolded her little sister in a hug. 'Shh, of course you can.' They sat on the floor adding their combined weight to the chest of drawers until the storm subsided and their dad gave the door one final kick before going downstairs.

The sisters cried before they slept, squashed together in the single bed, drawing comfort from each other.

It was one of many similar memories Amy could not forget, always there even though the girls rarely discussed their childhood and the violence they suffered. Beth, the younger and more spirited sister, seemed to antagonise their father without effort, suffering injuries no child should bear but hiding them as if the shame was her own. Amy remembered it all with a degree of ignominy. As the elder sister she should have looked after Beth – stopped their father's beatings – but Amy was a coward, it was easier to hide away in her bedroom. It wasn't that she didn't receive occasional beatings too, but she'd learned to keep her mouth shut, to avoid confrontation. Beth was too feisty and outspoken – their mother always said her lip would be the death of her.

I should have protected Beth. She was my little sister and I should have stopped him. The guilt hung over Amy now, every bit as much as it did then.

Long after Beth left and the light outside faded as dusk approached, Amy took a mug of coffee, wrapped up in her warmest coat and went into the tiny back garden to watch the day disappear. Sitting with her hands cradling the mug, her thoughts on the difficult day she'd endured and the painful memories which proved impossible to shrug off, Amy was treated to an unexpected delight as the sky was suddenly filled with a murmuration of starlings. It was a phenomenon she'd seen only once before and she watched transfixed as the birds swooped and dived, spontaneous yet as if choreographed. Thousands of wings fluttered to unheard music and the flock moved as one, each confident of their place in the group. It amazed Amy how they could fly so close together without crashing into one another – how unlike people who clashed and knocked into each other constantly, causing grief and pain to those around them.

TWENTY-EIGHT
SUNDAY 4TH DECEMBER

Callum had stayed away for most of Saturday. When he finally arrived home in the early evening he poked his head around the lounge door, said a quick 'Hi' and ran straight upstairs. Uninterested in her husband's activities, Amy didn't ask where he'd been. Whether he'd eaten crossed her mind until she reminded herself he was no longer her responsibility – Cal had made his choice and she no longer cared.

Sunday looked as if it would follow much the same pattern, an uneasy breakfast-time when the couple tiptoed around each other, until soon Amy was alone again in the house. After hearing the car pull away, she climbed the stairs and opened the spare bedroom door intending just to look, to see if Callum had started packing. He had. Two suitcases lay on the floor at the far side of the bed with clothes neatly folded inside. In spite of her determination to be strong the sight made Amy's breath catch in her throat and she wondered where he was going and when. They'd have to communicate at some point – would he be approaching a solicitor – should she? The last thing Amy wanted to do was go through protracted divorce proceedings, but to gain her freedom it seemed unavoidable.

Freedom. What would she do with it? What would it be like, but more pertinent, how long would it last? Amy had never felt entirely free – as a child at home there was always her father taking control, ordering her life, making her decisions; and then there was Callum. He didn't treat her badly as her father had but she still felt very much like she was not her own person, whoever that might be. Did she want to be alone or was it too late to do anything with her life – yes, it probably was. If Callum hadn't said he wanted out of their marriage, Amy wouldn't have made the effort to do anything herself.

Sitting on the spare bed, Amy tried to determine her feelings. Her marriage was over and Callum was leaving, probably for another woman, but there was nothing inside her other than a sadness at lost opportunities. If he'd died rather than left her, would she be grief-stricken? No, probably not.

Idly picking up one of Callum's shirts from the bed, Amy smelt perfume – something familiar which she couldn't quite place – not a fragrance she wore, and not aftershave, it was a scent which lasted, sweet and floral. So, there was another woman. A strange sorrow engulfed Amy, who held the shirt to her face, a sadness for what might have been. But it would soon be all over.

The phone's ring disturbed Amy's thoughts and she ran downstairs to answer it, pleased to hear Beth's voice.

'Hi, it's me. How are you today?'

'Oh, about the same. Callum's out again so if you want to come round you can help me feel sorry for myself.'

'You never succumb to such feelings! Sorry but I can't come today. Dave's messing with the van so I'm stuck in with him – lucky old me.'

'Oh well, have fun. I should really motivate myself to do something, make plans, I don't know. I suppose Christmas will be different this year, eh?'

'We can think about Christmas later. It's a good job we've no kids to consider, isn't it?'

No kids to consider!

'Perhaps things might have been different if we'd had children. You chose not to, but Callum and I didn't.'

Beth softened her tone. 'Well, seeing how things have turned out it's probably for the best.'

'Yeah, well – you go and enjoy your day, I'll probably have a lazy one so I'll be here if you change your plans.'

Amy was inexplicably upset. Beth appeared to view being childless as a positive whereas Amy had only ever looked upon her childless state as a negative, a sadness she'd never quite come to terms with. When they first married, Amy and Callum had a master plan. They'd enjoy five years of being together, save like mad for a house, and then think about children – two would be perfect. With the naivety of youth, they assumed the future was in their hands but the reality had arrived like a slap in the face. Amy managed to conceive but couldn't carry a baby to full term.

After the fourth miscarriage, the doctor told her she was suffering from antiphospholipid syndrome, a long name for a blood-clotting disorder. Amy cried for days while Callum appeared to shrug it off; perhaps he should have shrugged her off then as well – instead, they stayed together all these years and Amy couldn't think of a good reason why, and nor, she assumed, could Callum.

Beth and Dave *chose* not to have children. Sadly, Amy's sister married a man with the same attitude towards women as their father, a narcissistic misogynist. Beth accepted any beatings Dave dished out as normal, which her childhood experiences had endorsed. But bringing children into such a volatile marriage was unthinkable – Dave certainly wasn't the paternal kind.

Amy put the kettle on, without the energy or inclination to do anything else, and disappointed that Beth wasn't coming around to keep her company. Something was niggling at the back of Amy's mind, the perfume on Callum's shirt had unsettled her yet she couldn't think why – it wasn't jealousy for sure.

Before her coffee was drunk, Amy was asleep on the sofa, breakfast television playing to itself in the corner of the lounge.

Waking up an hour later, Amy shivered. Although tempted to pull a throw over her and go back to sleep, she didn't. Picking up the phone she tapped in Beth's number – wanting to hear a friendly voice. She'd ask her advice about a solicitor, a pretext for the call – Beth had a recently divorced neighbour and Amy hoped she'd pass on a name. Dave answered the phone with a gruff hello.

'Can I speak to Beth, please.' Pleasantries with her brother-in-law were virtually non-existent, they held a mutual dislike for each other.

'No, you can't. She's out – I thought she was with you.'

'Oh, maybe she's on her way, what time did she leave?'

'Can't say I noticed. I was changing the oil in the van.'

Amy put her phone away. If Beth was on her way she'd arrive soon although the buses were infrequent on Sundays. Looking out of the window she hoped to see her sister walking down the street. Five minutes later she sat back down, it appeared Beth wasn't coming yet it was strange for her to go out without the van, she didn't like using the bus.

TWENTY-NINE
MONDAY 5TH DECEMBER

Since Amy's redundancy, Monday mornings were no different from any other. This morning she woke only when the weak December sun shone through the curtains – 9am. Callum should have gone to work but noises in the kitchen told her otherwise. Dragging herself out of bed and padding downstairs, Amy stood in the doorway watching Callum frying bacon, at least he wasn't still expecting her to cook for him. 'No work today?'

Without looking up he replied, 'I've got an appointment with a solicitor. I suggest you find someone to represent you, too.'

'Isn't there a way we can do this without solicitors?'

'I don't know. Why don't you google it. You spend half your life on the laptop, and the other half watching telly.'

Amy ignored the snide comment. 'Solicitors are expensive and we don't have much spare cash, do we?'

Callum turned and looked at her. She could see his eyes were red, bloodshot. He must have been drinking yesterday – all day for all she knew – he didn't come home until late when Amy was already in bed.

'You suit yourself. I'm going.' Callum put the bacon he'd been frying between two slices of bread, smothered it with ketchup and took it with him. Amy automatically cleared up the mess left on the table.

If Callum insisted on a solicitor and Amy didn't, she could be left almost penniless. Things had been tight recently. With only one wage coming in they'd already stopped paying off the mortgage and were paying only the interest. Maybe Beth would be free to come over to talk and perhaps bring the name of her friend's solicitor. Amy took out her phone and found Beth's number.

'Hi, Beth. Sorry to have missed you yesterday, I thought you were staying in with Dave.'

'Oh, there was a change of plan. I popped to the supermarket. Er, was there anything special?'

'Yes, do you have the name of the solicitor Mandy used for her divorce? Callum's got an appointment with one this morning and I suppose I should find someone to represent me. If you'd like to come round, Cal's out now.' There was a moment's silence and Amy could hear Beth breathing. At the risk of sounding needy she added, 'I could do with the company.'

'Okay, I'll be with you soon.' Beth rang off and Amy sat down to wait for her.

Half an hour later, Beth pulled onto the drive. Amy met her at the door and the sisters embraced. 'You holding up?' Beth studied Amy's face.

Amy nodded and pulled away, suddenly struck by a ridiculous thought.

'What's that perfume you're wearing?'

'*Springtime*, why, do you like it?'

Amy felt sick and moved to sit on the sofa before she fell. 'It's the same perfume I noticed on Callum's shirt.' Staring at her sister, the thoughts buzzing around her mind were absurd, but Beth's face and her silence confirmed the notion, ludicrous though it might be.

Beth sat opposite her sister, apparently lost for words and Amy wondered if she was about to deny being Callum's *other woman*. After an awkward silence, a pale Beth almost whispered, 'I'm so sorry, Amy. We were going to tell you soon – it just – happened, neither of us meant to hurt you.'

Amy's head was spinning. Was she hurt? Or was it the shock making her feel disorientated. This couldn't be happening. Surely – not her sister. It was one thing to lose Callum, she could cope with that but not Beth – she was relying on Beth to help her through the next few months. A sudden urge to lash out took Amy by surprise. Usually the peacemaker, she now wanted to hurt her sister, to make her pay. 'How could you!' she screamed. 'After all I've done for you, you have to take my husband away!'

'But, you don't love him – and I do.' Beth defended herself but her words angered Amy even more.

'Have you no shame? Why do you always only think of yourself, Beth, because that's the way it seems. You're as bad as he is and probably deserve each other!' Amy's head throbbed and she feared embarrassing herself by bursting into tears – it was important to her to keep control, not to let her sister see her weakness. 'I think you'd better go now.'

'No, please! Let me try to explain.'

'I don't want to hear excuses, just go, leave me alone.'

But Beth seemed determined not to leave without a conversation and took control. 'I'm going to make us some tea while you stay there, then we'll talk about this.' She hurried into the kitchen before Amy could protest further.

Amy put her head in her hands and sighed. Tears would have to wait – she drew in several deep breaths to calm herself.

Perhaps she was in shock but it would take more than a cup of tea and a sisterly chat to process this news – Beth and Callum – no, heaven help her, no! She and Beth had been through so much together with only each other to rely on. And now as Amy was approaching her most difficult challenge of all, Beth was going to be with Callum!

Beth's marriage had been rotten from the start, Amy disliked Dave from the first time she met him. He was a bully and she recognised similar traits to their father in him but Beth was determined to marry Dave and couldn't be persuaded that he wouldn't change. But what would happen now? Had Beth told Dave? No, her sister would be black and blue if she had. And did this mean not only the end of her relationship with Callum but also with Beth?

Beth took a long time over making tea, eventually returning to the lounge with two steaming mugs. She sat facing Amy, who noticed her red eyes. Even though Amy was the one who'd been wronged, her heart ached for her little sister – the urge to look after her and protect her gnawed at the back of her brain and she found herself trying to think of a solution to this awful mess.

Amy spoke first. 'Does Dave know?'

'No! I promised Cal I'd tell him after he told you but the time has to be right – you know how he is.'

'There's never going to be a right time, Beth. Dave will be furious whenever you tell him.'

'I know,' Beth's eyes filled with tears, 'I'm so sorry, Amy. I didn't want to hurt you; do you think you'll ever be able to forgive me?'

'That's a big ask. You're right, I don't love Callum anymore and his leaving is almost a relief but this has thrown me. I don't know what to think anymore. You're my sister – the only family I have. Give me time to get my head around this, will you?'

Beth accepted her sister's wishes and stood to leave, the

usual warm atmosphere between them distinctly frosty. Once alone, Amy finally gave way to tears. The look on Beth's face, the pleading in her eyes, stirred up the guilt Amy still felt for one of the worst moments of their childhood and the awful feeling of letting Beth down washed over her again...

THIRTY

It was the worst row Amy could remember. Dad was drunk but not so drunk to be incapable, and he was furious. Beth was fourteen and Amy almost sixteen at the time, and one of his mates had told him he'd seen Beth with a boy. Like most things Beth wanted to do, seeing boys was forbidden. Dad arrived home early that night, anger seeping from every pore.

'Where's the little slut?' His voice boomed through the house – Amy felt sure the whole street could hear. The girls were in the kitchen – the only way to escape to their rooms was blocked by their booze-stinking, raging father. He burst through the kitchen door and grabbed a pan from the rack, raising it above his head.

'Dad, no!' Beth shouted as she scurried to the corner. Amy made a grab for her father's arm. 'Please leave her alone, what's she done?'

Pushing Amy to the floor, he shouted his accusations. 'She's a bloody little slut – snogging in the street like a whore!' He reached down and grabbed Beth, pulling her to her feet and striking her back and legs with the pan. 'No!' both girls cried together but the battering continued as he dragged Beth from the kitchen into the hall where he opened the 'glory hole' cupboard under the stairs and threw her inside as if she were a discarded toy.

Amy heard the clatter of buckets and brooms combined with Beth's sobs as she stumbled into the cold dark space.

'You can stay in there all bloody night until you learn not to embarrass me in public! And you,' he turned to Amy, 'don't even think of letting her out or you'll take her place!' This was their father's last word on the subject. He threw the bolt on the outside of the cupboard door with such force Amy thought it would break but it didn't, then he lumbered upstairs and Amy heard his bedroom door slam. Their mother had been upstairs during the commotion but didn't come down. Amy didn't wonder why at the time, they were used to her hiding from family confrontations, whether from fear or indifference she was never sure.

Amy sobbed throughout the night, afraid for her sister and herself and disgusted at not possessing the nerve to stand up to their dad. It was February and Beth would be freezing in the small space, cramped and frightened – how could a man treat his daughter in such a way? In the morning, Amy went downstairs and found her mother in the kitchen.

'Can I let Beth out now?' she asked.

'Best not to. Your dad said he wants her to stay there today until she's learned her lesson.'

'But you can't leave her there! She'll be freezing and hungry – and what if she needs the toilet?' Amy was horrified.

'He's made up his mind, love, and you know he won't change it. Now get ready for school and tell the teacher Beth's not well today – blame it on her monthlies if you like.'

Amy's mum wouldn't even allow her to take Beth some food or let her out to use the bathroom, even though her dad had gone to work. For the first time she realised just how afraid her mum was of her husband.

Before leaving for school and when her mum was safely in

the bathroom, Amy tapped on the cupboard door. 'Beth, are you okay?'

'No, please let me out!' Beth whimpered.

'I can't, you know he'd only do something worse...' Her sister's sobs gripped at Amy's heart and she left for school with tears streaming down her face.

School dragged and Amy paid no attention to the lessons, her mind back at home, wondering how Beth was coping. At 3.30pm she dashed home, hoping Beth would be out of the cupboard – but she wasn't! It was nearly two hours later when her dad arrived home and their mum asked if Beth could be released.

'Only if she's learned her lesson.' He disappeared upstairs and Amy ran to pull back the bolt. Beth almost fell into her arms. She was shivering and her jeans were wet with urine. As Amy held her, Beth sobbed, the tears staining her bruised and swollen face. With her mother's help, Amy managed to get her sister upstairs and into her room where she helped her off with her clothes, shocked at the number of bruises on her slim body. Beth was stiff from being folded double for hours and as Amy wrapped her in a quilt she said, 'Shh. It'll be okay now. When he's gone out, I'll run you a hot bath and you can have a soak to warm up.'

'I need a drink...'

Amy ran downstairs to fetch a warm drink. 'Make her something to eat, some scrambled egg perhaps,' she asked her mother then returned upstairs.

'Why didn't you come and get me?' Beth sobbed – the haunted look in her eyes was one Amy would never forget, coupled with the feeling of cowardice at again letting her little sister down. Amy knew she would never forgive herself.

THIRTY-ONE
MONDAY 5TH DECEMBER

Another day wasted, Amy thought to herself. After Beth left and she'd managed to shake those unwelcome memories from her mind, the remainder of the morning and early afternoon had been spent on the sofa – daytime television followed by procrastination on her laptop – and Amy felt exhausted. Since the brain tumour diagnosis, she'd wondered if the constant lethargy over the last few months could be connected to the illness. Perhaps reproaching herself for laziness was too harsh – but what did it matter now?

Amy missed the routine of going out to work, it had been the one thing which made her feel like a useful human being, not that filling in spreadsheets was going to change the world, but work drew her out of herself. Her colleagues had been mostly younger than her, unmarried and with social lives way beyond anything Amy had ever experienced. Nightclubs, alcohol and men featured in the tales she listened to after every weekend, and she missed the camaraderie. With nothing in common other than their jobs, Amy quickly lost touch with her former colleagues, other than to keep up with their posts on Facebook. Perhaps she lived vicariously through reading about their lives, yet rarely posted herself, having nothing witty or interesting to say which others would like or share.

Callum arrived home in the middle of the afternoon, opening the door quietly. Amy wondered if he was hoping she'd be out, but they needed to talk. Snow was falling in huge flakes, covering the streets in a crisp white blanket. She listened as he removed his coat and boots and set them to dry. On entering the lounge, her husband's hangdog expression told her he'd already spoken to Beth. Without a word he sat down and raised his eyes, as if waiting, she thought, for a tirade of abuse.

Amy shook her head solemnly. 'What happened to us, Cal? Why have we wasted so much time and sacrificed any happiness we could have had?' Her husband could offer no answer, nor could she. 'Aren't you angry?' he asked.

'I'm too tired to be angry, but you should have told me it was Beth. Have you any plans – like telling Dave?' Her tone was more sarcastic than she intended.

'Beth's going to tell him tomorrow. I offered to be with her as she's afraid of his reaction but she wants to tell him alone, some misguided notion about owing him as much.'

'Did you see the solicitor?'

'Yes, an initial enquiry. You were right about the cost; the only ones who'll come out of this well will be the solicitors, I couldn't believe their rates, over £200 an hour!'

'We can work something out without them, can't we?'

'That would be great, Amy. It doesn't have to get nasty, does it? We're all adults.'

'Yes, we are.' Amy switched on the television, a hint for Callum to leave her alone.

Beth had been truthful when she told Amy she hadn't wanted to hurt her and hoped her sister would believe her. Amy was perhaps the only friend she still had and the last thing Beth wanted to do was spoil their relationship, but maybe it was naïve to think their bond could remain intact. Callum and Amy were probably the only two people in Beth's life who'd ever loved her. Even their mother was, at the very best, indifferent to her daughters but she was long gone, cancer had taken both parents years ago and Beth couldn't say she grieved their passing.

Dave was a poor choice of husband; it was clear now. Beth was as desperate to leave home as Amy had been and he was the first man to offer an escape from her parents. Living in a violent home had always been difficult but when Amy left to marry Callum, it became unbearable. Dave's proposition of a tiny rented house seemed attractive and Beth snatched at the offer without forethought. What was it her mother said, *marry in haste, repent at leisure?*

Her new husband quickly exhibited his true colours and once Beth was his wife, Dave treated her differently. No longer taking her out with him, he preferred to see his mates at the pub rather than spend time with her. Dave had expectations of a wife's duties – basically whatever he said was law. There was no question of him sharing responsibility for domestic chores and Beth took on the role of little more than a slave to her husband's whims.

Another side to Dave soon became clear – he was jealous. Not only of other men but of her friends. Dave insisted she gave up her job to stay at home and be a full-time wife. When she dared to put up an argument, his display of temper shocked her into submission. It was like being back at home with her father and Beth thought maybe this was all she could expect from life. Having friends was a thing of the past, Amy and Callum were the only people Beth saw with any regularity.

Twenty years later they were still in the same grotty house but without hope of a better future and with any past affection between the couple rapidly bordering on hate.

If she'd asked herself why she stayed in an abusive marriage, Beth wouldn't have known how to answer – perhaps it was just hard to get out of a rut, or fear of what Dave might do, or maybe it was because what she really wanted in life was not hers to have. Beth was in love with her sister's husband and had been for as long as she could remember. There was no point leaving Dave when Callum wasn't available. But now everything had changed. Callum offered her a second chance at happiness and Beth was certain she could make him happy – if only she could be as sure that Amy would forgive her.

Without a doubt Dave would be angry when he learned she was leaving – not because he cared for his wife but his pride would be wounded, and also because he was lazy. Beth facilitated his idle lifestyle, afraid of his temper but not so much that she could be bothered to change the rut she was in. Better the devil you know, and she'd always thought Dave was better than her father had been.

The couple never had any money. With Dave having no intention of working, they lived on benefits which he spent on his precious drinking and darts nights. He blamed various health problems but Beth didn't believe him, assuming he exaggerated symptoms as an excuse to avoid work.

Yet now, things had changed and Beth smiled at the thought. Callum was willing to sort out any problems with Dave so she was determined to leave her husband.

Gazing around her home Beth saw nothing she would miss – ancient furniture, cheap ornaments and threadbare carpets. Most of their possessions had been bought second-hand, someone else's cast-offs – the story of her life. Even her clothes were bought at charity shops – it would be so nice to have something new for once.

Tomorrow, she and Callum could move into the rental flat he'd secured and when he and Amy sold their home, he planned to use his share to buy a house. Beth had made enquiries at the job centre and applied for Universal Credit which would also entitle her to housing benefit. They would manage, she'd look for a proper job, something Dave had always forbidden, insisting her role was to look after him. Could life really be starting to look promising for her? There were only two remaining obstacles to Beth's happiness – would her sister ever forgive her – and the most fearful – telling Dave she was leaving.

THIRTY-TWO
TUESDAY 6TH DECEMBER

Anticipation of the coming confrontation with Dave troubled Beth, guaranteeing a sleepless night. Having spoken to Callum the evening before – an intense and hurried conversation – he encouraged her to speak out as he had with Amy, but they both knew Dave's reaction would be very different from her sister's.

Callum had expressed surprise at how Amy had taken the news. 'She appears to have given up on everything and can't even summon up enough energy for a row, which would at least clear the air. She's being very sensible, almost too sensible. I've moved into the spare room until tomorrow, when we can finally be together. Amy's agreed not to involve solicitors in the divorce as well. I can't believe she's being so reasonable. When are you going to tell Dave?'

'In the morning, then he can storm off out and I won't have all night to suffer his temper. I'll pick the keys up and meet you at the flat when you finish work. I can't wait!'

'If you need me, Beth, call and I'll come straight round.'

And now morning was here. Beth was up and dressed long

before her husband, sitting at the kitchen table chewing her fingernails until they bled. Dave was moving around upstairs; the shower was running and Beth anticipated he'd be down in about five minutes.

Breathing deeply in an effort to calm her nerves, she silently repeated over and over that soon she'd be free and beginning a new life with Callum. Beth would tell Dave she was leaving and if he got angry, she could always walk out.

Thoughts of Callum kept her resolve strong. Beth had no regrets about leaving Dave – he deserved to be alone – but Amy was different altogether. Hurting her older sister was something Beth would prefer to have avoided. Amy was kind to Beth when not many other people were, but the discovery that Callum's feelings matched hers for him and the possibility of happiness was too much to resist, even at the expense of losing Amy.

For as long as she could remember Beth had envied her sister. Callum was so easy-going, she'd always liked him. He was her secret crush in those long-ago teenage years but Cal only had eyes for Amy – Beth was simply her annoying little sister. But over time her crush grew into so much more – and the excitement was heady. Amy and Callum's marriage was over. They should have separated years ago and maybe now Amy would be free to find happiness with someone else – Beth hoped so, it would certainly ease her conscience.

As kids, Amy tried to look after Beth – it was them against their dad and Beth knew she wouldn't have survived without Amy in the background, looking out for her. Yet she took advantage of Amy's feelings of responsibility, then, and even now. If she ran to Amy complaining about Dave, and sometimes she exaggerated his temper, Amy would try to make it up to her. Often this was by giving her money, although this hadn't been possible since Amy lost her job, or by taking her out to spoil her or buy her something nice. Guilt money, Beth thought of it, but took advantage nevertheless.

Suddenly Dave was in the kitchen, Beth, lost in thought, hadn't heard him come downstairs.

'What the hell are you doing? Daydreaming? Where's my breakfast?' Typical Dave, thinking only of himself, his stomach, even though it was nearer to lunchtime than breakfast. Taking a deep breath and holding an image of Callum in her mind, Beth looked directly at her husband.

'I'm not making your breakfast anymore. I'm leaving you, Dave. My only regret is that I didn't leave years ago.'

Dave's face darkened, his eyebrows melded together as he growled at Beth, 'You're going nowhere – so get any thoughts of leaving out of your stupid little head and get me something to eat!'

'No, Dave. I mean it. I'm leaving you – I'm going to get a divorce on the grounds of your cruelty and abuse – I've had enough.' Beth's body trembled. Her arms hung at her sides, fists tightly balled until they hurt, but she was determined to do this, to rid herself of this vile man who'd ruined her life.

'Why... you ungrateful bitch!' Swiftly Dave lunged at her, his open hand swiping across her face with such force that Beth screamed in pain and fell to the floor, hitting her head on the corner of the table. Momentarily stunned, when she looked up Dave stood over her, unfastening his belt, ready to thrash her. Panicking, she tried to roll away, to scramble to her feet and dash to the lounge but Dave was too quick and Beth was still dazed from the bang on her head – he grabbed her hair and threw her down again.

'No, please!' Beth struggled to her knees and attempted to crawl towards the door, to get help, but Dave was kicking her, the pain in her side excruciating. Beth covered her head with her hands but he laughed, enjoying inflicting such agony. This level of violence was new, she'd suffered the odd slap and a few thumps before but nothing comparable to this. Beth was terrified.

In an almost foetal position, Beth rolled behind the sofa seeking a place of refuge but Dave came towards her from the other side, grinning and slapping the belt into his free palm with a look of madness on his face. The small side table was the only thing between them and Dave kicked it over to reach her, knocking the lamp on top of Beth. Without thinking of the consequences, she grabbed the stem of the lamp, pulled herself to standing and with strength she didn't know she possessed, hit her husband on the side of his head with the heavy onyx lamp base.

'Arghh!' Dave covered his head with his hand and staggered backwards. He looked at his hands, covered in blood. 'You bitch! You'll pay for this!' With hatred in his eyes he staggered towards a retreating Beth, blood oozing from his head, but after only two steps he fell to the floor writhing in agony. Beth had never been so frightened and watched, petrified, as her husband bled all over the cream rug. What the hell had she done?

Collapsing onto the sofa, Beth clutched the lamp, trembling but ready to attack again if Dave stood up. The writhing lasted for little more than a minute then he grew still and looked at her, barely able to focus. His mouth formed the word *help*.

Beth grasped the lamp to her chest, white knuckles almost fused to the metal stem, unable to look away from the horrific sight of Dave and all the blood. His eyes may be closed but his chest rose and fell – *he was still alive.*

What the hell had she done? Her husband was unconscious on the floor in front of her – should she call an ambulance? Beth was unable to move and incapable of making a rational decision.

Was she in shock? The ticking of the mantel clock marked the passing minutes, the only other noise was her own breathing in time with Dave's rasping efforts to suck in air. Beth's eyes closed and she remained motionless on the sofa.

THIRTY-THREE
TUESDAY 6TH DECEMBER

'Bye, George, see you tomorrow!' Callum Cooper left Blacketts spot on 5pm, wrapped up in his old parka, gloves and a woollen hat, his boots crunching through the heavy snow. The sky was grey – skyglow they called it, didn't they – light pollution which prevented Callum from seeing the stars above. Even in the dark and cold, Cal enjoyed the walk at the end of his working day. It gave him time to think and presently there was much to think about. His concentration throughout the day had been lacking, his mind not on the job as he constantly checked his phone, expecting a message from Beth, a message which didn't arrive. Now, as his breath curled into the freezing atmosphere, he pulled out his phone, unable to wait any longer.

'Cal?' A dazed-sounding Beth answered after several rings.

'Beth, what's happening, where are you?'

'Oh, Cal! I'm at home, please come round, quickly...'

'Are you okay? Is Dave there?'

'Yes but he's unconscious... I hit him.'

'What, how long's he been unconscious?'

'I don't know, since breakfast-time, I think. I must have passed out too.'

'I'm on my way, Beth, hang in there, love.' Callum ended the call, changed direction and picked up speed. If he walked quickly enough he could be with Beth in twenty minutes but what he'd find there he couldn't imagine, she sounded confused.

Turning the corner onto the street where Beth lived, Callum saw the van parked outside. At least she was still there. He sprinted the last few yards to the front door and without knocking, opened it and stepped inside.

'Bloody hell, Beth, what happened here?' Callum's eyes travelled from Beth to Dave's body on the floor – he felt sick at the sight of the blood.

'He hurt me, Cal. He was going to use his belt so I hit him with the lamp... I think he's dead!'

Callum kneeled on the carpet beside Dave, careful to avoid the blood which was now a sticky brown mess. 'He still has a pulse... if it was self-defence we can call an ambulance, tell them what happened.'

'But they'll want to know why I didn't do that sooner.'

'And why didn't you?'

Beth looked hurt. 'I don't know – I was afraid – I think I must have passed out too, unaware of time.'

'How long has Dave been unconscious?'

'I don't know, Cal! Why all the questions – he hit me... took off his belt...'

Callum sat beside Beth on the sofa and drew her into his arms. 'I'm sorry, love. It'll be all right, we'll think of something.' But nothing came to mind.

'What can we do, Cal?' Beth sobbed and grasped at his sleeve.

'Shh, it'll be okay, let's think about this logically.' But he was afraid, unsure whether to call the police or not. 'Let's go in the kitchen.' Cal couldn't bear to look at Dave any longer, he couldn't think straight and all the blood was making him gag. Beth moved obediently on trembling legs, automatically righting the kitchen chairs which had been knocked over earlier.

'Have you eaten at all today?'

'Damn it, Cal, I can't think of food at a time like this.'

'You need to at least drink something. Make some tea while I decide what to do.'

With quivering hands, Beth moved automatically to do as she was told. Callum went back into the lounge, his mind spinning, thoughts crowding in on him. Above all else he needed to protect Beth – having just *found* her, he didn't want to lose her again. If only she'd called the police as soon as this had happened.

As Callum clenched his fists and tried to think logically, Dave twitched and a gurgling sound came from his throat. Cal stared at him for a few moments, mystified as to his next move.

Back in the kitchen, Callum took Beth in his arms. 'I'm sorry, love, but Dave's dead.'

Beth gasped, 'Oh, Cal – I've killed him! I should have called for an ambulance – what can we do?'

Callum sat her at the table and pushed the mug of tea she'd made towards her. They were both stunned by the events of the day. Tears flowed down Beth's cheeks. 'I can't go to prison, – it'll kill me!'

'I know. We'll make sure it doesn't come to that.'

'But how?'

'Shh, let me think.' Callum was shaking, his mind in turmoil. It should never have come to this – why didn't Beth just leave Dave without telling him – Cal should have insisted on it but it was too late now. What the hell could they do?

'Look, Beth. If we can get Dave's body out of here and take him somewhere in the country, maybe we can make it look like he was run over – with this bloody weather it's feasible that a car might skid and knock him down. If we find somewhere to roll him off the road, perhaps he won't be found for a few days.'

'No! Nooo! I can't bear to touch him!' Beth dropped her head onto the table and sobbed bitterly. Clearly she'd be of no use to him. 'But I'll need help, Beth. I can't lift him into the car on my own.'

'Isn't there someone else who can help you?'

'That would be crazy – we can't let anyone know about this!'

Beth pulled a tissue from her sleeve and blew her nose. 'What about Amy? She's always helped me in the past and even though she's mad at me now, she won't want me to go to prison.'

Callum's eyes grew wide. 'I can't ring Amy!'

'Please, Cal, I need my sister!'

With a heavy sigh Callum took his phone from his pocket and fumbled for his wife's number.

THIRTY-FOUR
TUESDAY 6TH DECEMBER

'What the hell's going on?' An angry-looking Amy stood on her sister's doorstep. She'd been dozing when Callum rang – when he *insisted* she went straight to Beth's yet would give no details as to why and refused to answer her questions. On the journey Amy's anger turned to concern and now she was confronting her husband on her sister's doorstep without a clue as to why she was there.

'Is Beth okay and why wouldn't you tell me what this is about on the phone?' She pushed her way into the house. 'Where is she?'

'Calm down, Amy. I've put her to bed, she's had a shock. Come into the kitchen and I'll explain.' Grasping her arm, Callum dragged her through to the kitchen, steering her to a chair.

'What's that awful smell?' Amy was feeling uncomfortable, she needed to know what was happening. 'Are you going to tell me or shall I go up and ask Beth?'

'It's not easy, Amy and you'd better prepare yourself for a shock.'

Amy pressed her lips together and frowned. *How many*

more shocks can I take? Her eyes fixed on Callum, willing him to hurry with an explanation.

'Beth told Dave she was leaving him this morning and, as you might guess, he was angry. He attacked Beth and in self-defence she hit him with a lamp which had fallen on the floor. Beth didn't know what to do – shock must have set in and she didn't help him at all. By the time I called her after work and managed to get here, it was too late – Dave was only just alive but died soon after I arrived.' Callum paused and looked at Amy for her reaction.

'No! It can't be true! Why the hell didn't she call the police? If it was self-defence she'd have been in the clear. Are you saying she waited all day before she did anything?'

'Yes. Since breakfast-time, at least. Perhaps she passed out herself, I don't know, but it's happened, and we have Dave's body in the lounge.' Cal ran his fingers through his hair. Amy noticed fine lines around his eyes and mouth, lines she'd not seen before. Stress.

'Are you sure he's dead?'

'Of course I'm bloody sure – you can smell it, can't you? That awful metallic smell of blood?'

'Let me see.' Amy stood and dashed into the lounge.

'Don't. It's an awful sight!' Callum reached for her but she pulled away. A few steps and Amy was confronted with a vision which would give her nightmares for weeks to come. Gasping, she covered her mouth and nose with her hand.

'You have to call the police!' Amy almost ran back into the kitchen.

'No!' Beth appeared at the bottom of the stairs – dishevelled with a tear-stained face. 'Please, Amy, no! I killed him and I'll go to prison.'

'It was self-defence – he attacked you!'

'But I let him die. I sat and watched when I should have

helped him...' Beth stepped into her sister's arms and cried like a baby, with Amy holding her and making shushing sounds as if to a child. Callum looked at his wife over Beth's head, an expression of hopelessness on his face, his body stooped, weary.

When Beth's tears were exhausted, the three sat in the tiny kitchen and discussed what could be done. Amy noticed her sister's face, red and swollen with a fresh bruise forming beneath her eye. It took her back to their childhood when Beth's poor face was often covered in bruises and she felt a strange combination of love for Beth and hatred for Dave.

Callum repeated his idea of finding a quiet road and running over the body to make it appear to be a hit-and-run, but Amy still favoured going to the police and telling the truth. The latter suggestion, however, sent Beth into a fit of hysterics, terrified she'd go to prison, even if they accepted it was self-defence. By 7pm the three occupants of the kitchen were exhausted and still perplexed.

'Okay,' Amy finally decided – clearly it was going to be down to her what would happen next. 'We'll go with your plan, Callum. I have nothing else. Do you, Beth?'

Beth shook her head furiously. 'But... I can't touch him!'

'We'll do it.' Amy sounded more confident than she felt and the other two looked at her with surprise in their eyes – she was taking charge which astounded even her. 'Drive Dave's van round the back, Cal, while we wait inside, the less activity around the house the better.'

A narrow lane ran along the back of the houses and Callum drove down and stopped outside Beth's home. The lane was deserted; the bad weather and time of night working in their favour. Amy had unlocked the back gate and Callum opened the back of the van, then followed his wife back inside.

Dave's body was on the edge of a large cream rug, a rug splattered with blood. 'We'll have to put a coat on him – no one will believe he was out in this weather without a coat.' Callum grabbed a parka from the hook beside the door and the two began to pull it on Dave's body. 'He's beginning to stiffen!' Callum pulled back from their task, turning away from Dave's bloodied face and fighting the bile rising in his throat.

'Then hurry before we can't move him – roll him into the centre of the rug and we'll wrap him in it to carry him.' Amy was focused and hardly noticed Beth was no longer downstairs. She was all efficiency now as Callum rolled her dead brother-in-law up like a bakery item. The blood was no longer flowing so they decided to lift the body into the van as quickly as possible then attempt the clean-up afterwards.

With Callum taking the brunt of the weight, the pair half lifted, half dragged the rolled-up rug outside. Snow was falling again – the criminal's friend in this case. With a strength Amy didn't know she possessed, she helped Cal to heave the body into the back of the van. 'I'm going to drive round to the front. If anyone tries to get down the lane, they'll get out of their car to ask us to move.' Cal did so and Amy went inside the back way.

Beth was sitting chewing on her lip, a sheepish look on her face. 'Thank you, Amy. I don't know what I'd do without you – both of you.' She squeezed Callum's hand and Amy swallowed hard, turning away from the sight.

'Any ideas where to go?' she asked Cal.

'Let's drive south, there are some quiet country lanes in that area, we'll find a suitable place.' Callum pushed his chair back, keen to get the deed over with. 'Stay here, Beth, we'll be as quick as we can.'

Before leaving, Amy drank a glass of water, her head was pounding with the unfamiliar exertion. Callum drove but it was impossible to relax, Amy's body was tense and her jaws ached from clenching them. She wanted to ask what would happen next, what he would do with Dave's body and how they would proceed afterwards but the silence was too thick to break and her voice wasn't to be trusted.

Several miles out of town the roads grew increasingly difficult to navigate. Snow was piled to the sides with room for only one car. Amy prayed no one would be coming in the opposite direction. Huge white flakes were falling again, a sight which might have appeared beautiful in any other situation and one Amy would usually enjoy. The delicate flakes seemed to deaden all sound and cover the imperfections of the ground on which they fell. If only they could cover the sinister imperfections of the day – the blunders and horror of the crime they were committing.

Callum switched on the wipers which squeaked in protest as they struggled to shift the snow. Suddenly he lost control as the wheels skidded and the car took on a mind of its own. Amy gasped, holding her breath to control the pounding in her heart. Callum regained control – they were okay – he tutted at Amy and shook his head.

Amy closed her eyes and momentarily allowed her thoughts to slip into the dark area of what if... *If the car crashes into the side of the road, we may not be able to get it out. With a body in the back, we could hardly call for assistance. And what if someone passed us and stopped to help? We'd then be placed at the scene; someone would remember us being out in such atrocious weather.*

Thinking the worst was no comfort. Amy opened her eyes and attempted to steady her breathing. Callum leaned over the steering wheel, his face contorted in concentration. Another skid sent Amy's heart racing but the van almost bounced off the snow at the roadside and Cal seemed unconcerned as he continued without comment. About fifty yards past a group of three houses, the road narrowed even more and it was clearly going to be difficult to continue.

'We'll have to do it here. It's a safe distance from the houses – just past this next bend, okay?'

'Okay,' Amy croaked as he depressed the brakes and the van slewed to a halt. 'What now?' She was almost afraid to hear the answer.

'We'll drag the body out and run over him with the van.'

Amy gagged, sure she would throw up.

'We can't back out now, you agreed to this!' Cal scowled at her.

'I know, come on, let's get it over with.'

It didn't take long. Together they dragged the body from the back. With them both pulling at the edges of the rug, Dave's stiff form rolled onto the road in front of the car. Cal bundled the rug up and threw it into the van. Amy stared transfixed at Dave's grotesque bloody body. *What in heaven's name have we done?* Looking at Callum, she shook her head. He would have to do the next bit, she wasn't physically up to it.

Amy took a few steps away from the van, turning her back and gazing into the white fields. She heard the soft thunk as the door closed. The short distance between her and the van didn't protect her from the grating of the engine and the ensuing awful crushing noise – Dave's bones breaking? Glad of the freezing air, Amy managed to hold on to the contents of her stomach, but only just. This must surely be a nightmare; it couldn't be real!

When the gruesome deed was done, Cal jumped out of the van and called her name. Together they rolled the battered body into the side of the road where, with a low thud, it obligingly dropped into a shallow ditch. They were both breathless. 'The snow should soon cover the body and give us more time.' Callum turned to go back to the van and Amy scrambled quickly into the passenger side. The return drive to Beth's house was as silent and uncomfortable as the outward journey.

THIRTY-FIVE
TUESDAY 6TH DECEMBER

Beth was anxiously pacing the room when they arrived, hugging her body, clearly agitated. 'Don't tell me, I don't want to know!' She spoke before the others had a chance to say a word. 'It's over now, thank goodness.' She sat on the kitchen chair.

'Beth, it's only just beginning.' Amy took her sister's arms and squeezed, attempting to calm the woman but also return her to a sense of reality. 'We've disposed of a dead body – a crime in itself. And have you thought of what we do next? Will you report him as missing to the police?'

'I... I don't know if I can. What do you think?' Beth looked from her sister to her lover.

'We need a plan, that's for sure.' Callum flopped wearily beside Beth and Amy took the other vacant chair, her legs barely able to hold her up – no one wanted to go into the lounge.

'There's a mess through there to clear up for a start.' Callum nodded towards the door. 'We'll have to take the carpet up and get it to the tip. I'll put the rug inside it and chuck them out together.'

'Might it not be better to burn them?' Amy suggested.

'A bonfire in this weather will look suspicious and when we report him to the police as missing, they'll be round here looking for signs of something amiss. When they find the body, they'll be looking to identify it.'

'Oh, hell, what a bloody mess!' Beth rested her elbows on the table and sighed. Amy kept her mouth shut. It was a mess of Beth and Callum's making – part of her resented them for involving her, but another part was screaming that this was her chance to make it up to Beth for all the times she'd failed her in the past.

Oddly the knowledge she was dying was quite empowering – in many respects Amy was untouchable – nothing could hurt her now. Perhaps this was a chance to recompense Beth – to give her a better life. And Callum, too. Amy didn't owe him anything but she'd loved him once; if he could make her sister happy...

'First things first. I'm going to take the carpet up.' Callum looked from a jittery Beth, chewing her nails, to Amy, pale and exhausted – neither looked fit to help. 'I suggest you make something to eat and a hot drink. It won't help if we're all weak with hunger. I'll do the heavy work. We need to reach a decision and reach it tonight.'

Callum set to work in the lounge while the women did as he suggested. Using Dave's Stanley knife, he cut the carpet into manageable strips and piled them in a corner. There was blood splatter on the wall and his next job was to clean it off with a bleach solution. Exhausted, he finally sat at the kitchen table and readily ate the scrambled eggs Amy put before him. The coffee was strong and sweet, Amy knew what she was doing.

Beth had been quiet but ate as instructed and hugged her mug for the slightest comfort and warmth it could offer. 'Promise me you won't go to the police?' she blurted out.

Amy looked at Callum and sighed. 'I think that ship has

sailed. We're beyond doing the right thing, so we have to decide what we *are* going to do. You really should go to the police, Beth, to report Dave as missing.'

'No, I couldn't!'

Callum grasped Beth's hand. 'You'll have to at some point. We might have a day or two before someone finds the body but it'll look suspicious if you don't make the effort to find him. Maybe Amy will go with you – it would be natural for your sister to support you at such a time.'

'Let's think of the immediate practicalities,' Amy interrupted. 'How were you intending to get rid of the carpet, Cal? You can't leave it piled up in the corner – and there's the rug in the van.'

Callum stroked the stubble on his chin. 'I'll load it into the van and take it to the tip first thing in the morning.'

'If the police find Dave and don't swallow the hit-and-run theory, they'll search the van and the house, looking for a possible crime scene. Take the van to be valeted afterwards. There may be signs of blood which we can't see, but forensic searches can find the slightest trace.' Finally watching so much television was paying off.

'But why wouldn't they believe it was a hit-and-run?' Beth looked horrified. The others exchanged a knowing look.

'We're just trying to second-guess what might happen.' Callum spoke soothingly but Beth's tears erupted again.

'I can't have the police here – they'll know I'm lying!' She turned to Amy. 'What can we do? Help me, Amy!'

'Beth, you're tired and not thinking straight. Go to bed and let Cal and I decide what to do. Go on, scoot...' The chair scraped on the kitchen floor, setting Amy's teeth on edge. A plan was forming in her tired mind but she needed to discuss it with Callum before sharing it with her sister.

Watching her husband tenderly lead Beth upstairs, Amy had a strange feeling of being energised. Perhaps she read too many books and watched too much television but she could do this, and in the execution of her plan, make it up to Beth for her past failings.

THIRTY-SIX
WEDNESDAY 7TH DECEMBER

In the early hours of Wednesday morning, Callum sank onto the chair beside his remarkably calm-looking wife. 'Bloody hell, Amy, what have we gotten into and what unearthly hour is this to be trying to think rationally? You know in the light of day everything we've done will seem ludicrous – we'll never get away with it.' With elbows on the table, he rested his head on his hands as if it was too heavy to hold up.

Amy felt remarkably strong, a second wind she supposed, or perhaps the new medication was finally kicking in. 'You have to go back to where we left Dave's body, Cal.'

'No bloody way! I don't want to revisit a corpse – I'll be having nightmares for months to come as it is! Why would I want to go back?'

'Tell me, do you still want to be with Beth?' Amy watched as Callum lowered his eyes and his cheeks turned red.

'Of course I do. I'm sorry, Amy, but I love her.'

'Don't be sorry. I needed to know that this mess hasn't changed anything and you'll take care of her. So, listen. How much are you worth?'

'Damn it, do we have to talk about money now? You know everything I have...'

'I don't mean what you have in the bank – we both know it's a paltry sum – but how much are you worth if you die?' Amy shook her head as Cal stared at her, not grasping what she was implying. 'If it was you who was dead, not Dave, there'd be a tidy sum coming from Blacketts, wouldn't there?'

'The insurance? Yes, I suppose – but it's *not* me who's dead, it's Dave, and they have even less than us.'

'What if we passed the body off as you? It's bound to be found sooner or later, so if we put something in his pocket to suggest it's you, I could report *you* as missing, not Dave. Then when things settle down, there'll be a nice fat insurance payment coming our way.'

'Coming to you, you mean.'

'Semantics, Cal. You may not believe me but I really don't want the money. You and Beth could use it to make a fresh start – move away somewhere you're not known. That's why you need to go back to where we left Dave.'

'Amy, it's a ridiculous idea! We'd be found out, someone would see me and know I was still alive.'

'Which is why you'd have to move away. Let's face it, there's not much in New Middridge for you both, is there? And the only family you have is your mum who's away with the fairies and Mike in New Zealand who you've all but lost touch with. As for being in trouble, we've already committed a crime by hiding a body – they can't punish us much more – and if we do get away with it you and Beth will be considerably better off.' Amy rubbed her gritty eyes, beyond tired now, and with the plan she'd hatched buzzing around her brain, she thought she'd never sleep again. 'If you go back to the body and put your wallet in Dave's pocket, when he's found they'll assume it's you. You're a similar age and build, so I'll report you as missing and then identify Dave's body as yours. If they accept the hit-and-run theory we'll be in the clear and you'll be in the money.'

'It's rightfully your money, Amy. I couldn't take it and leave you with nothing.'

'Well, then leave me the house. I'll sell it and get somewhere smaller, okay?'

'We need to think about this and discuss it with Beth.'

'There's no time to think about it, Cal, but we can go up and see if Beth's awake. I'm sure she'll jump at the idea – it gets her out of reporting Dave as missing which she's clearly obsessed with.'

Beth opened her eyes as they entered the bedroom and pulled herself up to a sitting position. 'I can't sleep,' she moaned.

'We need to talk, Beth. Your sister has an idea but we need to be in agreement to make it work.'

'What is it?'

Callum sat on the edge of the bed and took her hand, then looked at Amy, waiting for her to outline the plan. When this was done there was a moment of uncomfortable silence when no one wanted to speak. Amy broke the hush. 'There's no time to dither! If we're going to do it we need to hurry – Cal, you'll have to get back to the body quickly, then come here to load the carpet into the van ready to take to the tip as soon as it opens. What do you think, Beth?'

'Will it work?' She looked at Callum who nodded solemnly.

'I think it will. Once the body's found it's bound to be an awkward time. At least doing it this way we'll come out of it with the means to start a new life.'

'Right.' Amy stood, taking charge again. 'Choose what you're going to leave as identification on the body and get away with you. When you're finished call in at home and get whatever you need to move in with Beth. You become Dave Moorhouse from tonight onwards. With this new plan, you can use Dave's van to dispose of the carpet and then get it valeted. Maybe then we should all try to get some sleep. I'll have to report *Callum* as missing tomorrow – the police might think it suspicious if I leave it any later.'

'Perhaps you should take a photo of Dave to give to the police? They'll probably ask for one of Callum.' Beth was wide awake again and clearly thinking more rationally. She climbed from her bed and went to a drawer in her dressing table. 'Here. This is a couple of years old but it'll have to do – I don't have many photos of Dave.'

Amy took the image and looked at it. Dave was actually smiling for the camera and a pang of something shot through Amy's body, a twisting stab of guilt perhaps? She pulled herself together. 'Right, I'm off. Callum, from now on you can't let anyone see you – the neighbours here or anyone else. A sighting of you alive will ruin the whole plan. We'll keep in touch by phone.' Amy turned, went back downstairs and let herself out. Saying *goodnight* seemed totally inappropriate.

At 8am, Amy rang Beth's number. Callum answered which made her furious. 'Cal, you can't be answering the phone – it could have been anyone ringing! You have to be Dave now and don't let anyone see you.'

'Huh, I knew it would be you.'

'Don't assume it again, right?'

'Okay.'

'Did you go back to the body?'

'No.'

'What? Why the hell not? I thought we'd agreed.'

'When you left I decided perhaps leaving my ID on the body wasn't such a good idea. If the police somehow find out it's not me, having the ID will throw suspicion on us, whereas if there's none on the body, we have no connection.'

'This is getting so confusing. You might be right but it's too late now. Have you been to the tip?'

'Yes, I was there first thing and before you ask, I chose a skip with hardly anything in it, so it should soon be covered in plenty of other rubbish.'

'Good. And how's Beth this morning?'

'Still in bed. Neither of us got much sleep. By the time I loaded the van, Beth wanted to talk. I think it was 4am before we finally slept and then I was up early. But I suppose you didn't sleep either?'

'You suppose right. I kept going over every possible way this could work out. I still think we've a good chance of pulling it off, although it won't be easy. Anyway, I'm going to report you as missing this morning. I'll tell them as little as I can get away with without raising suspicion. Tell Beth I'll ring her when I've done it.'

'Okay, and thanks, Amy. I can't believe you'd do all this after what's happened...'

'Forget it. We're in it together now, we all have to play our part.'

PART 3

PRESENT DAY

THIRTY-SEVEN
FRIDAY 16TH DECEMBER

Sam arrived at New Middridge police station with a knowing smile on her face and a distant look in her eyes, to notice that, for once, her team were mostly in before her.

'Hi!' She glanced around the room. Jen blinked and studied her boss – usually, if Sam was running late, she'd be grumpy.

'You look happy, have you discovered who our mystery body is yet?'

Sam's grin widened and she motioned for Jenny to follow her into her office where she closed the door and sat down with a sigh. 'Ravi proposed to me last night!'

'What? D'you mean – as in a marriage proposal?'

'What else?'

Jenny's eyes widened as she flopped down in the visitor's chair and leaned onto the desk. 'Tell me everything.'

Speaking quietly, Sam began with the tandoori chicken...

When she'd described the proposal but not why she'd arrived late, Sam pushed back her chair and announced, 'Enough excitement, we have work to do. Gather the team, Jen.'

Ten minutes later, Sam asked what news the morning had brought. Kim was eager to start with her update. 'I spoke to two women last night, both of whose husbands went missing just before we found our John Doe. They sent me photographs which I've enlarged to compare.' All eyes turned to the whiteboard, where an image of the unidentified cadaver hung alongside two new images. Callum and Amy's photos had been removed, they'd wasted enough time chasing a motive for Callum's death and now he was back to a misper Sam hadn't abandoned hope of finding him alive. She stepped forward and squinted at the new photos. 'There's certainly a resemblance but after getting the wrong ID before, I want to be sure. Did you ask for a DNA sample – comb or toothbrush, Kim?'

'I did and they're sending them off ASAP.'

'Good work, Kim. Get them to Rick as soon as they arrive – it's a priority. How did the wives react?'

'Tearful – both of them – the one in Bristol wanted to come and see for herself but I persuaded her to wait and told her the ID would be confirmed one way or another as soon as possible. I did wonder if we should do another misper search for dates further back.'

'You're right, Kim, good thinking. Start with local reports and then widen the search area. Maybe Layla would help you as I don't think there's much more we can do until we get an ID. We'll consider a media appeal if we don't strike lucky by the end of the day. Paul, I'd like you to work on the Baxter case. Collate all the paperwork for the CPS and give the Baxters a courtesy call to see if there's anything we can do – within reason. I'll be visiting again, maybe tomorrow.'

Kim raised her hand. 'What will happen to the other boys, will they be charged?'

'It'll be up to the CPS who'll work with the youth offending team and I think the trauma they've already suffered will go in their favour. It's to be hoped the experience will be sobering for them and we'll have two less young hooligans on the streets.'

As the team dispersed, Sam told Jenny she was going out for a while. Jenny raised her eyebrows at her boss's enigmatic smile. Twenty minutes later it was Jenny's turn to smile as Samantha returned to the office with a tray of coffees and a huge bag of doughnuts.

'Ooh, are we celebrating?' Layla asked.

'You could say so. I've no ring to show you – yet – but as of last night I became engaged to Ravi.' Sam wasn't usually one to draw attention to herself unless it was to let a difficult suspect feel her presence in an intimidating way.

'Hey, congratulations!' Paul shouted, relieving her of the bag of doughnuts. The rest of the team joined in with their good wishes.

'Hmm, early elevenses, a great way to start a miserable Friday.' Jen grabbed Paul's arm before he disappeared with the whole bag.

'Ten-minute break,' Sam declared. 'And then back to work, we have much to do, folks.'

THIRTY-EIGHT
SATURDAY 17TH DECEMBER

With their plans completely skewed and a sense of depression descending, Amy Cooper wanted to visit her sister and Callum again to see how they were holding up. Talking on the phone wasn't the same. It was impossible to judge her sister's mood without seeing her face and Amy was getting antsy; she didn't trust using the phone.

Having been awake since 5.30am, Amy set off early and arrived at her sister's home at 8.45am. A dishevelled Beth opened the door a fraction, then stepped aside to allow their visitor in. 'You're early.'

'We need to talk. Where's Cal?'

'In the shower. You should have rung first.'

'Huh.' Amy marched into the lounge, annoyed with the casual manner Beth was demonstrating. Didn't the woman realise what trouble they were in? The bare floorboards gave a hollow feel to the room, an echoing reminder of the most horrific night of Amy's life, and an image of Dave's dead body crept unbidden into her mind.

'I'll tell Cal you're here and then get dressed.' Beth wandered from the room.

How can she stand to be in this house?

As Amy sat down to wait, a strange feeling spread throughout her body – something similar to jealousy perhaps? No, she wasn't jealous of Beth having Callum, they were welcome to each other. Maybe it was their togetherness – something she'd never experience again – Amy had no future to look forward to. All there was left for her to do was ease Beth's life, to make up for the times in their past when she'd let her down.

'I thought we might be better keeping away from each other for a while.' Callum had entered the room and Amy flinched, turning to look at him. His hair was wet and a whiff of the familiar aftershave he favoured reached her nostrils. It was an effort to steer her mind from the thought of Beth and Cal sleeping together, from the closeness they were sharing, an intimacy Amy hadn't experienced for years. Mentally shaking away the intrusive thoughts, she replied.

'It would be suspicious if I didn't see Beth when my husband's *missing*.'

'Who's going to know – surely the police won't be watching you. Have they been in touch since Thursday?'

'DC Gupta rang, not with any news but just to see how I was coping.'

Beth joined them fresh from the shower and dressed in jeans and a sweatshirt. Looking around the room she shivered. 'Let's sit in the kitchen and I'll make coffee.'

Seated around the table, hugging their coffee cups, Callum turned to Amy. 'It's as well I didn't put my wallet in Dave's pocket like you told me to. Now they know it's not me it would tie us to the body – as it is the police have no reason to connect us, we could have been in a right bloody mess if I'd done what you wanted!' His voice was tight, barely controlled as he spat out the words.

'And you can't resist gloating, can you? It's hardly my fault they discovered the body wasn't you, I didn't expect all those tests; you'd think identification from me would have been enough. And who knows, maybe if you *had* put the wallet in his pocket the police wouldn't have run those tests.' Amy refused to accept full responsibility. 'At least they seem to have accepted we made a genuine mistake in the identification. Even they admitted to a striking similarity with the photograph I gave them.'

'Yeah, but what happens now?' Beth interrupted. 'Is there a plan B?' A moment's silence followed.

Cal turned to Amy for an answer, his eyebrows raised, undisguised anger in his words. 'Let's face it, plan A wasn't brilliant. Any other ideas?'

'It appears we're committed to you remaining missing. The police know you as Dave now so there's no way we can say you've come home. They'd want to see you – ask where you've been.'

'But without my body, there'll be no insurance money which leaves us all in a mess – I can't even go back to work, can I?'

Beth looked hopefully from her sister to Callum. 'We could still go away, start somewhere new?'

'I don't think you have an alternative, Cal. If you stay in New Middridge, you can't hide away forever and if you venture out, someone's bound to recognise you. In another town you could try to find work and make a life together.'

'The only bloody trouble with that plan is that I'll have to assume Dave's identity permanently.' Cal looked glum and an intense atmosphere saturated the room as they each silently considered the implications.

'Damn your stupid idea, Amy!' Cal thumped the table and stood up, knocking his chair over.

'I can't remember you having a better one!' Amy didn't have the strength or inclination to argue but she didn't want Cal to get the better of her. 'Pointing fingers won't help. We need to think constructively.'

'How long does someone have to be missing until they can be declared dead?' Beth's question surprised the other two.

'A good few years I think – it's not a viable option...' But Beth was scrolling Google on her phone. Amy assumed she was thinking if they did go away and Cal was eventually declared dead, they might be able to claim the insurance. 'Oh, it's seven years! Wow, a long time...' Beth's words gave Amy a jolt as it struck her again that there wasn't enough time left for her to plan even one year ahead, never mind seven.

'We need to give the situation some serious thought. I suggest you have the conversation as to what you want to do – my vote is for the going away option – I think it's the only chance we'll have of getting away with this. If Dave's not reported as missing, the police won't connect their unidentified body with him. It's not as if he has many friends who'll come looking, any who do we can stall, and if you move away, Beth, I'll tell everyone you've relocated to find a job. Anyway, it's not up to me, it affects you more. I'm going home now, let me know what you decide.' Amy rose and moved to the door; neither her sister nor husband said anything.

THIRTY-NINE

MONDAY 19TH DECEMBER

Sam's frustration at the lack of progress in identifying their body was offset by her personal life being on such a high. Both she and Ravi had Sunday off and true to his word he took her to the designer outlet near York to choose a ring. The day included a leisurely meal out and what felt like miles of walking as Sam was determined to see as many rings as possible before making her choice. Ravi was patient, even encouraging and Sam couldn't remember enjoying a day's shopping so much. Finally, she'd found the perfect ring – a white-gold diamond solitaire with only the slightest pattern on the shoulders. Her fingers were small and the ring looked perfect. The jeweller had her size in stock too, a bonus for Sam to be able to take it away there and then.

Having never considered herself the romantic sort, since Ravi's proposal Sam was existing in a surreal haze of something she couldn't describe. Without a doubt, she loved Ravi, but it wasn't the realisation of 'being in love' which made her feel this way, perhaps it was more a contentment at having her future decided. There'd been a time when Sam Freeman thought the police force might be her life. Although she loved her work, Sam had seen too many colleagues sacrifice relationships for the job and was determined this wouldn't happen to her.

Over the weekend, the couple shared their good news with their parents. Everyone was delighted and promises were made to visit. There would be much to talk about and plan and Samantha surprised herself by her almost childlike feeling of excitement.

Monday morning inevitably dawned, Christmas would be upon them soon but work was, as always, relentless. Sam gathered her team together for a briefing, yet there were no new developments to report to cheer the start of the working week.

'The DNA samples for the two possibles for our John Doe are with the pathologist. We should have results by Wednesday.' Kim Thatcher appeared to be scratching around for something positive to bring the DI.

'Thanks, Kim. Can you give the lab a ring and see if you can sweet-talk them into processing them any earlier? Play the sympathy card and say we're trying to ID this man for his family before Christmas – and grovel if you have to.'

'Yes, boss.' Kim smiled.

With no new information the team returned to searching for other possible mispers who might fit the criteria of their cadaver, other mundane duties and the inevitable paperwork. Her phone rang – it was the desk sergeant, asking if Samantha could see a Mr and Mrs Baxter. From the background noise and the note of pleading in the sergeant's voice, Sam gathered Sylvie Baxter was upset about something. Hurrying downstairs, her assumptions were correct and a relieved-looking sergeant grinned knowingly as she ushered the Baxters into the nearest vacant interview room.

'Why haven't you locked those boys up yet?' Sylvie wailed.

'That bloody Dennison woman's been shouting her head off about my Ethan being responsible for them fires! It was her son, not mine – Ethan was the victim here and they're acting like he did it to himself!' Kev Baxter tried to hold his wife, to sit her down, but shrugging him off she wagged her finger in Samantha's face. 'I want to know why you haven't got those little thugs locked up for what they did to my Ethan. Why are they still walking about the streets when he... he...' Turning into her husband's shoulder, Sylvie appeared to run out of steam and wept. Kev persuaded her to sit down and give Sam a chance to talk.

Samantha sat opposite the couple and waited for Sylvie to calm down. 'I know this must be very difficult for you both and I really am sorry about Ethan – the loss of such a young life is always tragic.' Sylvie looked at her, disdain in her eyes as Sam continued. 'We're still investigating both fires. Tyler and Tim have admitted to being present and having a part in the incidents and there will be consequences for their actions.'

'What kind of consequences? They need locking up!'

'Mrs Baxter, the boys have told us exactly what happened and their accounts seem to suggest it was Ethan who started the fire in which he died...'

'Of course they'd bloody say that, my boy's not here to defend himself is he! So, will they be locked up?'

'The case will be passed to the CPS for a decision on whether to prosecute, and there'll be intervention from the youth offending team. From what I've seen of both boys, they've learned a salutary lesson.'

'Intervention – what the hell does that mean? Getting them to say sorry and dig an old lady's garden? And when can we have Ethan back – I want to make arrangements to give him a proper send-off.'

'It shouldn't be long now but I'll chase it up for you. I'll have a word with the pathologist and give you a ring.'

Sylvie grew calmer, blew her nose and turned to her husband. 'I want to go home now.' Kev Baxter stood to usher his wife from the room, nodding at Sam as he left.

FORTY
MONDAY 19TH DECEMBER

Amy Cooper was in a half-asleep zone, her feet on the sofa, a throw over her body and a cup of tea going cold on the coffee table. Without the slightest desire to move, she couldn't even summon the energy to come out of her cosy cocoon and drink her tea. Yet although her body was immobile, her mind was spinning. Was it really only eighteen days since she'd learned her life was drawing to a close? So much had happened since – she'd done some incredible things and told so many lies – Amy barely recognised herself.

The same was true physically, so much so that she'd taken all the mirrors down in the house and covered the cheval mirror in her bedroom with a sheet. The only offending mirror left was in the bathroom, the mirrored cabinet. Amy took to leaving the doors open so her reflection wouldn't confront her every time she went in. It wasn't as if she was vain but no one wished to see their physical appearance change for the worse so rapidly. If her husband and sister had noticed, they undoubtedly put it down to the stress of recent events. They too looked nowhere near their best.

The phone on the coffee table rang and Amy turned her

head to look at it, not wanting to move any other part of her body. Deciding to pick it up in case it was Beth or Callum, she answered with a weak, 'Beth?'

'No, it's Fran. Have I called at a bad time?'

'Oh, Fran, hello. No, it's not a bad time, I was expecting it to be my sister.'

'I've been wondering how you were coping, Amy. Is there any news from the police about who killed your husband?' On Fran's first visit, Amy told her Cal was missing; on her second that his body had been found, but the women hadn't spoken since last Thursday before the police told her it wasn't Cal's body so her nurse wasn't to know.

'Well, yes and no. The police forensic reports and Cal's medical records have proved the body they have isn't Callum...' Amy stifled a sob.

'What? But hang on, that's great news! He might still be alive. Are the police continuing the search?'

'Yes, but with time passing, it may be scaled down.'

'How strange. The man must have resembled your husband, didn't you identify him?'

'I only saw him through a window and he was badly bruised and swollen...'

'Oh, how awful for you, I'm so sorry, Amy. Would you like me to come round?'

'No, I'm expecting Beth soon. Perhaps another time?'

'Okay, but I'd like to review your meds in the next couple of days – are you managing on the current doses?'

'Surprisingly, yes. I'm having a lazy day today, but some days I feel quite good, strong enough to potter about.'

'Great but don't overdo things, and you can always ring me if I can help.'

'Thanks for calling, Fran.' The call ended.

Did I really say I potter about? If only Fran knew what the last few days have been like. Amy almost laughed at the absurdity of what her life had become.

She'd lied to Fran, Beth wouldn't be coming, preferring to keep her head down these days and hide away at home with Callum, playing *happy families*. Amy often wondered what was going on in her sister's mind. Beth was almost hysterical at times, expecting Cal and Amy to sort everything out and make every decision, particularly the more unsavoury ones. On that dreadful night, Beth was panic-stricken when Amy arrived, calming down until the thought of being questioned by the police agitated her again. As had been the pattern of their lives, Amy tried to do what was best for her sister – constantly striving to atone for the past. When Amy suggested the plan to pretend the body was Callum, Beth was finally placated – the focus would switch from her to her sister – an idea which clearly appealed.

Initially, Amy wondered if Beth was strong enough to play her part and was surprised when Callum described how relaxed she'd been with the police. The visit to Beth's house caused Cal more angst than Beth, and he related to Amy the awful minute when they might have been discovered. When the two women detectives asked to speak to him while Beth made coffee, he noticed a wedding photograph of Dave and Beth on the bookcase. Thinking quickly, he placed his coffee cup in front of it and hoped the detectives hadn't noticed. Afterwards, he and Beth searched the house for anything else which might give them away. Their near miss visibly shook Cal.

Amy was also amazed and somewhat impressed by her sister's *performance* when the police showed up to inform them the body was not Callum. When Beth arrived, she appeared calm and rushed to Amy's side to comfort her. When asked about the positive identification Amy had given, Beth played the indignant card on her behalf. It was a tricky time and Beth, to her sister's astonishment, behaved appropriately.

The discovery of the body not being Callum was a huge disappointment and an obstacle to their plan. The question was, would it be an insurmountable obstacle? At least the police wouldn't be investigating Amy as a murder suspect, and as Dave hadn't been reported missing – in fact, the detectives had actually met *Dave* – they wouldn't make the connection. But their breakthrough caused other problems. When, Amy wondered, would they give up trying to identify the body? Would they dispose of it if they didn't discover the identity? Only then would Amy feel safe. And there was the problem of being unable to claim the insurance money – the main reason for switching identities. How the hell did they get into this mess? She couldn't blame Beth, as Amy had been the one to come up with such a crazy idea. If only they'd had more time to think instead of rushing into things, but life is never straightforward.

Amy was content that her own part in this was less serious than for Callum and Beth, yet the thought of trouble with the police meant that increasingly she viewed her impending death as a welcome event, a release from her present trials and confusion and a freedom from the pain which would intensify with time. Yet still, Amy was committed to seeing this through – it was as much of her making as it was Beth's, and a chance to give her sister the future she deserved.

FORTY-ONE
MONDAY 19TH DECEMBER

Beth and Callum lay wrapped in each other's arms, neither feeling the need to get up and face another day. Having talked long into the night, sleep had been fitful and in the stark light of day, their problems returned to again trouble their waking hours. In his heart Callum knew there was little choice except to do as Amy suggested – move away and start a new life where they were not known. Yet a niggling resentment festered in his mind – he would be giving up more than Beth, and it would fall on him to support them financially while taking on another man's identity.

The plan wasn't nearly as appealing as it would have been with the insurance money, but that wasn't going to happen now – Callum would have to live with the consequences. Staying hidden in Beth's less-than-attractive home was also becoming stifling. It felt at times as if Dave's ghost was watching him, mocking him for the complicated predicament they found themselves in. Beth at least could go out, and frequently did, just short trips for shopping, but even a grocery shop appealed to Cal after being cooped up inside for so long.

'So, are we decided on going away? Shall we tell Amy today?' Beth idly scratched her nails over Callum's chest, her voice pleading, girlish.

'It's more complicated than just deciding to do it.'

'It doesn't have to be; it can be exciting. And what have we got to stay for?'

Callum removed her hand from his chest and shuffled away from her. 'There's my mother. She's been told I'm missing and probably thinks I'm dead.'

'But she's away with the fairies most of the time and you rarely see her, do you?'

'No, but that's not the point. We need to be sure it's the right thing to do, and there's my brother too – the police have been in touch with him to let him know I'm missing.'

'You haven't spoken to your brother for years – you may as well be dead for all the concern he shows you or your mum.' Beth sounded snappy but then her tone changed. 'I'm sure it's the best way forward. I love you, Cal, and want to be with you. So, shall we do it?'

'We don't have an alternative, but there are things to decide first. I'll need to speak to Amy about money. She mentioned selling the house and getting somewhere smaller for herself – we need that even more now, so we'll at least have some starting capital.'

Beth grinned and swung her legs over the side of the bed. 'Good, I'll ring her and ask her to come round later today. Then I'll start packing.' She hurried off to phone her sister while Callum lingered in bed. Was this really what he wanted? Yes, he was attracted to Beth and their affair had been exciting, livening up his mundane life – but a man was dead and Cal was in the impossible position of being sought by the police as a missing person. Yet he couldn't be found – the police knew him as Dave Moorhouse, an identity he was stuck with. What an unholy mess this was turning into. And then there was Amy. Her actions and support had staggered him. His dowdy wife had devised such an audacious plan to assist him and Beth after they'd been cheating on her – what was that all about? Perhaps there was more to Amy than he'd realised. They say you can live with someone without fully knowing them, which was certainly true in this case.

Callum had snapped at Amy more than he should have done the last time she'd visited. He'd been angry and it was perhaps a reaction to her taking control of the situation. He regretted his anger and felt a new admiration for his wife, Amy didn't deserve to be dragged into his problems. Yet he was left with no alternative other than leaving her, probably never to see her again. Strangely the thought sat uncomfortably in his mind. And he'd noticed another side to Beth which he'd not seen before – she was so needy and perhaps even selfish...

The feasibility of taking another man's identity also troubled him. Would it work, could he find a job in Dave's name and continue being Dave Moorhouse for the rest of his life? Callum shuddered and pulled the duvet up under his chin as Beth flounced back into the room.

'Amy's coming round this afternoon. I told her we'd decided to leave and needed to discuss practicalities, okay?'

'Okay,' Callum echoed before turning over. 'Wake me when you're out of the shower.'

Amy rang the doorbell and walked into her sister's home. Outside was damp, cold and miserable – inside was barely warmer so she kept her coat on. Beth greeted her with a quick hug and Callum a nod. Amy felt ill. Tiredness had descended on her and her head ached terribly, so much so she'd considered refusing to come, but she was committed to help.

'So, you've decided to go, then?' Amy didn't want to waste time; being at home, alone with her television and painkillers was all she wanted.

'I don't think we have any other options.' Cal's voice no longer held the aggression she'd come to expect. 'I can't suddenly become myself again as the police know me as Dave. It appears I'm stuck with his identity so the best decision, the only viable one, is to move away.'

'When?' If Amy was reading the situation correctly, Beth was the more excited of the two. Callum's face betrayed reservations, perhaps even regret.

'As soon as we can pack,' Beth chipped in. 'We haven't decided where yet but I fancy the coast, down south maybe where it's warmer.'

'And more expensive,' Amy reminded them. 'Maybe Northumberland or Cumbria would be a better choice.'

'We haven't started looking yet but we wanted to talk to you about the house.' Callum cleared his throat. 'It's in joint names so I don't know how you'll stand legally, but we wondered if you could sell it so we can have some start-up money.'

'That was my intention and still is but I don't think I can do it while you're still *missing*.'

'And he can't be presumed dead until seven years have passed!' Beth wailed. 'What a bloody mess this is – how can we start a new life without money?'

'If only...'

'Don't bother with *if only*; it'll just drive you mad.' Amy said, stopping Cal before he stated the obvious. The last thing she wanted was to get into another argument with him. 'I'll come up with something, leave it with me.' She needed to get out, to go home and think. How could she raise money without selling the house? Amy couldn't think straight with her sister and husband's accusing stares. Shaking her head, she stood to leave, to go home. Neither Beth nor Callum walked her to the door.

FORTY-TWO
TUESDAY 20TH DECEMBER

DC Kim Thatcher knocked on Samantha's office door, chewing at a fingernail while waiting for her DI to acknowledge her presence. The door was open but Kim was reluctant to step inside.

'Hi, Kim. What is it?'

Kim entered. 'I've got the DNA results but it's not good news – neither candidate matches our cadaver.'

'Damn it! You'd better ring the families and let them know – at least they still have hope of their missing husband and father returning home – not much of a Christmas present but better than having a funeral to arrange.' Sam looked at the hesitant DC. 'And well done, Kim, for getting the results so early.' Kim left with a smile. Noticing Jenny hovering in the background, Samantha beckoned her into the office.

'We've drawn another blank with the ID of our body. Kim's ringing the families now to let them know there's no match. We'll have to widen the search – someone must know who the poor man is.'

'He couldn't have been homeless, could he? I mean, there

was no ID on the body, no phone and the clothes couldn't tell us much – generic supermarket buys with the effects of the weather making it difficult to determine their condition.'

'If that's the case then it could take forever to ID him, but my gut tells me he's not homeless. If it'd just been a hit-and-run, then yes, but a murder victim? Who's going to murder a homeless guy and then take the trouble to make it appear to be a hit-and-run? Besides we don't have much of a problem with the homeless in New Middridge.'

'You're right, boss – what do I know? Anyway, I came to tell you we've had a call from Kev Baxter – I took it a few minutes ago. He wanted to apologise for Sylvie's outburst yesterday. He says she's taken it badly, Ethan being their only child. Apparently, she's much calmer today and he thinks she'll accept Ethan's culpability given time.'

'It's good of him to phone. We all have our coping mechanisms and Sylvie's is obviously anger. I can only imagine how terrible she feels. I'll pay them a visit before Christmas, not that she'll be delighted to see me...'

'Good for you – if you want me to ride shotgun I'll happily do so.'

'Thanks, Jen, I'll probably take you up on that – but there is something else you could do for me.'

Jenny raised an eyebrow as Samantha stood up. 'Come up to the canteen and we'll grab a coffee.'

The canteen was quiet; it was late for a mid-morning coffee break and too early for lunch. Sam bought two coffees and joined her DS at a quiet corner table. She also carried two large cream apple turnovers.

Jenny's eyes widened as she licked her lips. 'Gosh, now I'm wondering what you want!'

'It's a big ask, I know, but feel free to say no, I won't be offended.' Samantha lowered her eyes and took a bite of her pastry.

'Oh, come on, boss, what is it?'

Sam's voice dropped to a whisper as she leaned in closer to Jenny. 'I'd like you to be my bridesmaid.'

'What!' Jen spluttered.

'You heard – don't make me have to repeat myself.'

'So, you're going for the big white wedding thing, are you?'

'No, we're going for a small-*ish* refined wedding but I still need support... so, if you're up for it?'

'Sure am! Wouldn't miss it for the world. Have you set a date yet?'

'No, we want both families to get used to the idea first. If it was up to me, I'd elope tomorrow but the trouble we'd be in isn't worth it.' Sam grinned, looking remarkably young. 'Ravi's family are from the Indian state of Gujarat and very proud of their heritage. I suppose I'm lucky they've accepted me and not insisted on a Hindu bride. If we lived in India I'd be expected to convert but Ravi's not a practising Hindu which his parents accepted a long time ago. They're happy for us to have a traditional English wedding but have asked us to include the ceremony of the knots.'

'Ooh, tell me more!'

'There are three knots to be tied in the ceremony, the first two by the groom to signify our commitment as a couple and his obligation to assure my well-being, and the third knot tied by the groom's sister which signifies the commitment between the two families. It sounds fine to me and if it keeps them happy then I'll go along with it.'

'It sounds romantic. Does Ravi have a sister?'

'No but I think the role will pass to his brother. So come on, Jen, you haven't given me an answer.'

Jenny reached over to squeeze Sam's hand. 'Yes, I'd be delighted to be your bridesmaid. So, what do you fancy for a hen night?'

Samantha rolled her eyes and stood to go back downstairs to work.

FORTY-THREE
TUESDAY 20TH DECEMBER

Amy spent Monday night wracking her brain in a futile attempt to find a solution to her sister's financial problems. When sleep finally claimed her, it was fitful, with strange dreams in which she was being chased by an unknown predator, ploughing through deep snow which slowed down her leaden legs as the predator closed in. When she finally reached her car, all four wheels were missing and Amy sat inside and cried, the tears freezing on her face. She could no longer see the predator but could hear his footsteps drawing closer...

On waking, Amy took a hot shower – no prizes for guessing where the dreams came from. After making coffee, food no longer appealed. Amy settled down at her laptop to research the only idea she'd come up with the previous evening, a long shot but one which might possibly work. Googling equity release companies, her first question was answered immediately, yes, they could still apply for equity release if they had a mortgage on their property, which they did. Half an hour of reading was quite enlightening – all they had to do was fill in the forms and it appeared several companies would be delighted to offer them a lump sum of equity for signing over part of their house. It seemed almost too simple but Amy was wise enough to know there would be catches. There was a hefty penalty for redeeming the *loan* which would be no problem; she wouldn't be around to redeem it even if she wanted to. The best part of the scheme was that Callum could sign the papers, even if it had to be done in person it could be arranged.

Under no illusion that she would be acting legally, Amy was beyond caring – was fraud any worse than disposing of a body and claiming her husband was missing when she knew exactly where he was? She almost laughed out loud. The last few weeks had turned her into a criminal and she had no qualms about doing whatever was necessary for her sister's happiness – it was too late for her own.

By lunchtime, she'd scribbled several notes and intended to visit Beth and Callum to outline her new plan when the doorbell brought her back to reality.

'Hello, Amy.' Fran's smiling face was simultaneously welcome and intrusive. Amy stood aside to let her visitor enter, deciding the company was wanted; she could visit Beth later. Coffee was made and the women settled in the lounge where Amy turned the gas fire on to supplement the central heating.

'How are you?' Fran asked.

'About the same as when we spoke on the phone yesterday.' Amy almost laughed and Fran smiled.

'Sorry, I get used to asking this when I'm visiting, but you do look tired, I didn't pick that up on the phone.' A frown crossed the older woman's brow. 'Try to get more rest, Amy. You're coping with a heavy load at the moment.'

'Sleep's impossible. Do you think you could ask the doctor to prescribe me some sleeping tablets? You're right, I'm sure I'd feel much better if I could sleep.' The look on Fran's face told Amy exactly what she was thinking. 'Fran, if I had any intention of doing myself in, there are plenty of ways to do it. I have a cupboard full of painkillers, remember? I just want some respite, and sleeping pills would at least give me a bit of rest.'

'I'll have a word with the doctor and let you know. We have to be careful with medication, Amy; it can be a fine balance.' Fran sat forward and clasped her hands together. 'Is suicide something you've ever considered?'

Amy answered immediately and honestly. 'Yes. Surely most people in my position at least think about it. But I'm too much of a coward to actually do it; death will come soon enough for me without helping it along.'

Fran nodded, seemingly satisfied. 'Okay. I have to say I admire your strength, Amy. It's not only the tumour you're coping with, it's this business with your husband too...'

'Don't be under any illusions about me. I muddle along but I'm certainly not someone to be admired!'

Fran appeared surprised at the irritation behind Amy's words and quickly changed the subject. Taking out a notebook she made a few notes, firstly to remind herself to ask the doctor about sleeping tablets and then to arrange a check-up at the hospital. Amy wondered why an extra appointment was necessary but didn't ask – her demise was secondary to the other problems of the day.

Finally, Fran left. Amy drank more coffee and forced herself to nibble on a biscuit before setting off to Beth's house.

FORTY-FOUR
TUESDAY 20TH DECEMBER

Rain had replaced the snow, heavy and continuous. Amy drove through the wet streets, the car wheels splashing through the puddles and the wipers on full to clear the windscreen. At least it was a few degrees warmer and the last of the lingering snow piled at the roadsides had finally been washed away.

Pulling up in front of her sister's house, Amy exited the car and dashed to the door. Beth opened it for her and the women hugged briefly before going into the lounge. Several boxes were piled around the walls, it was clear packing had started and as Amy sank into the sofa she asked, 'Have you found somewhere to go?'

Beth sat beside her; her expression unreadable. 'Yes. We spent the evening searching Rightmove for a reasonably priced rental. There's one in Wigton in Cumbria, a tiny one-bedroomed cottage which is only £400 a month. It looks in good condition and is partly furnished so we emailed this morning and it's available immediately. We've decided to take it.' Chewing on her lip Beth looked at Amy, studying her sister's face.

With a slow nod, Amy asked, 'So when do you go?' A feeling of finality washed over her – this was it – when they left, she may never see Beth again.

'Tomorrow. We can pick the keys up at the estate agents and be in for Christmas. Once we're settled, you can come to visit; it's not too far away.'

'We'll see.' As Amy swallowed, trying to process the news, Callum came bounding down the stairs, a pile of towels in his arms.

'Oh, you're here.' He dropped the towels on top of one of the boxes and sat facing his wife. 'Has she told you?'

'Yes. You seem to have it all mapped out. What are you doing about money?'

'We suddenly realised that if Cal adopts Dave's identity, he can carry on receiving his benefits. He emailed the job centre this morning to tell them we're moving. They'll pass his details onto the Wigton office and we'll even be entitled to housing benefit.' Beth smiled, clearly pleased at this sudden upturn in their situation.

'We'll struggle for a while but I'll be able to get a job and Beth wants to look for something too. Have you had any thoughts on raising capital on the house yet?'

'No,' Amy lied. Suddenly the idea of equity release lost its appeal. Why should she put herself through more angst and get into deeper trouble when it appeared Cal and Beth could manage on their own. 'Beth says you're leaving tomorrow.'

'Yes, the place is empty and we have to start paying the rent immediately so we may as well go. We've given the landlord here notice, although officially it'll still be Beth's for the next four weeks. We'll take Dave's van with as much stuff as we can load into it and maybe after Christmas make another trip down to pick up some more.'

'Wow, you've moved quickly once you made the decision.'

'There's nothing to hang about here for, and the sooner we leave the better. At least I'll be able to go out without fear of being seen.'

Amy thought she detected a sarcastic tone in his voice. Did he still blame her for the mess they were in? She looked at her sister whose eyes were focused on Callum with such devotion that despite her own feelings, Amy smiled. 'Is there anything I can do to help?'

'Thanks but we'll manage. Beth, write the address down for Amy.' Turning to his wife he continued. 'It might be best if we don't see each other for a while. Have you heard any more from the police?'

'No, they said they'd be in touch after Christmas. Apparently, missing persons often contact their families over the holiday season, which is what they're hoping will happen with you. So, this is goodbye then.' With no reason to linger, Amy stood to leave. Beth gave her sister their new address, walked to the door with her and hugged her tightly.

'Thanks for everything you've done, Amy. We'll let you know when we're coming back for more stuff. You will be okay, won't you?'

'Sure I will. Take care of yourself, Beth, and give me a ring when you're settled. Bye, Cal,' Amy shouted over her sister's shoulder, receiving little more than a grunt in response.

The rain was still teeming down. Amy arrived home with a strange and inexplicable mix of emotions. Dashing inside, she threw off her coat and switched on the fire. Snuggling down on the sofa, Amy pulled the woollen throw around her cold legs and sobbed in a way she hadn't done since she was a child.

FORTY-FIVE
TUESDAY 20TH DECEMBER

An artificial tree stood in the corner of the office looking somewhat sad rather than festive. Each year the team were asked to bring in baubles to decorate it; there was little storage space to keep such items in the station, and the budget didn't run to frivolities, but this year few had bothered. Samantha Freeman looked at it and smiled, remembering the previous evening when she and Ravi had put up their own tree. Opting for a real one, the satisfying scent of pine filled their lounge; it almost made her feel like baking mince pies... but she resisted the urge.

The evening was filled with laughter, helped no doubt by the bottle of wine the couple had shared. Ravi took responsibility for the top of the tree while the more vertically challenged Sam decorated from the bottom up. As with many things they attempted together, it soon transformed into a competition resulting in squabbles over the blingiest items and two breakages when things became playfully physical.

Jenny's voice brought her back to the present. 'So, are you off to visit the Baxters today?'

'I suppose – there's no time like the present. I thought I'd take Tom Wilson with me; it may not be an easy visit but he needs some experience of legwork. There's an email from the CPS with their decision and I know Sylvie Baxter won't be a happy bunny when we tell her what it is.'

The council estate was eerily quiet; even the hardened teenagers who usually hung around the street corners seemed to have been put off by the rain. The Baxters' house looked as bereft as its occupants must be. The weedy string of outdoor lights had been ripped down and trampled into the garden path and Sam noticed the absence of the tree which had stood in the window on her previous visit. It was understandable; she would feel the same. The doorbell chimed a different tune than their last visit, and Kev Baxter opened it wide to allow them in from the rain.

'Sylvie!' he called up the stairs, and was answered with an angry, 'What?'

'Visitors.'

Sylvie Baxter trudged downstairs looking anything but pleased to see Sam and Tom. 'Come to wish us happy Christmas, have yer?' She glowered at the detectives.

'Sylvie, that's hardly fair...' Kev admonished.

Sylvie suddenly looked as if any energy she still possessed had been sucked from her as she flopped into an armchair and muttered, 'Sorry.'

'This is DC Wilson, Sylvie. We wanted to see how you were and if there's anything we can do for you.' Samantha sat facing the grieving mother.

'That's very thoughtful of you but there's nothing, is there, Syl?' Kev responded. His wife shook her head, blinking back tears.

'I spoke to the coroner this morning and he's agreed to release Ethan's body so you can make your arrangements.' *Is this good news?* Sam wondered as she spoke.

'That's good, isn't it, Sylvie?'

Kev was clearly looking for the positives and his wife responded with a nod before asking, 'What about those two little thugs, what's happening to them?'

'We heard this morning that they'll both be receiving a youth offending supervision order and a conditional discharge.' Samantha was aware this wouldn't be enough for Sylvie.

'Wouldn't you bloody know it! They'll get away with this when our Ethan's dead – his future's gone – he was a bright lad, he could have done things with his life.'

'I know, Sylvie, and I'm sorry. But Tim and Tyler will learn from this experience, and a supervision order isn't *getting away with it*. There'll be intervention to help them stay out of trouble but if they commit any subsequent crimes, we'll revisit what's happened and it'll be taken into account.'

Sylvie sniffed and turned away from the detectives while Sam addressed her husband. 'This is the number for the coroner's office, Kev. If you'd like to ring and let them know which undertaker you'll be using they'll make the arrangements to move Ethan.' Sam passed a piece of paper to Kev Baxter who took it and moved to a sideboard behind the couch where he propped it up against one of several photographs displayed there.

Tom, idly looking around the room, was also studying the photos. Sam thought she must warn him not to appear so nosy in future until her DC turned to her. 'Boss – take a look at this.' Sam's eyes rested on the image Tom was holding. She took the photo from him and stared at it, open-mouthed. 'Kev – do you know Callum Cooper?'

'Who?'

'This man beside you here.' She tapped her finger on the frame. 'It's Callum Cooper, isn't it?' Tom was scrolling on his phone trying to find the image of Callum the team knew so well – the photo Amy had given them of her missing husband.

'No,' Kev looked puzzled, 'that's Dave Moorhouse. He's on our pub darts team, a fantastic player but he hasn't been around for a while.'

Tom found the image, held it against the photograph and exchanged an excited look with Sam. Thanking the Baxters, they left the house and hurried to the car, no longer noticing the still pouring rain.

FORTY-SIX
TUESDAY 20TH DECEMBER

Samantha fumbled with her car keys, impatient to get back to the station and share this latest information. Like the Lego blocks they'd bought for Ravi's nephew, everything was finally connecting, click click click...

'Are we going to make some arrests?' Tom was as fired up as his boss – he may as well have been rubbing his hands, Sam thought.

'Not yet. We'll go to the station and plan our next move – I don't want anything to go wrong.'

Paul Roper glanced at the two detectives as they hurried through the door. 'You two look as if it's Christmas already.' The answer was an enigmatic grin from Samantha and a request to gather the team together.

'Two pieces of good news.' Sam glanced at her wide-eyed colleagues. 'We've found Callum Cooper and we also know who our John Doe is.'

'But weren't you visiting the Baxters?' Paul frowned.

'Yes, and they've solved the mystery for us.' Sam couldn't help dragging it out, enjoying her team's bewildered expressions. 'Kev Baxter is a keen darts player and his photograph is displayed in his home with the man we know as Callum Cooper, who Kev informs us is actually Dave Moorhouse.'

'So, who is the body?' Kim asked.

'Dave Moorhouse!' Paul was ahead of her, banging the desk as he spoke. 'What the hell do they think they're playing at?'

'Leading us a merry dance, or when we arrest them, I'll refer to that particular charge as wasting police time and obstructing an officer in the course of their duty, and a few others I can think of.'

'So, the body in the morgue is Dave Moorhouse and the man living with Beth Moorhouse is presumably Callum Cooper?' Layla asked.

'Exactly.' Samantha waited for a moment to let the reality sink in. 'So, we get a warrant and first thing tomorrow we visit Beth and Callum to arrest them and then on to Amy Cooper's to arrest her.'

'Whatever were they thinking of?' Layla shook her head. 'And who killed Callum, I mean Dave Moorhouse – and why?'

'I think perhaps Beth and Callum are a couple – how long that's been going on is anybody's guess but as Amy's helping them she must accept the situation. My money's on either Beth or Callum killing Dave, or perhaps both of them. When we first visited Beth, she had significant bruises which I assumed the man she was with had caused. What if Dave Moorhouse was a wife-beater and that's why he was killed – whether intentionally or in a fight, who knows? Then they somehow get Amy on board to pretend Callum's missing so they can claim the insurance money. If we'd accepted her identification of the body without forensic backup, they may have got away with it. Alternatively, if the body hadn't been discovered their plan could also have worked.'

'But would Amy go along with such a complicated plot?' Layla asked.

'Maybe. If Beth and Callum had been carrying on for a long time and Amy knew about it – half the insurance money from Blacketts would certainly compensate for the loss of an unfaithful husband. Anyway, this is all supposition. Tomorrow we'll have the chance to hear their version of events and learn why they've been mucking us about. Paul, can you get on with some digging into Dave Moorhouse – find a photograph if you can to compare with the one Amy gave us, supposedly of Callum – and we can forget the search for a misper to match our cadaver.'

'Well, damn Amy Cooper and her *missing* husband! They've been playing us for fools,' Jenny said, expressing her anger.

Suddenly, Sam thought about Aiden Kent. 'Hell, the DCI will have something to say about more wasted time. Jenny, can you contact Rick and tell him our suspicions. Ask if he can get the medical records for Dave Moorhouse, it could be the same GP as the Coopers, and I think he'll find the doctor prescribed the medications he expected to find in Callum Cooper's notes.'

'On it, boss.'

As the team dispersed to their various tasks, Samantha stood before the whiteboard, hands on hips and sighed. 'What an absolute bloody waste of time,' she whispered under her breath. Taking down the photos and crossing out the now irrelevant jottings, she began to rearrange the board into the order of what they now believed to be correct.

When the necessary plans were in place for the arrests early the following morning, Sam sent the team home to rest before what would surely be a long day.

For once Samantha arrived home before Ravi and after a long hot shower, prepared a simple meal of omelettes and salad; even she couldn't go far wrong with eggs.

Ravi hugged her close when he arrived. He smelled of crisp fresh air and the woody aftershave he wore. Sam relaxed in his arms, her cheek against his chest, and counted her blessings. After a quick change, Ravi sat beside her to eat as she recounted the extraordinary events of the day.

'My fraud cases seem tame next to your exciting adventures. I suppose it's an early start tomorrow?' he asked.

'Oh, yes. I want to be outside the Moorhouses' home by 7.30 in the morning. We'll take them in first and pick up Amy Cooper later. I'll have a warrant by then for a full search of the Moorhouses' home which I'm sure will confirm it as our crime locus. I can't wait to hear how they'll explain their lies. With a bit of luck it'll be a quick confession and we can have it all tied up before Christmas.'

'If it's going to be an early morning, perhaps we should go to bed early?' Ravi's eyes twinkled. 'Leave the washing up – I'll do it in the morning after you've gone.'

'Now how can a girl resist such an offer?'

FORTY-SEVEN
WEDNESDAY 21ST DECEMBER

'More bloody rain!' Jenny shook her umbrella as she entered the office at the unearthly hour of 7am. 'I hate these dark winter mornings, it's so hard to drag myself out of bed.' Samantha was already at her desk, as was a hopeful-looking Kim Thatcher who'd dropped a couple of heavy hints about how she'd love to be in on the action of the day.

'Just be grateful it's not snow; we've had enough white stuff for one winter,' Sam reminded her DS. 'I've arranged for two marked cars with two uniforms in each to follow us to the Moorhouse home and a CSI team will be there soon after. The warrant is in order and I'm feeling confident we'll find this was the locus of the murder.'

Jenny slapped her forehead with her hand and sighed. 'Of course – there was no carpet on the lounge floor – the pretence of decorating now seems so obvious; how stupid are we?'

'Not stupid, Jen. We had no reason to suspect the man we were introduced to wasn't Dave Moorhouse. Right, is everything in place?' Samantha wasn't one for looking back to hunt for mistakes, preferring to focus on moving forward. The answer was an enthusiastic yes, so the team prepared themselves to arrest Beth, Callum and then Amy. 'You can ride with us, Kim.' Sam smiled at the huge grin which split the young DC's face.

The short drive through the wet streets of New Middridge was tense with nervous anticipation. The windscreen wipers worked hard to clear the pouring rain with an almost metronomic effect, lulling the car occupants into silence. The journey ended outside Beth's home. Sam, Jenny and Kim exited the Mini and peered at the house. It was still dark; curtains were closed and all was quiet – too quiet – with no sign of Dave's van parked in its usual spot.

When the marked cars pulled up behind them, Samantha beckoned the occupants to follow her to the door where Jenny stood with her finger on the doorbell. Sam looked through the letter box. There was no sign of life.

'Open up – police!' she shouted, but her gut told her there was no one inside. Frustrated, she gave the order to force the lock and moved back, fearing the worst. As the uniformed officers ran inside, announcing their presence and splitting up to search each room, Sam stood on the bare floorboards in the small lounge and mentally kicked herself.

'We couldn't have anticipated this.' Jenny stood beside her boss. 'I'll ring Paul, get him to put an APB out on the van. We'll find them.'

'Yeah, I know. I suppose I thought we'd have it sorted this week before Christmas, you know?'

'Could still happen.' Jenny took out her phone to make the necessary calls while Sam moved to stand down the uniformed officers, wanting them out of the house before the CSI team arrived.

'Shall we search the house?' Kim Thatcher asked.

'Just a quick look, and wear gloves. The CSIs won't want our fingerprints all over the place.'

'I think they're here.' Kim looked out of the window.

'Thanks, Kim. I'll have a word while you look around. See if clothes are missing and bathroom stuff, and then we'll get off to find out if Amy Cooper has done a runner too.'

'Do you think she will have?' Kim's eyes widened.

'Anybody's guess, but we'll soon know.' Samantha moved away to meet the CSI team and tell them what they were looking for.

'A forwarding address would be helpful.' Her disappointment was channelling into sarcasm. 'Failing that, bag up anything interesting for us to go through at the station. We're looking at this as the possible murder scene.'

Kim returned downstairs and shook her head. 'Just a few clothes left and virtually nothing in the bathroom. The fridge is empty and switched off too.'

Back in the Mini, a sense of frustration settled on the detectives, but Samantha used the setback to spur her on. She was keen to find some answers and Amy Cooper would be the best person to supply them.

FORTY-EIGHT
WEDNESDAY 21ST DECEMBER

'Why do we have to set off at this unearthly hour?' Beth pulled the duvet up under her chin and stared at Callum who was already showered and dressed. 'Bloody hell, Cal, it's only 5.30!'

'I want to get on the way before the traffic gets heavy. I have a weird feeling about staying here any longer than necessary, so get a move on while I pack the car. We can stop for something to eat on the way.' Cal watched Beth struggle out of bed, scratching her backside and yawning as she plodded to the bathroom. He swallowed hard, experiencing an emotion he couldn't readily identify – fear certainly but also a weighty regret – was the romance fading in their relationship already? Had this been nothing more than a stupid mid-life crisis?

Quickly, Cal zipped up his suitcase and lugged it downstairs. Hearing the rain drumming heavily on the windows he shrugged on his parka and unlocked the door. Outside, he shivered. Was it the cold or opening Dave's van which sent a chill through him? He threw the case into the back and returned to the house to start loading the boxes. Hell, he'd be glad to get away from this house – it was creeping him out.

Since being forced to hide out at Beth's, the place felt increasingly like a prison, the walls made him feel trapped, the space claustrophobic. Callum had hardly slept which wasn't any great surprise, he was sleeping in Dave's bed with Dave's wife, and memories of the man's body sprawled on the lounge floor disturbed him more than he could ever have expected. But now there was an urgency within him. He had to move swiftly, circumstances had committed him to this course of action and there was no way back. It galled him that he'd have to live with another man's identity for the rest of his life – Beth had even started calling him Dave, which he loathed – she said he'd get used to it but Callum doubted he ever would.

By the time all the boxes were in the van, Cal was soaked and there was still no sign of Beth. 'Are you ready yet?' he shouted upstairs, but the only reply was a grunt. Running upstairs Cal found Beth applying make-up, something she rarely did. 'What the hell are you doing?'

'Getting ready!' Beth matched his tone. 'If this is to be the start of my new life I want to feel confident. I don't want to arrive in Wigton feeling anything other than my best.'

Instead of arguing, Callum zipped up Beth's case and heaved it downstairs, mumbling almost to himself. 'We need to set off before the neighbours see us.'

By 6.30am the ageing white van was heading north on the A1. Callum expected the journey to take the best part of three hours, mainly because he'd keep well within the speed limits; getting stopped by the police didn't figure in his escape plan. He was confident no one had seen them leave, the rain proved to be a blessing. Even hardened dog walkers would probably wait until it eased before venturing out on such a shocking morning.

Beth dozed in the passenger seat. She'd been remarkably calm about the move, as if it was some big new adventure rather than a cowardly attempt to escape the heinous crime they'd committed. Cal glanced at her once or twice, again wondering how their life together would work out and if the grass really was greener on the other side – but it was too late for regret, he was tied to Beth by the crime they were running away from.

Beth stirred and opened her eyes. 'Are we nearly there?'

'About halfway.' Callum kept his eyes on the road.

'I'm starving. When can we eat?'

'I'll pull in at the next service station.'

Beth shuffled down in her seat. 'Great, wake me when we get there.'

FORTY-NINE

WEDNESDAY 21ST DECEMBER

Amy was unsure of her feelings concerning Cal and Beth's leaving. Today was the day, but it would be a low-key move, not quite a moonlight flit, just a walking away from their old life and the seemingly insurmountable problems of their current situation. No way would Amy be going to wave them off – there would be no fond farewells, tears and promises of keeping in touch. After the events of the last three weeks, it would probably have been better if Beth hadn't even told her where they were heading.

Amy put the kettle on to boil and looked at the clock on the wall – 9.25am – still early. There were no plans to consider, no responsibilities to prepare for, her life was drawing to a close with absolutely no purpose. *Will anyone even miss me?* It was a sobering thought.

Sitting close to the fire, the cold seemed to penetrate through to her bones these days, Amy cradled her mug and found her thoughts slipping back to Beth, to the past. Could this be because she had no future?

After the incident when their dad had locked her in the cupboard, Beth became unusually withdrawn. Perhaps her spirit had finally been broken; as a child, there was surely only so much cruelty she could take. Beth's appetite was gone and she lost weight rapidly, weight she could ill afford to lose. Amy tried to revive the old spirited Beth she'd admired so much but it seemed the light had gone from her.

The suggestion of taking Beth to the doctor met with a cold response from their mother who didn't dare ask her husband. For several weeks the family home was quiet but Amy would have preferred the old Beth back, the spirited, devil-may-care sister. School, which had always been a welcome escape for both girls, became an effort for Beth to attend and there were many days when she stayed at home, alone. As long as she was quiet and didn't make a mess, their parents seemed not to care.

One day when Beth couldn't muster the energy to go to school, their dad was at work and their mum had left Beth to her own devices, Amy came home to an eerily silent house.

Calling her sister's name as she ran upstairs, she instinctively knew something was terribly wrong, but was unprepared for the sight which met her in her sister's bedroom. Beth was slumped on the bed, unconscious, with an empty bottle of paracetamol beside her. Amy screamed, convinced her sister was dead but when she ran to the bed, Beth was still breathing. Amy flew back downstairs and dialled 999 – neither girl possessed a mobile phone – and from then, events were blurred. Paramedics dragged a sobbing Amy off her sister and set to work establishing the seriousness of her condition. Amy was tasked with contacting her parents and then allowed to accompany Beth in the ambulance.

At the hospital, Beth was treated with an intravenous acetylcysteine, which the doctors said would prevent liver damage. If Amy hadn't found her in time, she could have died. A barrage of questions were asked which Amy was afraid to answer;

why would her sister do this; was everything at home okay? It was almost a relief when her parents arrived and Amy was no longer the focus of attention.

After two days in hospital, Beth was allowed home. The incident prompted a series of visits from social services, which infuriated Amy's dad. The girls were interviewed on their own but fear of the repercussions which would surely come, prevented them from telling the truth about their home life – they dreaded being taken into care and possible separation, even more than staying at home. Beth managed to convince the authorities she'd taken the tablets accidentally for a persistent headache, unaware of how easily she could overdose.

Within weeks the family were left alone. If there were concerns about the girls' welfare, overstretched staffing probably swayed the social worker into deciding no further intervention was necessary.

Looking back, it was a sickening experience, one of the most frightening of Amy's life. If anything had happened to Beth, she would have been devastated, and from then on Amy kept as close to her sister as possible, developing an even greater sense of responsibility towards her.

Strangely, the experience also had an effect on their father. Maybe he feared interference from the authorities, but his temper mellowed and an uneasy truce reigned throughout the house. Perhaps this had something to do with his surprising low-key reaction to the fantasy of Amy's 'pregnancy' a few years later.

Gradually, Beth returned to her usual self. Her appetite increased and life became so much more bearable than before. The sisters never had the conversation as to Beth's intentions that day but the experience frightened Amy, even though the outcome proved positive.

Shaking herself back to the present, Amy refused to allow herself to slip into becoming maudlin. Having done as much as she could to secure a happy future for Beth, she wished her sister and her husband well. Briefly, Amy wondered when she would see them again, or should it be *if*.

Just as she was about to switch on daytime television, the doorbell rang. Amy sighed – *what now?* – she really couldn't be bothered to see anyone today.

FIFTY
WEDNESDAY 21ST DECEMBER

Ignoring the doorbell was appealing but not a feasible option. Amy's car was parked outside, whoever it was would know she was in. Wearily she dragged her aching body from the sofa and turned towards the door where a woman's shape could be distinguished through the decorative glass panel.

'Hi, Amy!' Fran's cheery greeting took her by surprise, it was so incongruous with the miserable weather and Amy's depressed mood. 'Sorry to call so early but I have the prescription for you – the sleeping tablets?' She smiled at Amy who must have looked vague, her mind was all over the place this morning. 'Are you okay to get it filled or would you like me to get them for you?'

Before Amy had the chance to reply a Mini drew up behind Fran's car, closely followed by a police car.

'Oh!' Fran's head swivelled from Amy to the cars, then back again as Samantha Freeman and Jenny Newcombe stepped out of the Mini and walked purposefully towards the front door. Amy watched them silently, feeling the cold damp air suddenly penetrating her body – this was not good news. Her legs felt unable to hold her up and she slumped against the door-jamb.

Fran grabbed her arm to steady her and prevent her from collapsing.

Sam reached the door first. 'Can we go inside, Amy?'

Amy turned towards Fran and offered a half smile. 'I'm okay.' She turned to go inside. Jenny flashed her ID at Fran who allowed them to pass. Then, not fully understanding what was happening, the nurse followed them inside.

'We've found Callum alive and well,' Samantha said first, 'but you already know he's alive, don't you?' Amy opened her mouth then thought better of it and closed it, remaining silent. A very solemn Samantha announced she was arresting Amy, set out the crimes in question and cautioned her, then Jenny took the woman's arm and led her outside to the waiting officers.

Turning to a very stunned-looking Fran, Samantha asked her name and connection to Amy. Fran gave a slight shake of her head and blinked, which seemed to jolt her back into professional mode.

'I'm a nurse. My name's Fran Jenkinson and I'm rather concerned about what's happening here. Amy isn't a well woman – I can't say much more, but as you appear to have arrested her on some very serious charges, I suggest you have her examined by a doctor as soon as possible.'

'Thank you for the heads-up, Ms Jenkinson, we'll certainly take medical advice before we interview Mrs Cooper. Perhaps you'd give your contact details to my sergeant and then leave us to continue here.' Fran produced her card and gave it to Jen before leaving.

Jenny turned the card over. 'Look at this, boss. She's a Macmillan nurse – do you think Amy has cancer?'

'Damn it, that complicates things. Ring Layla and ask her to arrange for the duty doctor to see Amy as soon as she arrives at the station. You'd better tell her to put her somewhere more comfortable than the cells, too. See if the rape suite's free. We'll have a quick look around here then get back to the station.'

Jenny took out her phone and made the call while Sam climbed the stairs. It was futile spending much time there, the place had been searched by them and the CSI team quite thoroughly, but it was prudent to check things were in order before they locked up. On one such occasion, Sam had nearly locked a cat in an empty house after arresting its owner, who never said a word about his feline accomplice. She shuddered to think what might have happened to the poor thing if she hadn't discovered it.

There was a small pile of paperwork on the desk in the back bedroom which hadn't been there before so Samantha bagged it to take back to the office and read later. Satisfied everything was in order, they left number 43 Cypress Close, their thoughts turning to the awaiting interview.

'Do you think Amy knows where her sister is?' Kim asked.

'I'd put money on it.'

Samantha pulled her Mini into the police station car park in time to see an ambulance pulling out, lights flashing. Layla was in the doorway, chewing on her thumbnail.

'What's going on?'

'Sorry, boss, but Amy Cooper had a seizure before we could get the medic to take a look at her. It appeared serious so we called the ambulance – she was unresponsive as they took her away. Paul's gone with her, he said he'll wait there until he hears from you.'

'Are you sure she wasn't faking it?' Jenny frowned.

'Positive, it was pretty scary, no one could fake that.'

'Damn it!' Samantha stormed towards the stairs to go to her office, Kim and Jenny following behind. Pushing open the swing doors and throwing her bag onto the nearest desk, Sam flopped down on a chair and ran her fingers through her hair.

'This is not the way today should have worked out. We should have the three of them in custody and be unravelling their lies. How the hell did this happen?'

'Sod's law.' Jenny sighed. 'So what now, boss?'

FIFTY-ONE
WEDNESDAY 21ST DECEMBER

Callum woke Beth as they turned off the A1 into a service station. He ordered a black coffee, unable to stomach food, while Beth chose a bacon sandwich and a latte. Callum was lost in thought and barely heard Beth's chatter; after sleeping for the first half of the journey she appeared much more animated and seemed unaware that Callum had tuned out.

Back in the van Beth complained of the cold and urged Cal to drive faster. 'I'm flooring it as it is!' he snapped. 'And the heater's on full blast. Don't blame me for the state of Dave's van...'

Beth ignored him and fiddled with the radio. 'How much longer?'

'Another hour, maybe more.'

'Great, I'm looking forward to seeing our new home, aren't you, Cal?' She squeezed his knee playfully, causing him to swerve the van.

'Don't do that! We'll see it soon enough.'

An hour later they entered Wigton. Cal drove into the town centre looking for King Street where the estate agent would be waiting with the key to their rental property. It was a small town, easy to navigate and King Street was fairly central, just off High Street. There was short-term parking nearby and as Callum exited the car he stretched his legs and rolled his shoulders to remove the kinks, glad to have arrived.

'It's a bit small, isn't it?' Beth took in the centre of their new hometown.

'We knew that. You said it looked pretty when we googled it – countrified – which was what you wanted.'

'It's pretty enough I suppose but there aren't many shops.'

Callum refrained from making another comment and headed in the direction of the estate agent. Beth tagged along behind.

There were no other customers in the agent's office and they were treated to the undivided attention of a smart, middle-aged lady who introduced herself as Marion.

'Welcome to Wigton.' She smiled. 'Lavender Cottage is beautiful and you're lucky to have seen it when you did, we've had loads of enquiries since you agreed on it.' Marion handed over the keys, gave a few simple directions as to the location of their new home and asked if she could help in any other way.

'Thank you but I'm sure we'll find our way around soon.' Callum didn't want to chat. They returned to the van and headed towards Lavender Cottage.

From the outside the cottage appeared almost exactly the same as in the photographs only without colour in the garden, but it was December. It was small with no near neighbours although they'd passed a few houses on the single-track road leading up to the cottage. Beth was keen to go inside, Callum was straining to muster any enthusiasm but followed on to view the place they would be living in for the foreseeable future.

Beth sniffed the stale air. 'Smells a bit musty, but I suppose it's been locked up for a while.' The layout was boxy; a lounge to the right of the door, a kitchen to the left and behind those were the bedroom and bathroom, a simple square building divided into four. It was clean, recently painted and the furniture looked dated but serviceable.

'Do you like it?' Beth turned to Callum.

'It's small but okay, I suppose.'

'We can make it cosy, can't we? Some colourful rugs and throws, a few plants and pictures... let's unpack the van and make the place our own.' Beth was animated. Cal thought she looked very young and excited as if they'd arrived at a holiday destination. 'Aren't you happy to be here, Cal?'

'*Happy*? That's not the word I'd use. This isn't some big new adventure, Beth. We've run away... it's not how we planned to be together.' Callum couldn't pretend he was comfortable with the situation, too much had happened to allow him peace of mind; he thought he'd never feel relaxed again.

'But we're together, does it matter how it happened? We're free of Dave and Amy – this is the start of our new life.' Beth spoke with excitement but Callum detected a coldness behind her eyes as she stared at him, almost daring him to argue. He turned without comment to return to the van and start unloading their possessions.

When everything was inside, Beth started putting things away, humming to herself as if she hadn't a care in the world. Callum struggled to remain calm – here she was playing house as if they were on holiday or on an exciting adventure. He felt suddenly very sick. Had he exchanged one prison for another?

FIFTY-TWO
WEDNESDAY 21ST DECEMBER

The hospital car park was full. Samantha reluctantly took a spot reserved for volunteer drivers and displayed her Police sign on the windscreen, silently hoping the place wouldn't be needed. To say the day hadn't gone to plan was an understatement, and now Sam wanted to speak to Amy Cooper to find out if the woman knew where her sister and husband were.

DC Paul Roper was seated in the emergency room and stood when he saw his boss approaching.

'How is she, Paul?'

'Unconscious, or sleeping, I don't really know – they won't tell me anything even though I've explained the situation.' Nurses and paramedics went about their duty and no one took any notice of the detectives. 'She's in that cubicle.' Paul pointed to a curtained-off space barely large enough for a bed. 'A doctor went in a while ago but I think she's alone now.'

'Thanks. I'll see what I can find out from the nurse at the desk.' Sam stood in front of a very young-looking nurse who appeared engrossed in her computer screen. 'Excuse me,' Sam eventually interrupted. 'Can I enquire about Amy Cooper?'

'Are you a relative?'

'No, I'm a police officer. I think my colleague has explained that we need to speak to Amy, who is technically under arrest, to see if she knows the whereabouts of her husband and sister.'

'I'm sorry, I can't let you see her without permission from the doctor.' The girl's eyes returned to the screen.

'Then can I see the doctor?'

'He's with a patient. I'll try to catch him when he comes out.'

Frustrated, Samantha sat down. 'Damn, I know they're busy but so are we! Keep an eye out for the doctor and grab him if he comes by, I'll get us a couple of coffees.' Sam wanted to keep moving. Hospitals weren't her favourite place, especially accident and emergency rooms, too much blood and pain for her liking.

Returning with the coffee, Sam found Paul on his feet. 'The doctor's in with Amy now. I didn't catch him on the way in but maybe we can talk to him when he's finished in there?'

Two minutes later a doctor swished the curtain to one side and left Amy's cubicle. They caught a glimpse of Amy, eyes closed, on the bed. Sam was in the doctor's face before he could escape, her badge in front of his nose where he couldn't miss it.

'Yes, I heard the police were here. Come with me.' The tall, long-limbed man hurried towards a room away from the beds, ushered Sam and Paul inside and closed the door. 'I don't know what you think Mrs Cooper has done but she's a very sick woman. This latest seizure was the most serious yet, she very nearly didn't regain consciousness.'

'When will she be discharged?'

'Good grief, woman, have you not been listening? There's no way you can cart her off to prison in her condition.'

'I appreciate the situation and I understand you can't tell me much more about her condition but Mrs Cooper has been arrested for attempting to cover up a murder by disposing of a body. There are several other charges pending too. I have no intention of *carting her off to prison* but she has accomplices who have disappeared. I'm keen to talk to Mrs Cooper to see if she can help me locate them.'

The doctor appeared to mellow. 'Ah, I see. I didn't realise the charges were quite so serious. I'll be keeping her overnight for observation and to run some blood tests. She's not entirely with it yet but when she's transferred to a ward, you might be able to see her for a few minutes, will that help?'

'It will, thank you. I'll also need to place a guard outside her room. Mrs Cooper is considered a flight risk.'

The doctor raised an eyebrow. 'Okay. Someone will let you know as soon as we can transfer her to a ward.' He hurried from the room leaving the door open behind him.

'Well, Paul, I don't think we both need to stay. I'll get back to the station and arrange a guard for the rest of the day and overnight. You hang around until someone arrives. Let's hope she'll be discharged tomorrow.'

'The doc wasn't giving much away, do you know how sick she is?'

'When we arrested her, she was with a Macmillan nurse, but we shouldn't jump to conclusions. I'm hoping now that Amy's been left to carry the can she'll be forthcoming about who did what and why. If there's any change before you leave give me a ring, or tell the officer guarding her to ring.'

She would be back first thing in the morning to speak to Amy and pick up the threads of this increasingly complicated case.

'I need wine!' Samantha greeted Ravi with the request as she walked into his open arms.

'A bad day, huh?'

'The worst. What should have been three easy arrests all went badly wrong and I ended up with no one in the cells.'

Ravi poured two glasses of wine and sat beside her on the sofa. 'Never mind – we can just talk about family, the wedding and our future.' His smile worried Samantha but she knew he was right. She gave more than her allotted hours to the job and they deserved some downtime.

FIFTY-THREE
THURSDAY 22ND DECEMBER

After an uncomfortable night, Callum was convinced the mattress on the bed was damp. Beth was up early. Cal could hear her in the kitchen, hell you could hear every sound in every room in this miserable place, with the kettle boiling and toast popping from the toaster. Dragging himself from the bed he showered then went into the kitchen.

'Good morning, Dave!' Beth laughed.

'Don't call me that! When it's just the two of us I still want to be Callum.'

'Okay but it might get confusing – can't you just get used to being Dave?'

'No, so drop it.' Callum helped himself to toast, the subject closed. They'd planned to go supermarket shopping that morning before finishing the unpacking although neither activity filled him with joy. Callum was growing increasingly uncomfortable with the decision they'd made and wondered if they'd acted rashly – the desire to escape prompting a panicked knee-jerk reaction. The reality was that their problems still existed, only in a different location. Callum was also feeling guilty for involving Amy and then leaving her to cope alone. Beth seemed to have forgotten about her sister.

'Perhaps we can ring Amy when we're out, from a phone box if you don't want to use your phone?' he suggested.

'Why, she'll be fine, she always is and I don't think they have phone boxes anymore, do they?' Beth poured more coffee into her cup and buttered another slice of toast.

'I thought you'd be missing her. You've always been close and she's looked out for you over the years. We owe her, Beth. I think we should at least ring.'

'I don't owe her anything. Oh yes, I know she felt guilty about not *protecting* me from Dad, but Amy was always a bit of a wimp – no backbone. Maybe if she'd answered him back like I did he wouldn't have been the bully he was.'

'Beth, that's not fair!'

'Who cares? So, what if she has been good to us? The only thing I've ever wanted from Amy was her husband – and now I've got you!' The smug look on Beth's face stunned Callum, leaving him speechless as Beth continued. 'Come on, let's clear up and get out to explore our new surroundings.'

Callum had often resented the way Amy appeared to consider Beth's needs before his, but for Beth to be so callous about it, so unappreciative... This was not the way he'd wanted things to turn out, what a bloody mess he'd gotten himself into.

The drive into Wigton gave them a chance to familiarise themselves with their new hometown. Beth's mood was somewhat more mellow and she was making an effort at conversation, an attempt, he assumed, to draw Callum out of his melancholy, but he couldn't relax. With little enthusiasm for the mundane task of shopping, Cal was eager to return to the cottage. When they eventually got back he decided it was time for a serious conversation.

'We've got to talk, Beth.'

Beth snaked her arm around his waist and pressed herself close to him. 'Really, I thought you were a man of action, not words.'

He pushed away from her. 'I'm serious. Are you in denial or something? This isn't a holiday, Beth.'

'In denial about what? Isn't this what we wanted, to be together away from our dreary little lives? Lighten up, Cal, what do you want me to do, go around miserable all the time like you seem to be?'

'No, just get real. Yes, we wanted to get away from Dave and Amy but not like this – not with Dave dead and me assuming his identity; this was never part of the plan. I've been drawing his benefits illegally, and you want me to look for a job in his name, but what happens if the police discover the body is Dave? Hell, Beth, we'll be in serious trouble.'

'But you told me you'd sort it. It was you who wanted to get rid of the body, you and Amy, with all your talk of insurance money. Don't turn on me now!'

'It was you who wouldn't let me call the police when it could have been considered self-defence! You should have waited until I was with you to tell Dave you were leaving, as I said, but oh no, you wanted to do it your way and look how it's worked out!'

Beth's nostrils flared and her eyes narrowed. 'Don't blame me for everything – you were a willing partner as I remember. So, what do you expect me to do now?'

'We have to at least keep in touch with Amy to know what the police are doing. If they discover it's Dave's body, we're in trouble and we'll probably have to move on again...'

'But why? Amy won't tell them where we are.'

'Maybe not but they'll be looking at us for murder then and won't give up. We need to get rid of the van for a start, it can be linked to Dave and they could find us if we keep using it.'

Beth turned away and put her hands over her ears. Callum was stunned, she was behaving like a child. Would she stamp her feet next until she got her own way? The weight of everything he'd done lay heavily on him and looking incredulously at the back of Beth's head, Callum made the decision as to what he must do next.

FIFTY-FOUR
THURSDAY 22ND DECEMBER

DI Samantha Freeman was at the hospital by 8.30am. Knowing their routine started early, Sam didn't think she'd be in the way and if the nurses were busy it could be a good time to talk to Amy.

Sam stopped at the nurses' station to speak to the sister, explaining what she wanted.

'Ah, yes – and then perhaps you can take your policeman away with you. We don't encourage unnecessary people on the wards these days, he's in the way.'

'I'm sorry but he'll have to remain until Mrs Cooper's discharged. She's technically under arrest.' Sam smiled her best smile.

'The doctor won't be here for another couple of hours at least – he'll decide then if discharge is appropriate.'

'Can I see her now?'

'Okay. In the circumstances, we had to put her in a private room. She's at the end of the corridor in the room where your man's sitting.'

'Thank you.' Sam tried to be polite but the sister was already staring at her computer screen. The officer on guard duty stood when he saw Sam approaching. 'Sit down – have you had a quiet night?'

'Yes. Mrs Cooper slept all night. I think they gave her something, but I know she's awake now, they've taken breakfast in.'

'Why don't you go and grab yourself a coffee and a sandwich while I talk to her.'

'Great, thanks. I'll be back in fifteen?'

'Fine.'

Amy was sitting up in bed, wearing a pink hospital gown and looking less than pleased to see Samantha.

'Good morning. How are you feeling today?'

'As if you care.' Amy's stare was cold. Sam chose to ignore the barb.

'We need to talk, Amy, and I'd like the truth this time. Can you tell me where Beth and Callum are?'

'No – not now, but I will talk to you when I'm out of here. Will you be taking me into custody?'

'Yes. Assuming the doctor is happy to discharge you and you're well enough to answer questions, and I would advise you to contact a solicitor to accompany you.'

'I won't need a solicitor. I'll tell you whatever you want to know.'

Samantha felt a frisson of excitement run through her – was Amy finally going to tell the truth? Maybe she'd get the case wrapped up before Christmas after all. An image of how pleased Ravi would be if this was the case almost made her smile. 'Thank you, but for now perhaps you can tell me where to find your husband and sister.'

'No. When I'm out.' Amy was determined and it hardly seemed appropriate to argue with a hospital patient. Sam reined in her frustration – she'd have to wait.

'Perhaps you'd tell the officer outside when you're discharged and I'll come and pick you up.'

'Okay. Now if you don't mind leaving, I'm feeling tired.' Amy shuffled down the bed and closed her eyes.

Fine! Round one to Amy, but this is only just beginning.

Samantha left the room and sat to wait for the uniformed officer. Excitement and curiosity ran equally through her mind, it would prove difficult to wait but hopefully the doctor would discharge his patient today.

The constable came hurrying along the corridor, his to-go coffee in his hand. 'Sorry, there was a queue.'

'It's okay. Our prisoner's not talking but says she will at the station.' Sam gave the constable her card. 'I want you to ring me as soon as they say she can leave. I'll come back to take her in myself.'

'Yes, will do.' He grinned. 'Sorry, I should have asked if you wanted a coffee.'

'No, I'm fine. I'll be off now. If you're relieved before she's discharged, pass on those instructions to the next officer – I don't want anything going awry.'

Once back in her car, Samantha rang Jenny to update her.

'Do you think she'll be discharged today?' Jen asked.

'She looked okay to me and they don't keep patients any longer than they need to these days. Better reserve an interview room for this afternoon and make sure it's one with heating. We're going to have to tread very carefully with this one. Maybe you could let the DCI know that Amy's promised to talk. It might go some way to making up for losing Callum and Beth.'

'Will do, boss!'

Sam ended the call and returned to her mental gymnastics of wondering what would transpire from the interview with Amy. She could hardly contain her excitement.

FIFTY-FIVE
THURSDAY 22ND DECEMBER

Amy Cooper sat on the edge of the hospital bed wearing the clothes she'd had on the previous day and looking frail. Clutching a bag of medication and a discharge letter, she had no other possessions when Samantha arrived to escort her to the police station.

'How are you feeling?' Sam asked.

'Okay.' At least this time she took the question at face value, Sam thought.

A nurse followed her into the room pushing a wheelchair. 'Hospital policy!' She smiled and manoeuvred the chair beside the bed. Amy rolled her eyes yet obediently climbed into the chair.

'Can you manage?' The nurse addressed Sam who nodded and took charge of the chair. The two left the ward without fuss and entered the lift to descend to the ground floor.

Amy looked up at Sam. 'No handcuffs?' she asked.

'Do you need them?'

Once inside the car – Sam had selected a more comfortable pool car to use rather than her little Mini – the pair drove the short distance to New Middridge police station in silence, each anticipating the coming interview. Sam checked if Amy had eaten lunch, she didn't want her to faint with hunger, and she herself had managed a bacon bun earlier, washed down with coffee. Taking Amy straight to the interview room, they found Jenny already waiting, adjusting the radiator as the room was now too hot. Jen asked after Amy's health and received the same one-word answer, *okay*.

A constable followed them into the room with three coffees and a plate of biscuits – they were determined to do everything by the book. Jenny switched on the recording equipment and reminded Amy of the charges against her and that she was still under caution. Samantha then took over.

'Amy, I asked you earlier if you wanted a solicitor and you declined. Would you like to change your mind?'

'No.'

'Right. When we came to your house yesterday, we'd already been to Beth's to arrest her and Callum but they weren't there. A quick search established they'd left – can you tell us where they are.'

'They were heading north I think but I haven't heard from them since they left.'

'And when was that?'

The answer was a shrug of Amy's shoulders. Samantha decided to leave the whereabouts of the others – she was keen to learn what Amy had promised to tell her. 'You said you'd tell me everything I wanted to know. The tape's running. Perhaps you'd like to start at the beginning and tell me how Dave Moorhouse died and the role you played in it.'

Amy took a sip of her coffee then placed it back on the table, running her fingers around the edge of the mug. 'I killed him.' Her words were flat, it didn't appear to Sam that she was trying to shock them or mislead them. If anything there was regret in her voice.

'I didn't mean to, it wasn't planned, it just happened.' Another sip of coffee was the only movement in the room. Jenny appeared to be holding her breath, choosing not to interrupt the confession they were hearing. Even Samantha managed to wait quietly without prompting Amy to continue. The woman seemed to need time and space.

'It was Tuesday, the seventh of December. I went to visit Beth. She didn't know I was coming, it was a spur-of-the-moment thing. It was mid, maybe late morning when I arrived and I heard the shouting before reaching the door. You have to understand that Dave was a violent man – he regularly hit Beth. Oh, he apologised afterwards, blamed his temper or too much to drink and Beth believed him and forgave him.

'We grew up with a violent father. Beth took the brunt of his anger, so I think she assumed it was normal behaviour between a man and his wife. I tried to tell her to leave Dave – she didn't love him – but she refused – said there was nowhere else to go, but she could have come to us! Callum had offered to sort him out in the early days but Beth wouldn't let him, kept insisting Dave didn't mean to hurt her and the making up was worth it. But he was a mean, lazy bastard – he didn't deserve her.

'When I arrived that Tuesday morning they were in the middle of a blazing row. Beth's nose was bleeding and her eye was red. I literally walked in on them – they were making so much noise they didn't hear me arrive. Beth was on her knees and Dave was thrashing her with a belt! I was horrified – this was my sister he was beating. Without thinking I waded in. There was a lamp on the sofa table and I instinctively picked it up and hit Dave over the head. He appeared stunned and came after me. Beth was screaming and Dave was spitting obscenities; he raised the belt to me so I hit him again.

'It stopped him and he fell to the floor, bleeding. He seemed only semi-conscious so I thought it was safe to see to Beth. She was dazed and hurt. I took her into the kitchen and cleaned her up then made her have a drink. Her eye wasn't the worst of the injuries, Dave's belt left terrible welts on her back, raw and bleeding. I bathed them, dressed them and we sat, neither of us knowing what to do.

'I could hear Dave's occasional moans but at that moment I hated him so much I had no sympathy for him – for all I cared he could die! I wasn't thinking straight and Beth looked to me to know what to do. With hindsight I can see it would have been better – the right thing – to call the police or an ambulance, yet I couldn't stop trembling and my mind wouldn't focus. We did nothing. I know now it was unforgivable but I wanted Dave to suffer. Perhaps I was transferring all my hate and anger for our father onto him – I don't know – but I did nothing. There was a sense of satisfaction in knowing Dave was in pain – the tables had turned – he usually inflicted the pain but now he was the victim. It seemed like karma.' Amy was fiddling with her empty mug. 'Do you think I could have another coffee and maybe a short break?'

'No problem.' Jenny stated the time for the tape and switched it off. 'Would you like to visit the bathroom?'

'Yes, please.'

Jenny led the way, leaving Samantha trying to figure out if the woman was genuine or spinning a very credible lie.

FIFTY-SIX
THURSDAY 22ND DECEMBER

When Jenny returned Amy to the interview room, she and Samantha left her with a PC while arranging coffee, and to allow time for her to rest.

'Wow!' Jenny sighed, looking at her boss for a reaction.

'Yeah, wow. She's clearly thought this through, it's all very neat and tidy, isn't it?'

'It is, but that's good surely. Everything Amy's confessed to fits in with the forensics so far – we need to move on to the disposal of the body next.'

'Yes, but we should ask her again if she'd like a solicitor. With Amy's medical condition she'll be charged and released on police bail. I'll feel more comfortable if she has someone fighting her corner. Initially, I thought it would be a manslaughter charge if she was protecting her sister as she said, but then by her own admission they virtually left the man to die – it'll have to be murder.'

'So, you do believe Amy did it?'

'When we find Callum and Beth and hear their story, I'll feel happier about making a judgement. Come on, let's grab a quick coffee before round two.'

They settled for what passed as coffee from the machine in the office so they could catch up with any developments from the rest of the team. 'She's confessed to killing him,' Jenny told Paul and Layla.

'Really? What part did the others play?' Paul wanted to know the full story.

'We haven't got round to all the details. Amy claims to have interrupted Dave Moorhouse beating Beth and instinctively hit him with the first thing which came to hand.'

'That wouldn't happen to be an onyx lamp base, would it?' An *I know something you don't know* grin crept onto Paul's face.

'Forensics?' Jenny's eyes widened. Paul passed over the interim report which Samantha grabbed with both hands. She scanned the pages, seeking the salient points and then passed it to Jenny.

'We were right. Dave Moorhouse was killed in his own home – the living room. Their efforts to clean up were good but not good enough. Rick has more than enough to put an accurate scenario together – he's working on it now according to his notes – hell, that man lives and dreams blood splatter. The lamp base is apparently a perfect match to the head wounds and there are traces of blood which match Dave's – Amy was telling the truth about that much.' Samantha pushed away the coffee Jen had placed in front of her and took a swig from a bottle of water in her bag. 'Right, round two, Jen. Let's get going.'

On their way back to the interview room, Samantha told her DS they needed to draw more detail from Amy. Her illness meant she needed to be treated carefully but questioning would have to be stepped up – specifics in particular – to ensure Amy was telling the truth.

As Samantha entered the interview room, she experienced what was almost a wave of pity for Amy Cooper who looked thoroughly exhausted. Jenny switched on the tape and reminded Amy she was still under caution then Sam took over.

'Are you able to continue, Amy?'

'Yes, I'm fine.'

'We can always fetch a doctor if you need one.'

'No, thank you. I'd just like to get it over with.'

'Again, I would advise you to have a solicitor present. We can halt the interview while we arrange one?'

'No.' Amy's tone was determined.

'Okay. Can we move on to what happened later in the afternoon of Tuesday the seventh of December?'

'I can't remember the exact timings – Beth was upset and I was still reeling from the shock of what I'd done. I tried to call Callum a few times but his phone must have been switched off, there was no answer. I remember shutting the kitchen door so we couldn't hear Dave's groans. I suppose I didn't consider that he might die, I expected him to eventually stand up and then we'd be in for it. Beth was in pain so I gave her paracetamol and we drank tea. At about five, I called Cal again and he answered. He came straight to Beth's but by the time he arrived, Dave was dead.' Amy stopped and gulped in air as if reliving the trauma again.

Samantha waited, giving her time to compose herself before asking, 'And what was Callum's reaction?'

'He wanted to call the police but the suggestion sent Beth into near hysteria – she was afraid – for me I suppose. We were all stunned, but it was me who came up with the idea of taking Dave's body out of town and making it look like a hit-and-run. Callum refused at first but I talked him round. Beth was in a state so we put her to bed. We made sure Dave had nothing to identify him in his pockets and together we put him in the van and took him away.' Amy paused and finished the coffee in her mug. She shuddered even though the room was warm.

'It was only later that I had the idea of pretending Callum was missing – and I persuaded the others to go along with it.' Amy's words weren't flowing as freely, her hands were moving under the table, picking at the skin on her fingernails and she looked tense.

'Are you okay to continue?' Jenny asked.

'Yes.' Amy sat up straighter in the chair, linked her fingers together to stop fiddling and began to speak again.

'Callum and Beth were having an affair. I'd known about it for months – they were planning on leaving together when she could get away from Dave. You may find it hard to believe but I didn't mind. I haven't loved my husband for a long time and things were only getting worse between us. When he told me about him and Beth it was almost a relief. My sister deserved a better life and if she was happy with Callum then good luck to them.

'Again, it was me who suggested reporting Callum as missing – then when the body was eventually found, we could identify it as Cal and claim the insurance money from his work. They'd have a nest egg to start their life together and I'd be comfortable too.' Amy looked from one detective to the other as if waiting for a reaction.

Jenny, remembering Sam's earlier words to draw more detail from Amy, asked, 'Going back to when you arrived at Beth's, did you not think to get help rather than wade in yourself? You're not in good health are you, Amy?'

'Um... I didn't stop to think, my sister was being beaten up...'

'But there are houses nearby, neighbours to call on, or you could have rung the police?'

'You don't stop to weigh up the options in a situation like that... you just do what you have to.'

'And later, what time did you say Dave died?'

'I don't know. When Callum arrived, he was dead, I hadn't been to look at him for a while before that.'

'How long is a while, Amy?'

'I don't know!'

'Minutes? Hours? You must have some idea. And how did you manage to lift Dave's body? The man was no lightweight.'

'Cal took most of the weight.' Amy's eyes filled with tears.

'Do you need another break?' Jen asked. Amy shook her head but Jenny sat back and looked at Samantha.

'Amy. I think we're going to leave the questions for today. Before we can let you go home, DS Newcombe will formally charge you. Because you've been charged, you'll be released on bail with conditions. An officer will drive you home and collect your passport. Do you understand?'

Amy nodded and Samantha stood to leave.

FIFTY-SEVEN
THURSDAY 22ND DECEMBER

Ravi was on the telephone when Samantha arrived home, his face serious as he glanced in her direction. Dropping her bag on the floor and shrugging off her coat, Sam snuggled beside him on the sofa and wormed her way under his arm, enjoying the warm comforting nearness of his body. He jumped as she wriggled her cold hands under his shirt.

'Of course I'm disappointed, but it doesn't make any difference.' Ravi squeezed Sam's shoulder as he spoke into the phone. 'No – tell them I'm sorry they won't be coming but it doesn't alter the fact... right, I'll leave it with you and we'll speak later.' He thumbed off his phone and sighed.

'What's wrong?'

'That was my mother. She's been in touch with my grandparents in India and they're not happy about the wedding. Apparently, they won't be coming over for the big day.'

'Oh, Ravi, I'm sorry. This is because I'm not Hindu I suppose?'

'Yeah, but don't worry. If they had their way, they'd find me a *suitable* wife from India who'll stay at home and give me lots of babies.'

'Wow, I didn't realise they were so traditional – so I'm not considered suitable then?'

'You'll do for me.'

'Should I convert to Hinduism?' Sam wasn't sure herself if she was serious or not, but being the cause of division in Ravi's family was an upsetting thought.

'There is a process you could go through called Ghar Wapsi, a kind of purification to become a Hindu – but by the look on your face it's not an option!' Ravi laughed. 'Seriously, it isn't an issue for me. My grandparents are old, they're never going to change now and as I've only ever met them in person a handful of times, I can live with their disapproval. They know I'm not a practising Hindu – and anyway, it's more about tradition for them than religion. My parents are happy with our marriage which will do for me.'

'It won't cause problems for your mum, will it?'

'No. Neither of my parents observes the rites of Hinduism – it would be hypocrisy for them to have expectations of us and they know it. Don't worry – I mean, they're celebrating Christmas, aren't they? Not very Hindu-ish I'd say. Now, tell me how your day went. Have you got your confession?'

'Yes...'

'And what's the *but*?' Ravi appeared to read her mind.

'I'm not entirely convinced. Amy Cooper has admitted to killing her brother-in-law. She's given us a believable motive and the facts concur with forensics but I feel I'm missing something.'

'Like the two accomplices?' Ravi raised an inquisitive eyebrow and grinned. Sam thumped his arm.

'More than that – you know what it's like – when things just don't feel right even though the facts stack up. We've released Amy on court bail, keeping a sick woman in the cells isn't an option. I'm not sure how seriously ill she is and she's not giving much away on that front. We'll bring her in for more questioning tomorrow but her condition limits us as to how much pressure we can apply. Jenny seems to think it's all cut and dried but I need to dig a bit deeper before I'll be entirely satisfied. Anyway, enough shop talk, what's for dinner, I'm starving?'

'There's curry in the freezer, I could do some rice, or would you like to go out? It might be good to have an evening out alone together.'

'Fine by me, as long as I get to choose the venue. And you can tell me all about your grandparents in India while I eat the most expensive dish on the menu. I'm curious to know what kind of family I'm marrying into.'

'It's a deal.'

FIFTY-EIGHT
FRIDAY 23RD DECEMBER

Amy Cooper arrived at the police station at 10am as previously arranged with Jenny Newcombe. Samantha and Jenny took coffee in for them all, Amy was hardly their usual murder suspect.

After the formalities, Sam asked, 'How are you this morning, Amy?' The women were sitting opposite each other with a table in between.

'Okay.' Amy shrugged, her words belied the dark circles beneath her eyes and the droop of her mouth. Samantha thought she looked so much older than the previous day.

'It may not seem relevant but it would be helpful if you could explain the nature of your illness. It's not our intention to cause you any unnecessary discomfort, so perhaps if we had a better idea of the problems you're facing?' Sam paused while Amy appeared to consider her request. Almost a full minute passed before she decided to speak.

'I have a glioblastoma, grade four brain tumour. It's inoperable but I'm on medication. The seizure on Wednesday was due to the tumour – I don't get any warning and their frequency is increasing.' Amy pressed her lips tightly together, it seemed she'd said all she wanted to on the subject.

'I'm sorry to hear that, Amy. Please let us know when you need breaks during our interviews or if we can make you more comfortable in any way. Have you heard from Callum or Beth since we last spoke?'

'No.'

'Have you thought any more about where they might be?'

'No.'

'If you do know, or hear from them, it will be in your best interest to tell us. Their testimonies could support what you've already said and help us to get this sorted out swiftly. Clearly there'll be charges for them to face but staying away to avoid them will only mean more trouble in the long term.' When Amy didn't respond, Samantha asked if she could go over the sequence of events on the day Dave Moorhouse died.

'I told you all this yesterday, why do I have to repeat it?'

'Because until we find your sister and husband, you're the only witness we have as to what actually happened that morning.'

Amy rolled her eyes and started her story again.

Less than half an hour into the interview, Amy was showing signs of fatigue so Samantha called a halt to the questioning. She and Jenny left Amy with more coffee and a constable and went to Sam's office.

'She's saying pretty much the same as yesterday – is that indicative of the truth, do you think, or a rehearsed lie?' Samantha wanted her sergeant's opinion.

'Well, they say if you stick to the truth you'll not slip up, and what she's said so far matches her confession yesterday. I'm inclined to believe her but as you're asking me, does that mean you don't?'

'I'm still unsure. And why have the others done a runner if she was the one who struck the fatal blow?'

'Yes, but they're guilty of conspiracy to hide a body, attempted fraud and possible other charges.'

'Hmm, I still think there's more we need to know. Are we tracing calls from all three?'

'Yes, Paul's got that in hand. He's waiting for a list from Callum and Beth's mobile phones too, then we may be able to verify Amy's story. And hopefully, if they use their phones we may even get a location.'

'Good work, Jen. I'm not sure how profitable this interview with Amy is. Considering her health, I think we'll keep it short and let her go home, I don't want it to appear we're bullying the woman. Did she drive here, do you know?'

'No, she's not allowed to drive since having the seizures. I'm not sure if she's been sticking to that, but she did come on the bus today.'

'Good. She's not for telling us how serious this tumour is but it could have a bearing on what she is telling us.'

Jenny looked puzzled. 'How do you mean?'

'Well, let's say it's terminal – if so, maybe Amy's taking the blame for Dave's death to protect her sister. That would explain Beth's sudden disappearance which seems a rushed decision, and Amy's got nothing to lose.'

'But can't they operate for tumours these days? And if it is terminal, she could still have years left, surely?'

'Yes, they can do wonders, I know, but she was seeing a Macmillan nurse – aren't they only for terminal cases?'

'I'm not sure. My aunt had breast cancer and changed visits from a Macmillan nurse for the duration of the illness, but it wasn't terminal, in fact, she's as large as life now.'

'Glad to hear it. Still, I think we need to go carefully with

Amy. A few more questions and then we'll get someone to take her home.'

Jenny gave a mock salute. 'Yes, boss.'

FIFTY-NINE
FRIDAY 23RD DECEMBER

Beth woke and stretched luxuriously. With a full day ahead, no commitments to worry about, and Callum to keep her company, life was looking good. It was almost daylight; the rain of the previous day had eased and Beth could hear birds singing in the trees outside. Callum must be up and about but she decided to have a few more minutes dozing, there was nothing to get up for.

Whoever would have thought she'd actually be living in Wigton with Cal? Yes, things could have gone better – Beth was glad Dave was dead although regrettably it meant police involvement. Still, at least it had the effect of mobilising Callum into action. Hopefully he'd soon find a job – he *was* a skilled joiner – and then he'd look after her as he'd promised.

The cottage was okay as a temporary measure; a bit small maybe but in summer it would be lovely and they could spend hours in the garden. Beth had always wanted a garden. Not a gravelled forecourt like their old place (a giant cat litter, Dave had called it) or a concrete backyard but somewhere she could grow flowers, maybe try her hand at vegetables too, live the good life, like that old programme on the telly – maybe even keep chickens.

As she rolled onto her side and snuggled down into the warmth, thoughts of her sister popped into her head. Beth supposed Cal was right and they should be grateful to Amy. She knew her sister didn't want him anymore but it must have been a shock to find out who *the other woman* was. It was a bit of a giggle really, although Callum didn't see the funny side.

Beth had waited a long time for Callum. As a teenager she'd envied Amy, coveting her handsome witty boyfriend, but she was too young to do anything about it, and then the lovebirds got married when Amy told everyone she was pregnant. It was only after the so-called miscarriage that Amy had told her the truth – there'd never been a baby. Callum must have really loved her sister to risk their dad's wrath by faking a pregnancy – Beth envied that kind of devotion.

Dave had never lived up to her expectations – in any department. He didn't love her, but lusted after her in a way she'd initially found flattering. Desperate to escape from home, Beth agreed to marry him. It appeared the sisters were fated to make parallel mistakes.

It was after a drunken barbecue that Callum first seemed to notice Beth. The couples rarely spent time together, it was only Amy's insistence which led them to endure the occasional foursome, and the barbecue at Amy and Cal's house was one such time. Dave made a pig of himself with the food and the beer – it was free – so, true to character why wouldn't he? An hour of overindulgence took its toll and Dave ended up sick as a dog before passing out on the sofa in the lounge. Amy went inside to tidy the kitchen, annoyed at her get-together being ruined by Dave, which left Callum and Beth alone in the garden.

The September heatwave and the beer must have gone to

their heads. Well, perhaps Beth still knew what she was doing but Cal didn't. Her low-cut summer minidress hadn't gone unnoticed and it delighted her when Cal couldn't keep his eyes off her. Sitting close together, their bodies hot and sticky, it seemed the most natural thing in the world to kiss – and when they started, they didn't want to stop. But they had to – they were not alone. In a drunken passion, the couple made furtive plans to meet, and the clandestine relationship was ignited. By October, Callum was infatuated with Beth's attentions, blinded by this new excitement in his life and ready to agree to her plans for a new life together.

Wigton was the commencement of this new life and as Beth lay reflecting, she smiled at her good fortune. With every confidence that Callum would look after her and keep them from being found, she relaxed. Amy too would keep their hideout a secret. Perhaps Beth should ring her sister occasionally. Callum was right; Amy had done much for her over the years, but her constant interference, which Amy clearly saw as being protective, was stifling. Beth was almost as pleased to get away from her sister as from Dave.

Throwing one leg out of bed, Beth called out to Callum. No answer. Struggling into her robe she went to the kitchen then the lounge but he wasn't in either room. The bathroom door was open – he wasn't in the shower. Perhaps he'd gone to the shop for some milk or something. Beth decided to shower and then make him a full breakfast to come home to. It was then she noticed the folded piece of paper propped up by the kettle.

Beth,

This has all been a huge mistake. I'm so sorry but I can't stay here with you. I don't know what I'll do or where I'll go but I hope you'll forgive me. What we've done was wrong and I can't forget it. Being with you will always remind me of our deceit and I can't do it any longer.

I've taken the van which I'll dump somewhere so the police can't trace you and I've left you as much cash as I can spare.

I wish you well,
Callum

Beth screwed up the paper and threw it to the other side of the room. With her fists balled she hammered on the kitchen wall until the pain made her stop. Looking out of the window confirmed the van was gone and covering the few steps to the bedroom established that Callum's clothes were gone too.

The bastard! When had he managed to get away? Maybe that was the reason he'd persuaded her to finish off the bottle of wine last night. Beth wanted to scream and shout, to find Callum and scratch his face until it bled.

Instead, she threw herself on the bed and sobbed.

SIXTY
FRIDAY 23RD DECEMBER

Amy had expected more from the police. Her interview had lasted barely an hour in total, hardly the grilling she'd anticipated. The consideration of the two detectives was also a surprise – she'd admitted to being a killer – surely such an admission warranted removing the kid gloves? And then the DS arranged for a lift home when she was quite prepared to catch a bus.

And Fran was a disappointment too. Amy hadn't heard from her nurse since her arrest. Were Macmillan nurses forbidden from supporting criminals, she wondered. Only time would tell. At least she wasn't in custody which would probably be the case if not for her tumour.

The house was quiet; the silence had taken some getting used to when Cal first left but being alone was something Amy was starting to appreciate, even crave. With only herself to care for she could be a slob whenever she felt like it, which was increasingly the case at the moment. With nowhere to go, she'd changed into pyjamas after lunch and by 4.30pm the curtains were closed and Amy was indulging in a glass of wine. Alcohol may be a no-no with her medication but who was going to take her to task when she was going to die sooner or later anyway? Sooner was looking increasingly preferable.

Sprawled on the sofa flicking channels on the television, Amy settled on a repeat of *The Repair Shop* which would take her nicely up to *Pointless*, but her viewing was interrupted by the doorbell. Maybe it was Fran, it would be good to have someone to talk to. There was only one way to find out, so she pulled her robe around herself, tied the belt and went to answer the door.

'Callum!' Amy staggered back as he hurried inside. He was the last person she'd expected to see on her doorstep. 'What the hell are you doing here, and where's Beth?'

'It's good to see you too, Amy.' Cal frowned, moving towards the fire to warm his hands.

'You know the police might be watching?' she warned. Callum sniggered thinking she was joking. Why would they be watching her?

'I was careful, no one saw me.'

Amy noticed how cold he looked and so much older than his years. This bloody mess was taking its toll on them all. 'You haven't told me, where's Beth?'

'In Wigton, playing house.'

'Why isn't she with you – does she know you're here?' Amy was considering all the possibilities as she looked at her husband. He was clearly distressed – had something happened – something else that is? 'Tell me, Cal!'

'I've left her. I can't do this, Amy. It was a mistake to get involved with Beth and to do what we did... with Dave.'

'But you said you loved her; you were going to take care of her!' Amy's protective instinct came into play, she was worried for her sister. 'Does Beth know you've come back here?'

'No. I didn't even know I was coming back, I left without a plan... it's been a confusing time, Amy.'

'You're telling me! You do know the police are looking for you?'

'Hell, no! Why, what's happened?'

'They know everything, Cal. They discovered the body was Dave and that you'd assumed his identity. I've been charged with his murder and they're looking for you and Beth as accomplices – then there's the fraud angle with the insurance money – they've worked most of it out.'

'Damn it! But why've they charged you with murder? Surely they should be looking for Beth?'

Amy lowered her eyes, unable to meet Callum's. 'I confessed.' Her voice was barely a whisper.

'You did what? But why – you weren't even there? Isn't this taking protecting Beth a little too far – and she doesn't appreciate it you know – she...' Callum stopped, unable to tell Amy the truth about how her sister felt, he couldn't disillusion her in such a cruel way after all she'd done for Beth.

'Beth needs me, she's vulnerable and I've let her down in the past, I'm not going to do it again!'

'No! You can't do this to yourself, Amy. You'll go to prison – you'll never cope with being locked away.'

'Don't worry about that. It's not going to happen.'

'Don't be stupid, Amy. If you've confessed to murder they're bound to send you to prison, even if they only charge you with manslaughter. You should have told them it was Beth, and it was self-defence – she might get away with it if we told them about the abuse Dave inflicted on her. But you could get fifteen years for murder!' Callum looked horrified and Amy could almost believe he cared. Chewing on her bottom lip she decided the only thing to do was to tell him the truth.

'There's something else.' Again she lowered her eyes.

'What?' Was he angry with her or himself, she wondered.

'I'm ill, Callum. I have a brain tumour and its terminal. You see, I won't be going to prison, so why not let the police think it was me?'

'No – you can't have – it's not true!' Callum had been standing by the fire during their exchange but now sat beside his wife on the sofa and took her hand. Amy gave a hollow laugh at the absurdity of the situation and the unexpected tenderness in his eyes.

'Yes, it's true. Strangely enough I found out shortly before you told me you were leaving. I was considering when, or even if I should tell you, but events sort of overtook me.'

'Oh, Amy, I'm so sorry. But this isn't how things should be. You'll still have to go to court, to prison even... I mean... how long have you got left?'

Amy shrugged. 'Anybody's guess. Probably not too long the way things are going. I'm considering stopping the medication – well, not the pain stuff, I'm too much of a coward for that!' She laughed again – gallows humour.

'You can't!' Callum was insistent. 'You have to fight this, Amy.'

'What for? I have no life, no husband, no children...' She burst into tears then, sick of being the strong one, of holding things together when all she really wanted was to go to sleep and never wake up. Callum held her to his chest making shushing noises and waited until her tears ceased.

SIXTY-ONE

FRIDAY 23RD DECEMBER

An hour later and with Amy once more composed, the couple ate tinned soup and drank strong sweet tea.

'What are you going to do, Cal?' Amy put her spoon down on her empty plate.

'Quite honestly, I don't know. I suppose now the police know I'm not Dave I'll have to revert to being myself – which is something of a relief – but do I keep on running? I wonder what the penalty is for hiding a body. Maybe I should give myself up and take the punishment. What I'm more concerned about is you. Even if you don't have long left, do you want to spend your time waiting for a court date, maybe even be remanded in custody? You need to tell the police the truth.'

'No. My mind's made up. If the police prosecute me maybe they'll leave Beth alone and she can come home too. Do you think there's still a future for you and her as a couple?'

'I doubt it. I was infatuated – a stupid mid-life crisis which should never have happened. I'm sorry, Amy, can you ever forgive me?'

'Damn it, Cal. It's too late now! What we had wasn't so very bad, was it? Perhaps we should have worked at our marriage earlier instead of letting things slide. Yes, I know we were young and foolish and our relationship wasn't solid enough to withstand the problems of life.' Amy thought briefly about her inability to have children and again wondered if having a family might have made a difference. 'It's crazy how it's come to this but we've created the problem. It's down to us to respond in the best way possible – and I decided that confessing was the way.' Callum opened his mouth to contradict her. 'No, don't! You may not agree but I have nothing to lose and the police may even consider my actions to be self-defence. I don't want Beth to suffer any more than she already has and you were dragged unwittingly into this too. Please, let me do this.'

Before Callum could reply, the telephone rang and Amy answered.

'Is Callum with you?' Beth's angry voice took Amy by surprise and she hesitated, thinking how to reply.

'He bloody is, isn't he? Well, you're welcome to him – he's nothing but a pathetic excuse for a man. All those promises he made and at the first hint of trouble he runs away...'

'Beth, calm down. Tell me where you are.'

'Why? So you can tell the police?'

'No, but we need to talk. Things have happened, there are things you should know...'

'I've done all the talking and listening I want. Tell Callum he's missed his opportunity – you two deserve each other and neither of you will be hearing from me again!' The phone went dead. Amy looked at it with astonishment. Where had all that anger come from? But Beth had always been feisty and Amy hoped she didn't mean her closing words.

'She doesn't know the police have identified the body as Dave! Do you think she'll call again? We need to tell her.' Amy was trembling from the ferocity of her sister's tirade.

'I think she'll be in touch with you, maybe not me. I can't say

I blame her – leaving without a word was a cowardly thing to do but she'll need you, Amy. She'll come round.'

Amy looked at the clock – 8.20pm – she was exhausted and her head ached terribly. 'I hope you're right. For now, we need to make some decisions. What do you want to do?'

'I want you to tell the police you're not guilty.'

'It's not going to happen, Cal. I mean about you. Are you going to disappear again?'

'I don't know what I want – turn back time maybe so none of this ever happened?'

'If only! Look, I think you should stay here tonight. The spare bed's still made up and you need time to think. I have to report to the police station again tomorrow morning but they're being very considerate and I don't think they'll keep me long. We might both feel better in the daylight and be able to think more rationally.'

'Thanks, Amy, it's very generous of you. My life seems to consist of hiding away these days, but I'll not stay long, I don't want to get you into any more trouble.'

Amy could have laughed at his words – was it possible to be in this any deeper?

SIXTY-TWO
FRIDAY 23RD DECEMBER

After discovering Cal had left her, and when Beth could cry no more, her feelings turned to anger. How could Callum do this to her – he'd promised to care for her – they were going to be happy, but he'd turned out to be no better than any other man she'd known; selfish, immature brutes, all of them!

Briefly she wondered if Cal had gone back to New Middridge but even he wouldn't be so stupid as to go there. Then she tried to persuade herself that she didn't care where he was – she could manage without a man, couldn't she? Dressing quickly, Beth decided to make her own plans. Cal had paid a month's rent in advance on Lavender Cottage so she at least had a place to live and there was still money in the bank to draw on, so why not enjoy herself?

Attempting to push thoughts of Callum from her mind Beth set off to walk into town. Cal's presumptuous decision to get rid of the van left her without transport but the day was fine, although cold, and the walk would clear her head and present an opportunity to think.

It was unnerving to be alone, to have no one to discuss plans with. Maybe she should call Amy to ask her advice and her sister may even be able to send her some money. Beth decided it was important to think about herself and to do what she wanted to do but the problem was, she was unsure what she wanted.

It took less than half an hour to arrive in the centre of Wigton and Beth thought she'd treat herself to a coffee and cake before a little retail therapy. It was almost Christmas, time to spoil herself for once.

After a pleasant half hour in the coffee shop, Beth headed towards the bank. Staying outside, she used Dave's debit card to draw the maximum £300 from the machine. The notes felt good between her fingers, clean and smooth. She also had Dave's credit card. He'd never allowed her to use it before and the thought of what he'd say if he knew gave her a thrill. Yes, perhaps she'd use it today and keep the cash for emergency use.

There was no way anyone could get lost in Wigton. Was that a positive, Beth wondered. There seemed to be more bookshops than anything else, so she thought maybe a browse in one would be fun, to choose a book to occupy her now lonely hours. It didn't take long and next she moved on to a clothes shop. The prices surprised and pleased Beth and temptation won the day – she came out of the shop with two carriers containing several new outfits. Passing a bakery, there was also no reason to resist, so another bag of cakes and pastries was added to her cache.

Normally a few hours of shopping would delight Beth but somehow having no one to share the day with wrung all the pleasure out of her purchases. A fleeting desire to have Amy with her lodged in her mind as she turned away from High Street and started the walk home.

By the time she arrived Beth felt incredibly grumpy. Self-pity took over and she felt thoroughly sorry for herself.

Naturally, it was all Callum's fault with Amy designated to share some of the blame.

Opening the cottage door, the musty smell hit Beth first followed by the silence, neither of which improved her mood. She decided then to move on – perhaps there was a chance of a refund on the rent – although it was unlikely.

The rest of the day was spent feeling miserable. Her new purchases couldn't lift her mood and even the cakes and pastries she gorged on made her feel worse, not better. Beth tried dozing through the afternoon and even attempted to read a chapter of her new book but nothing held her attention. Her mind returned constantly to her uncertain future – what could she do?

A city would offer more opportunity. Wigton was great if you wanted the quiet life but she wasn't ready for that, Beth wanted to live a little. No, she wanted to live a lot! She'd need transport. Damn Callum for getting rid of the van, he was too bloody cautious. Perhaps if she knew where he'd abandoned it, she could reclaim it, there were spare keys somewhere. The problem with this was getting in touch with Cal. Maybe it would be worth ringing Amy who may have heard from him, so as evening was drawing in, she decided to call her sister.

Amy answered the call but when Beth asked if Callum was there, the silence left her in no doubt that he was. Suddenly she was furious. How dare they do this to her, she'd been made a fool of and in that moment Beth hated her sister and ex-lover. Amy wanted to talk and said there were things she needed to hear but Beth wasn't in the mood to listen and slammed the phone down. It was only afterwards she realised her chance to ask Cal about the van was lost, due in no small part to her own stupid anger.

SIXTY-THREE
FRIDAY 23RD DECEMBER

As Friday afternoon wore on, Samantha's thoughts were more on the impending visit to Ravi's home than her current workload. She'd met Ravi's parents on a couple of occasions previously but this would be the first time she'd be staying at their house as his fiancée. Nothing much intimidated Samantha Freeman, but there was a distinct brewing of nerves in her stomach at the idea of being under scrutiny. They were lovely people and had been nothing but pleasant with her in the past, yet would this be different now she was to be their daughter-in-law?

'Penny for them!' Jenny interrupted Sam's train of thought.

Sam screwed up her face. 'Just anticipating going to Ravi's and the dubious pleasures of being confined with the future in-laws.'

'You'll be fine. They'll love you if you make Ravi happy, which must be the case if he wants to marry you.'

'I know. I wish his grandparents felt the same. It's more important to them that he should marry a nice Hindu girl rather than who he chooses. It's their culture I suppose, and I'll have to respect them for their beliefs.'

'But you'll probably never meet them. You're not planning on India for your honeymoon, are you?'

'No way – at least *I'm* not. We haven't talked about it yet but I rather fancy Mauritius. Anyway, you didn't come to ask me about my future plans, did you?'

'No. I wanted to discuss how to proceed with Amy Cooper. I thought we should hang back with any more interviews, give her time to consider her confession.'

'Sounds good to me. She'll be reporting to the station again in the morning but then it's Christmas – we can't drag her in too often when she's so ill and I don't think Amy's a flight risk now. Let's see how it goes day to day and make any changes as and when necessary.' Sam looked at the clock on her office wall. 'It's nearly four, Jen. Why don't you take the chance to knock off early and begin your holiday?'

'Thanks, I might just do that while the shops are still open, I've a few things left to get.' As Jenny turned to leave Sam's office, she almost bumped into an animated Paul Roper who deftly swerved to avoid knocking her over.

'There's been a withdrawal made on Dave Moorhouse's debit card!' He paused, looking from Jen to Sam who stared back, waiting for him to continue. 'It was this morning at a cash point in Wigton, £300, and then his credit card was flagged up as used in a clothes shop also in Wigton.'

'Good work, Paul.' Samantha's day was suddenly looking up. It was then she noticed DC Kim Thatcher hovering outside the room. 'Come and join us, Kim.' She motioned for the girl to enter before noticing the tears in her eyes. 'What is it?'

'It's to do with Paul's, I mean DC Roper's news... I er, I came across an address in Wigton when going through the paperwork from Amy Cooper's house. It was written on a scrap of paper and I didn't think anything of it at the time...'

Samantha counted to five before answering. Bawling the young DC out wouldn't help anyone. It was a mistake which had lost them a couple of days in the search for Beth and Callum but probably one Kim would learn from. 'Don't dwell on it, Kim. Have you got the address?'

'Yes, I dug it out of evidence.' Kim handed over a small piece of crumpled paper which Sam read and passed to Jenny.

'Sorry about the early finish, could you ring Cumbria constabulary and ask for their assistance? With any luck the day should end with two arrests.'

'Right on it, boss. And I'm happy to stay until we know what happens.' Jen was pulling her phone from her pocket as she left the room.

Samantha looked at Kim. 'I'm not going to bite your head off, Kim, but it was a basic mistake when you knew we were looking for two people who'd flown the coop. Put it behind you, we've all made similar errors of judgement and it should make you more conscientious in the future.'

'Yes, boss, it will.' Kim left the room and Samantha turned to Paul.

'With luck on our side our colleagues in Cumbria should find Callum and Beth at home. I can't believe they'd be so stupid as to use the cards, but then they probably don't know we've identified the body as Dave Moorhouse yet.'

After Jenny's call to Cumbria it took only an hour before the team at New Middridge received the news that the police had been to Lavender Cottage and arrested one suspect. Beth Moorhouse.

'Damn it, where's Cooper?' Samantha turned to Jenny.

'According to the arresting officers, Beth told them he'd left her and she had no idea where he was.'

'I suppose one of them is better than none. Look, I'll hang

around here and process Beth when she arrives, you get off and start your holiday and I'll see you in the New Year.'

'Okay, thanks! Enjoy your trip away with Ravi, you deserve it. Merry Christmas, Sam.' Jenny grabbed her bag and coat and set off home.

SIXTY-FOUR
SATURDAY 24TH DECEMBER

Callum opened his eyes and for a few delicious moments was unsure where he was. The familiarity of the spare room soon enlightened him and he rolled over and groaned. Sleep was a welcome escape from reality and he'd had the best night's sleep since before Dave died. But it was time to get up, to face the world and its considerable problems.

Cal smiled at the thought of Amy being downstairs. He was appreciating her calm common sense more than ever, and couldn't help comparing her to Beth whose company had become increasingly exasperating as time progressed. But being with Amy was temporary – in more ways than one. Cal had been shocked by the news of her illness. He'd noticed a considerable weight loss and she looked somewhat ashen and drawn but he'd attributed these changes to the situation they were in rather than illness.

In some way he understood what she was trying to do and admired her for it, but Cal was convinced she was wrong to sacrifice herself. Even if she was going to die, to be thought of as a killer was absurd – everyone wants to be remembered for the good they've done, not for something as wicked as taking another person's life. But Amy was adamant and Cal had been unable to change her mind. What she was determined to do shamed Callum – would she ever know how guilty it made him feel?

Cal's next thought was that it was Christmas Eve. Christmas had never been important in their marriage and he suspected the season pained Amy as a reminder that they'd never had a family. It wasn't as important to him as his wife, and perhaps he'd not given her the chance to express her feelings on the subject. With the benefit of hindsight Cal could see he'd been a rotten husband. If only he had the opportunity to make it up to her – but Amy's days were numbered – the reality made him incredibly sad.

Downstairs, Callum entered the kitchen where Amy turned and smiled at him. 'Coffee or tea?' she asked.

'Whatever you're making.' He sat at the table.

Amy poured tea for them both and pushed a plate of toast towards him before sitting opposite. 'Do we go straight into serious conversation mode or pretend all's right with the world?'

Callum shrugged. 'If only we could. This must be the strangest Christmas ever.'

'Gosh, yes, it's Christmas Eve, I'd forgotten.'

'Did you have any plans for the day?'

'Only reporting to the police station. How about you?'

'Nothing. Could I stay here a couple of days? It's not the best time to be travelling and to be honest, I still haven't decided what to do.'

'Yes. I don't think anyone's going to be visiting today or tomorrow but maybe it's best to keep away from the windows – the neighbours are in a tizzy over all the police attention I'm getting. They'd love to have something else to gossip about.'

'Thanks – I'm getting used to hiding... Amy... are you okay?'

Amy clearly was not. Her eyes appeared to roll back and her

head shot backwards. Her face drained of all colour with a sheen of sweat on her pale skin. Callum was on his feet in a second, reaching for her arms to stop her falling but it was too late. Her body became rigid as she dropped heavily from the chair onto the floor, arms and legs flailing. Amy was in full seizure mode and Cal was terrified.

'Amy, Amy!' He shook her by the shoulders but it was clear she wasn't responsive. Callum grabbed the phone and dialled 999. 'An ambulance – my wife's having a seizure!' He listened to the call handler's instructions and answered her questions. He moved furniture away from Amy in an effort to prevent her hurting herself as instructed. 'She's still thrashing about!' he cried.

'An ambulance is on its way, sir. Please, just make sure your wife can't hurt herself and that her airways are open. When she's still, she'll need to be put in the recovery position.'

Callum could hardly concentrate but the words *recovery position* snagged in his mind, remembered from his Boy Scout days, but Amy was still fitting and he felt helpless. After five minutes which seemed much longer, Amy's thrashing ceased yet she remained unconscious. He rolled her onto her side. Cal heard sirens and rushed to the door, running outside to flag the ambulance down.

'The seizure's only just stopped but she's out cold!' He ran back into the house followed by the two men.

'What's her name?' the paramedic asked.

'Amy Cooper, she's my wife.'

'Perhaps you could stand back, sir, while we assess your wife's condition.'

Cal stepped back and watched, impressed with the speed and knowledge of the two male paramedics and was relieved to allow them to take over the responsibility.

'How long did the seizure last?' the older man asked.

'About five minutes.'

'We'll be taking her to hospital, perhaps you'd get a few essentials together for her and you can travel with us in the ambulance.'

Callum was only too happy to have something practical to do. He'd never felt so useless in his life. Gathering toiletries and nightclothes from her bedroom felt almost intrusive, but he did so quickly, anxious to get back to Amy.

SIXTY-FIVE
SATURDAY 24TH DECEMBER

During Callum's absence, the paramedics attached monitors to Amy's body and a cannula was inserted into her arm. The paramedic called Jim was bringing in a trolley. 'How is she?' Cal dared to ask.

'She's very poorly I'm afraid. We'll get her to hospital as soon as possible – the team have been notified we're coming.' He squeezed Cal's shoulder briefly before wheeling the trolley close to Amy's still body. The two men lifted her onto it and wheeled her to the ambulance.

Callum had never travelled in an ambulance before. The equipment was impressive, as was the calm professional way the paramedics carried out their duty. The ambulance travelled at speed with sirens blaring, a bumpy ride which thankfully was not too long. Amy remained unconscious.

The Accident and Emergency department was an experience which shook Callum, and one he hoped never to be subjected to again. Trolleys were backed up in corridors, paramedics standing beside them like sentries. Amy was wheeled past several other patients, an indication of how serious her condition was. Cal tried to keep close but eventually a nurse asked him to wait outside a curtained cubicle while Amy was assessed by a team of doctors and nurses.

Finding a seat in a corner where he could watch Amy's cubicle, Cal gratefully allowed the hard chair to take his weight. Only then did he realise he was trembling. His fingers felt stiff and cold but he couldn't keep his hands still and his right leg bounced up and down of its own accord. A light-headed feeling made him nauseous and for one embarrassing moment he thought he might pass out. Putting his head in his hands helped and soon Cal's breathing steadied and he tried to clear his mind to think.

Cal felt he should be ringing someone, but the reality was there was no one to ring. A sadness swept over him for his wife. Maybe he should ring Beth, but what could she do anyway? She didn't know about Amy's illness and yesterday's call had left Cal in no doubt that she didn't want to see him or her sister again.

Amy was expected at the police station – would she be in trouble for not attending? Could he ring anonymously to inform them she was in the hospital? No, someone would come to check and he'd have to make himself scarce. He didn't want to do that, Callum needed to be close to Amy – to be certain she was going to pull through.

The clock on the wall moved slowly. Callum watched the red minute hand jerk between the numbers, tick, tick, tick, an almost mesmerising action which added to the surreal feeling of being in a dream. The swish of a curtain claimed his attention as a doctor and several nurses exited Amy's cubicle. Callum stood to approach the little group; he needed to know what was happening. The doctor met his eyes and intercepted Cal before he reached the cubicle.

'Mr Cooper? I'm Dr Brookes, shall we go somewhere private?' He steered Cal by the shoulder, silent until they came to a small empty room. Callum couldn't form the questions he wanted to ask and stared at the doctor, then he sat on one of the more comfortable chairs as requested.

'I'm so sorry, Mr Cooper, but your wife didn't recover from the seizure. It's not uncommon with the type of tumour she suffered from, as I'm sure her consultant has explained...'

Callum heard no more. This man was giving him the worst possible news – Amy was dead – he would never see her again. 'Can I sit with her?' he asked.

'Of course. If you'll wait a few minutes someone will come and get you. Can I fetch anything for you, a coffee maybe – or call someone?'

'No, thank you, there's no one.'

Fifteen minutes later a nurse opened the door quietly and spoke Callum's name. He stood and followed her in silence, not back to the cubicle but to a private room where Amy lay on a high bed, motionless. The monitors and cannula had been removed and as Cal pulled a chair closer to her he thought she looked peaceful. Her features were relaxed and her face had taken on some of its previous youthfulness. Taking her hand Cal was surprised at how warm it was and how soft her skin.

'I'm so sorry, Amy!' Tears now coursed down his face. 'I let you down badly – you didn't deserve any of this.'

Callum could find no more words. Sitting in silence for another ten minutes he weighed up his options and made the decision about what to do next. It was unthinkable that Amy should be remembered as a killer – she shouldn't have her memory sullied by actions instigated by him and Beth.

Callum arrived back home – he still thought of Cypress Close as such – without any awareness of how he got there. Amy was dead. It hadn't fully sunk in. After the dramatic events of the last two or three weeks, Cal assumed his life couldn't become any more complicated and depressing than it was. But now his wife was dead; it was worse than he could have imagined.

The house held no greeting. It felt cold and hollow as he opened the front door. Callum's instinct was to listen for signs of Amy's presence, to become aware of which room she was in, but she would never inhabit their home again, the thought chilled him to the bone. In his hand he clutched a batch of leaflets the nurse had given him as he'd left the hospital. Cal dropped them on the table. His eyes filled with the tears he'd been holding back all day, he couldn't read them now.

With his coat still on, Cal sat on the sofa and finally gave way to his emotions. Unaware of time, his own hunger, or what needed to be done he cried like a child. Finally, when there were no tears left to shed, he stood up and went into the kitchen – Amy's domain. After switching the kettle on to make coffee, he checked the fridge to see what was there and decided to fry an egg to make a sandwich, something to line his empty stomach before he went out.

Callum forced himself to eat then picked up the house phone and dialled Beth's number. He'd take the risk of the call being traced; it didn't matter now and she needed to know about Amy. The phone rang out. *Damn Beth,* he thought and tried again. Still there was no answer and satisfied he'd at least tried, Callum Cooper set off for New Middridge police station. Running away was no longer an option; it was time to tell the truth.

SIXTY-SIX
SATURDAY 24TH DECEMBER

Callum pushed open the heavy doors to the police station, entered and looked around. It was mid-afternoon on Christmas Eve and unexpectedly quiet. Moving to the reception desk, Cal concentrated hard to make his legs work and stop the trembling throughout his body. Today would go down as the worst day in his life, followed closely by the day he tried to hide Dave's body. The regrets he carried weighed him down.

'Yes, sir?' A smiling sergeant looked up from his computer. 'How can I help you?'

'I'd like to speak to DI Freeman please.'

'I'm not sure she's still here.' He picked up the phone. 'What name is it, sir?'

'Callum Cooper.'

The sergeant stared at him, recognising the name. 'Please take a seat.' Callum did as the man asked, ignoring the strange and frightening sense of his life being no longer his own. Whatever happened to him now would be determined by other people, his recent actions had forfeited his right to a future.

DI Samantha Freeman was sitting in her office, reading the transcript of the previous evening's interview with Beth Moorhouse. With Paul Roper, Sam had spent an exasperating hour with a suspect who apparently remembered nothing and had only done what her sister and her lover told her to. Beth's story was confusing – she admitted to pushing her husband when he attacked her but claimed events afterwards were a blur. Amy and Callum Cooper were both mentioned as being there at some point on the day in question but Beth couldn't collate the events to any coherent order. As to the role of her sister and lover, Beth couldn't say, having either not been with them or unable to recall due to her distress.

Paul was as baffled as Sam. Fragments of Beth's story concurred with what Amy Cooper had confessed to, but as to Beth's own role, the waters were certainly muddied. Due to the lateness of the hour, Samantha suspended the interview and Beth was accommodated in the cells overnight.

On Saturday morning the detectives continued the interview which proved every bit as frustrating, and with Beth claiming to feel faint, it was again cut short. Although Samantha generally possessed an intuitive insight into these situations, Beth confused her and time was not on her side.

The detectives conferred over the case and lack of progress and as Beth could only be held for twenty-four hours without charge, they decided to charge her later that day with concealment of a body. She'd then be held on remand, clearly a flight risk having already disappeared once. With her safely in custody, they'd have time to continue the search for Callum Cooper and interview Amy Cooper again now her sister had been found.

Another twist to their investigation was that Amy had not reported to the station that morning – a blatant breach of her bail conditions. At lunchtime, Sam sent a couple of uniformed officers to her home but she wasn't there and there were no signs of anyone at the property – the case which had been coming nicely together was again falling apart.

Samantha's phone rang and the desk sergeant asked for her immediate presence downstairs as a man by the name of Callum Cooper was asking to see her. Sam almost fell off her chair. 'What?' she shouted but the sergeant didn't repeat it, she was already on her feet.

'Paul, with me, now!' she yelled and her surprised DC jumped up to follow. 'Callum Cooper's in reception waiting to see us!'

'No!'

'Yes. I don't know what's going on with this case but with a bit of luck, he'll hold the key to sorting this mess out.'

When she saw Cooper sitting waiting in the lobby, Samantha was tempted to come out with a sarcastic remark – the last time she'd seen the man he was impersonating his dead brother-in-law. But something about his demeanour halted her – an aura of sadness surrounded him which almost made her sympathetic – and presumably he was there to turn himself in for whatever part he'd played in Dave Moorhouse's death. Perhaps now they could get to the truth. A frisson of excitement ran through her body at the prospect of finally wrapping up this case.

'Good afternoon, Mr Cooper. Would you follow me please?' Sam led the way to the nearest vacant interview room. 'Please, sit down.' She pointed to the chair on the far side of the table while she and Paul took the two opposite. Paul switched on the tape recorder while Sam explained the procedure and asked if he wished to have a solicitor present.

'No. I've come to tell you the truth – but first, you need to know that my wife, Amy, died this morning.'

SIXTY-SEVEN
SATURDAY 24TH DECEMBER

Samantha was stunned. This was the last thing she'd expected to hear and the news threw her slightly. Paul recovered composure first and looked at Callum with genuine sympathy. 'I'm sorry for your loss, Mr Cooper. Please accept our condolences.'

'Yes, I'm so sorry, Callum. We were aware she was seriously ill but this is a shock; do you want to tell us what happened?'

'Amy suffered a seizure this morning. I called for an ambulance but she didn't regain consciousness – it was sudden, I'd only found out she was ill yesterday.'

It was tempting to jump in with the many questions spinning in Sam's mind but clearly, the man needed time to process his thoughts, so she remained silent.

'I shouldn't have run away – there's much I shouldn't have done – but if I'd known about Amy... anyway I decided to come back yesterday. Being on the run isn't the life I wanted. I didn't know you'd discovered the body was Dave, Amy told me, but whatever, I was sick of it all. I can give you an address to find Beth – she's the least culpable of us all. It was me who killed Dave.'

Samantha showed no reaction to his confession and made a snap decision not to tell him that Beth was already in their custody. Before she could ask for any details, Callum spoke again.

'I know Amy confessed to killing Dave but she didn't, my wife wasn't even there until after Dave was dead.' Talking about Amy appeared to upset Callum, his voice cracked and tears filled his eyes.

'Callum, before we continue, I want you to consider again whether you'd like us to call a solicitor for you. Perhaps you need some support and advice? We're going to take a short break and then we'll fetch some coffee, okay?' Sam was conscious of the dangers of taking a statement from a man without a solicitor and one whose wife had died on the same day. Callum Cooper nodded and after Paul switched off the tape, the detectives left the room.

While Paul organised the coffee, Sam returned to her office. Jenny was on leave but Sam knew her DS would want to be updated on the case so she rang Jen's number.

'How's family time going?'

'Don't ask! I'm at Mum and Dad's and the tension's mounting already – but why are you ringing – did you get anything from Beth?'

'No, she's saying very little and is either genuinely confused or acting the part quite convincingly. I'm sorry to disturb you but I was sure you'd want an update.'

'I'm all ears.'

'Firstly, Amy Cooper died this morning...'

'Hell, no! I didn't think she was so ill.'

'Apparently it was another seizure but this time she didn't recover.'

'Damn it, now we'll never be sure if she was telling the truth until we find Callum Cooper.'

'Ah, well – that's the next piece of the conundrum – we have Callum Cooper in custody.'

'Callum! Where did you find him?'

'In the lobby downstairs – he handed himself in. He'd come back to New Middridge and was hiding at Amy's. He's confessed to killing Dave Moorehouse.'

'What! But I thought Amy or Beth killed him?'

'Yes, so did I but I think Amy's death has really shaken Callum and he clearly has regrets which appear to have prompted his confession. We've given him time to consider having a solicitor although he's already refused. Paul's getting him coffee, so I'd better get back.'

'Ring me later to keep me in the loop, won't you?'

'You're supposed to be on holiday.'

'Yes but I won't settle until I know – you'd be just the same!'

Sam smiled. Jen was right, so she agreed to ring later with more details.

The interview resumed. 'Have you considered having a solicitor present, Callum?' Samantha asked.

'I don't need one. I'm guilty and I've come to terms with accepting my punishment.'

'We don't have to do this today. It's a difficult time for you...'

'Please, I need to do it now!'

As he was so determined, Sam was satisfied it was prudent to continue and after making it clear he was under caution, began her questioning. 'Callum, you said Amy told you she'd confessed to killing Dave Moorhouse – can you tell us exactly what she said?'

'Amy was surprised to see me when I arrived yesterday, I'd left Beth, it was never going to work out. She told me you knew the body was Dave and I'd taken on his identity, and that she'd confessed to killing him. When I asked why, Amy explained about her illness. In an effort to protect Beth, something she'd been doing all her life, Amy thought if she confessed, Beth wouldn't be charged.'

'And you're saying that Amy wasn't at the Moorhouse home when Dave died?'

'That's right. Amy only came when I rang her after Dave was dead.'

'What time would that be?'

'Around 6pm – I'm not sure.'

'Okay, so can you take us through the events of the day, Callum?'

Cal nodded. His hands were clasped together on the table, the knuckles white as he haltingly told his side of the story. 'Beth was going to tell Dave she was leaving him, that we were going to be together. I wanted to be with her in case he became violent – he frequently did – but Beth insisted she'd tell him on her own. I was at work and waited all day for her call. When she hadn't rung by 5pm, I rang her. Beth was confused and asked me to go straight around, which I did.

'Hell, I should never have let her do it alone.' Callum ran his fingers through his hair and shook his head. 'Beth was distressed. Dave had taken the news badly and attacked her – she was severely bruised but managed to fight him off, and during the argument, she'd hit him with a table lamp – in self-defence. When I arrived, Dave was unconscious and Beth was in shock. I think she might have passed out, she was very confused with no concept of time. Beth was so afraid of what may happen – it hadn't occurred to her to phone an ambulance.'

Sam wanted to ask why he didn't call an ambulance but was reluctant to interrupt his flow, so allowed him to continue without interruption.

'I took Beth into the kitchen, away from Dave. She was in a state so I told her to make a drink and we'd think about our next move. Her concern was that she might go to prison and the thought terrified her.

'While Beth made tea, I went back into the lounge. Dave was conscious and making an awful gurgling sound. Suddenly, I suppose I was frightened and without thinking picked up the lamp and hit him over the head. He stopped moving and when I checked, his breathing had stopped as well. I'd killed him. Beth knew nothing about this; she still thinks she killed him and coward that I am, I let her go on believing it.'

'Is this the same lamp Amy claimed to have used?' Paul asked.

'Yes, you'll find my fingerprints on it but you won't find Amy's.'

As Callum appeared to be growing increasingly agitated, Sam decided to end the interview at that point. 'Thank you, Callum. We'll take a break now and an officer will be here shortly to take a DNA swab and your fingerprints. We'll be keeping you overnight and resume this interview in the morning.'

Callum nodded resignedly and Samantha and Paul left the room.

Samantha sighed wearily and rolled her tense shoulders as they walked back to the incident room. 'Hell, what a day this is turning out to be. It's like *Murder on the Orient Express* here, everyone's had a hand in it. Well, maybe not Beth. I find her a strange one – a bit of a manipulator if you ask me – as tricky as a box of frogs. It's not that she isn't talking, it's just almost impossible to get a straight story out of her.'

'But what about Callum, do you believe him?' Paul asked.

'Yes, I think I do. Apparently, Callum did leave Beth – he came home to Amy and was with her when she died – then turned himself in this afternoon. Now they've been charged we can keep them over the holiday weekend and possibly on remand after that. They've both proved to be a flight risk.'

'So, it's tying up loose ends tomorrow. I suppose there's the attempted insurance fraud too – it's all rather complicated...'

'Hang on, Paul. Our trio might have been planning to defraud the insurance company, and this may go some way to proving a motive, but no claim was ever made. We can't charge them for *thinking* about a crime – if we did that, half the population would be behind bars. Concentrate on Dave Moorhouse's death and we'll consult the CPS on any other charges.'

'Sounds like a plan to me.' Paul smiled as he grabbed his coat to head for home.

Perhaps the outcome of this investigation hadn't turned out quite as they'd hoped but it was a result. Samantha would go upstairs to update DCI Kent and no doubt make his Christmas, then she'd ring Jenny to update her and finally go home to Ravi.

SIXTY-EIGHT
SUNDAY, CHRISTMAS DAY

It wasn't the first Christmas Day Samantha had worked and wouldn't be the last but she'd try to finish early, hopefully in time to cook the traditional Christmas meal Ravi was looking forward to. Jenny, Paul and Layla were now on leave, Kim Thatcher and Tom Wilson were the only others in the office with Sam, who arrived with decent coffee for them all – Christmas Day wasn't the time to drink what passed as coffee from the office machine.

After a briefing to update the detective constables, Sam went downstairs to enquire if Callum Cooper had been okay through the night. As a precaution, she'd put him on suicide watch, the man was clearly depressed and the last thing they needed was for him to harm himself. The duty sergeant reported an uneventful night with Cooper remaining quiet throughout.

Samantha would interview Callum later and perhaps take Tom Wilson in for the experience, but the day would mostly be spent writing up reports ready to send to the CPS. It wasn't her favourite part of the job, a necessary evil, but Sam was grateful the case was wrapped up in time for her to go away. She didn't need to worry about work over her holiday, spending time with Ravi's family was concerning enough.

The day proved surprisingly quiet, something of an anticlimax after the hectic few weeks of late. Sam and Tom conducted only a short interview with Callum Cooper who still declined to have a lawyer and Sam outlined the process and what would happen to Callum.

'He seems resigned to his fate,' Tom commented when the interview was finished.

'Yes. Callum Cooper is a man with regrets and it appears the only way he can live with his actions is to co-operate with us and accept his punishment.'

It was becoming clear that Beth hadn't been responsible for her husband's death so she would be charged with prevention of the lawful and decent burial of a body, perverting the course of justice and withholding information – all serious charges. The court would decide if she could be released on bail and Samantha tasked Kim Thatcher with preparing the paperwork for the charges.

Time passed quickly and by mid-afternoon, Samantha was satisfied with the completed paperwork which was ready to go to the CPS. It was a relief to be able to take her holiday without an unfinished case hanging over her head. Wishing her colleagues a happy Christmas, Sam left the office for home, thinking about the coming week rather than her current caseload and mentally preparing a turkey dinner rather than solving a thorny crime. When she realised this she laughed out loud, perhaps there was hope for her to become a domesticated wife after all.

Boxing Day

When Samantha woke on Boxing Day, Ravi lay beside her, propped up on his elbow and smiling.

'What?' She grinned.

'I'm just thinking how fortunate I am to have you – brilliant detective, sexy lady and chef extraordinaire!' He laughed as Sam poked him in the ribs.

'At least I tried!'

'You did, but I didn't realise sprouts were meant to be burned and what were those lumps in the mashed potato?'

'Next Christmas you're cooking!' Sam rolled out of bed and went into the bathroom. Yes, Christmas dinner had been a disaster – the turkey was dry, the carrots hard and she wanted to erase her efforts at roast potatoes from her mind.

The day was spent relaxing. They were setting off to Ravi's family home later in the evening. Sam had wrapped their gifts and the packing was almost finished. A knot of anxiety was growing in her stomach but she refused to acknowledge it, her future in-laws couldn't be any scarier than the criminals she dealt with on a daily basis, could they?

SIXTY-NINE
TUESDAY 27TH DECEMBER

Samantha woke up in the unfamiliar bedroom in Ravi's parents' home on the outskirts of York. Hearing Ravi in the en-suite shower she turned over to enjoy a few more minutes in the luxurious king-sized bed. The room was of the standard Sam would expect to find in a five-star hotel, in fact, the whole house had taken her by surprise the previous night as they drove through the gates and crunched up a gravelled drive. Yes, a gated driveway. She was completely unprepared for the size and opulence of Ravi's family home and wasted no time in lecturing him for not warning her. Ravi laughed at her awestruck expression, her complaints disregarded.

Now, as she snuggled under the expensive duvet, Sam considered Ravi and all the things she had yet to learn about him and his family. Divya and Arjun Patel had greeted her as warmly as they always did and Sam was struck again by how beautiful Divya was. Dressed in an emerald-green sari, Ravi's mother appeared to have stepped straight from a beauty salon, hair and make-up immaculate, and for an instant, Sam regretted wearing her usual jeans and jumper and being without make-up. But the young couple were welcomed with affection, Arjun hugging his son and slapping his back as he congratulated them on their engagement. Divya enthused over Sam's ring and any awkwardness quickly vanished.

Later, when they were alone, Sam had another moan at Ravi. 'You should have told me your parents were rich. I wasn't expecting such a beautiful house – what exactly does your dad do?'

'I've told you, he's in finance. He's the CEO of a wealth management company and very good at his job.' Ravi spoke with pride. 'He expected me to follow into a career in finance too, I suppose we have the same kind of brain, wired for numbers! That's why I majored in business admin and finance at uni but then I was seduced into joining the police force.'

Sam knew Ravi had a PhD and DBA in accounting whereas she'd never been to university; after A levels she followed her lifelong dream and joined the police.

'Didn't Arjun mind when you joined the police?'

'Initially yes, but secretly I think he's proud of my work. One day I'll inherit the family fortune – which includes a herd of a thousand cows back in India.'

'What! What on earth would you do with a thousand cows?' Sam noticed the grin Ravi was trying to hide and thumped him on the arm. 'You're winding me up, aren't you?'

'Sometimes you can be so gullible!' He laughed.

As Sam snuggled down in the bed, smiling at the memory, Ravi appeared from the shower, a towel wrapped around his waist. 'Good morning.' He flopped beside her on the bed. 'Sleep well?'

'Absolutely. We should get one of these king-sized beds.'

'And whose wardrobe will we throw out to fit it in the room?'

'Yours of course!' Samantha rolled over and kissed Ravi. 'I'll jump in the shower and be with you in a couple of minutes – don't go down without me.'

'Hurry up then, I'm starving.'

The day was surprisingly enjoyable. Samantha's anxieties about staying with her future in-laws were alleviated by the easy manner in which Divya included her in the preparations for Ravi's brother and family. Sam felt comfortable enough not to grumble when Ravi went off to the local country club with his dad for a pre-dinner drink. Thinking of her own dad who enjoyed going down to the local to meet his pals brought a smile to her face – Ravi's world was so different from her own.

When Ravi and Arjun returned, Divya was showing Sam the family photograph albums. Ravi snatched at the book but she pulled it away. 'Oh no! You promised you wouldn't do this, Mata.'

'No, I said *we'll see*, it's not a promise, Ravi.' Divya smiled at her son and continued turning the pages.

By the middle of the afternoon, Samantha was feeling quite at home with the Patel family. Ravi's sense of humour clearly came from his father, and his mother was the glue which held their family together. Ravi's brother and his family would arrive the following morning and Sam hoped she'd feel as comfortable with them as she did with his parents. It came as something of a surprise to Samantha that she hadn't thought about work all day.

SEVENTY
WEDNESDAY 28TH DECEMBER

Ravi's brother was an older, shorter version of Ravi and proved as convivial as their parents. His wife and children were also delightful – it all seemed a bit too perfect and Sam found herself waiting for something to go wrong. The visit she'd been so apprehensive about had surpassed everything she could have wished for.

When it was time for the couple to leave on Wednesday morning, Samantha was surprisingly reluctant to go. Yet a few days at home with Ravi would set her up to face more family gatherings – this time her side of the family for New Year.

Thoughts of work briefly flitted through Samantha's mind. In the Cooper/Moorehouse case there were still t's to be crossed and i's dotted, which Jenny and Paul were more than capable of doing. Having the case virtually sorted had helped Samantha relax – not that she wouldn't enjoy returning to work – she'd be refreshed and raring to go.

Packing her belongings, Samantha stroked the beautiful mohair jumper which Divya and Arjun had given her. It was probably the most extravagant garment she'd ever owned, a beautiful pale blue which fitted her perfectly. Embarrassment warmed Sam's face as she recalled the Marks and Spencer chocolates and Christmas plant arrangement which had been her gift to them. Still, Ravi had added a rather good bottle of wine and the gifts were received with genuine enthusiasm. What do you buy the couple who have everything?

'You ready yet?' Ravi bounded into the room, keen to set off early as the weather forecast predicted more snow.

'Yes. Here, you can take my case now. I'll go and find your mum and dad to say goodbye. Samantha trailed downstairs behind Ravi. Voices from the kitchen led her to Divya and Arjun who were chatting animatedly while making coffee.

'Oh, can't you stay for coffee?' Divya asked when she saw Samantha wearing her coat.

'I think Ravi wants to get away and beat the weather. It's freezing out there.'

Divya moved to hug Sam and when Ravi joined them, she drew him into the embrace. 'Don't be long in coming back; it's not too far you know.'

'Yes, Mata, we know!' Ravi hugged his father and then the couple went outside followed by his parents. 'Don't stand out here, you'll catch cold,' he told them, but they ignored his words and waved as the car pulled away and out of sight.

'Is it time for the post-mortem now?' Ravi chuckled.

'You only dare ask because you know how well it's gone. Your family are amazing – they've been so kind to me, I couldn't have asked for more.'

'Great. Let's hope New Year goes as well then!'

'Hmm, yes.' Sam lapsed into a thoughtful pause as they entered the dual carriageway, a satisfied smile on her face. Life was good.

A sudden honking of horns caused Ravi to swerve to avoid a large truck which had veered onto the wrong side of the road. Samantha braced herself, holding in a scream as the vehicle, apparently completely out of control, hurtled towards them at speed, and in a trajectory which would force them off the road. As Ravi turned the steering wheel sharply, Sam was thrust forward in her seat with such force that the airbag activated – she could see nothing but heard her own voice, an echoing scream as the car rolled over and over, bouncing like a rubber ball. A horrendous sound of grating metal pierced her ears and then nothing! Sam's world went black.

Snow was falling heavily. A shivering Samantha stood by the ditch and stared at the gaping scar in the earth where a body was gradually disappearing beneath the white carpet. She strained to see the man's face but her legs refused to move and her arms hung stiffly at her side. Blinking away the soft flakes of snow from her eyelashes, Sam leaned forward to identify whether the body was Callum Cooper, or Dave Moorehouse and a sudden gust of wind gave her the answer. The face became clear – it was Ravi! Sam screamed but no sound left her lips. Tears froze on her cheeks before darkness engulfed her again.

It was two days before Samantha woke up. Light stung her eyes as the room swayed and she felt nauseous. Turning her head to the side she retched but there was nothing in her stomach. Someone was beside her, holding her shoulders and making soothing noises like her mother had done when Sam was a child.

Turning back to lie on the pillow, Sam realised it was her mother – but why – where was she?

'Mum?'

'Shh, just rest. You're in York Hospital, Samantha. There

was an accident, but you're okay; a broken leg and a few bumps and bruises, you'll be fine.' Her mother's voice didn't sound very confident.

'Where's Ravi, Mum? Is he okay?'

Sam's mother hesitated.

'Mum, where's Ravi?' she repeated more urgently.

'I'm so sorry, love. Ravi didn't make it...'

'No, you're lying! I want to see him...' Samantha struggled to rise, tears clouding her vision. It couldn't be true, not Ravi, not her beautiful Ravi!

A nurse appeared at the foot of the bed. 'I'll give you something to calm you down, Samantha.'

'No, I don't want anything, I want Ravi!'

The nurse injected her patient and Sam quickly lapsed back into a state of unconsciousness. Her mother remained at her side where she'd been for the last two days.

EPILOGUE

DI Samantha Freeman had encountered death before, even violent death, but until Ravi died, she'd not actually *experienced* death – the searing pain, the aching agony and the depth of sadness which the loss of a loved one can bring.

Initially, Sam refused to accept Ravi's death, her enquiring mind demanding answers, and it wasn't until she learned every detail of the horrendous crash which took him from her that a reluctant agonising acceptance settled over her.

Samantha escaped the accident with a broken leg, dislocated shoulder and various cuts and bruises and was hospitalised for a few days, during which there were many times she wished she had also died. Sam's leg injury required surgery and the surgeon told her she was lucky to have escaped any internal injuries – *lucky* – that was the last thing she felt!

Jenny was one of her first visitors. Sam's friend and colleague sat beside the bed and held her hand. The first visit could be described as an empathic one. Few words were spoken between them; Jenny didn't mention work or their current cases and Samantha didn't ask.

Her mother insisted on moving into Sam's house to take care

of her, and her daughter couldn't deny she was in need of help, so accepted gratefully. But returning to the home she'd shared with Ravi deepened the pain and loss. Knowing he would never again walk through the door, wiggle his eyebrows in the silly manner which always made her laugh, or hold her when she needed a hug, was unbearable. But what choice was there other than to bear it? Sam's bed felt empty – cold. It became the private place to shed her tears, alone and bereft.

DCI Aiden Kent also visited York Hospital and insisted Sam remain off work until her leg was out of plaster. Half-heartedly, Sam protested but saw the sense of his argument. After the enforced leave, Samantha returned to work.

Work would never replace Ravi, but it would fill the void of empty time, keep her brain active and perhaps one day, Samantha would come to terms with the sorrow of her loss. Naturally, her team were delighted at her return to work and continually watched her back – they were friends as well as colleagues.

The CPS were clear regarding the charge they would bring against Callum Cooper – murder. He had deliberately attacked a man who was unable to defend himself and although Dave Moorhouse would likely have died from the injuries inflicted by Beth and the lack of treatment, there was no doubt it was Callum who struck the fatal blow. The fingerprint evidence backed up his story. Pleading guilty counted in his favour, as did turning himself in, and he was sentenced to life imprisonment with a recommendation to serve at least six years before being eligible for parole. Callum accepted his punishment, even welcomed it as warranted. Clearing Amy's name had been uppermost in his mind and in that respect, he'd succeeded.

Beth Moorhouse was stunned to learn of her sister's death and Callum's confession. With a period in remand, a Christmas she would never forget, Beth had time to think and reflect on her life and her actions. Having previously thought she had no true feelings for her sister, Amy's death revealed otherwise – it affected her deeply. Beth's grief was genuine. Remorse became her companion, regret at what she'd done to Amy, who was probably the only person who had ever truly cared for her.

Beth was almost certain Callum would want nothing more to do with her and consequently felt very much alone in the world, a situation undoubtedly of her own making. But by the end of January, Beth discovered she was pregnant – a huge shock. Dave had had a vasectomy shortly after they married as neither of them wanted children but on discovering she was pregnant with Callum's child, her whole way of thinking was unexpectedly reversed.

Charged with conspiracy to conceal a body, to which Beth wisely pleaded guilty, the CPS decided there was insufficient evidence to bring any other charges relating to the shocking events surrounding her husband's death. By the time of the sentencing hearing, Beth was seven months pregnant and in consideration of her condition was given a four-year suspended sentence.

Was this a chance for Beth to make the new start she'd so often dreamed about? Gratitude at the leniency shown to her and the support offered by social services humbled Beth, giving pause for thought. Can a leopard change its spots? Beth's feelings for the new life growing within her had certainly amazed her. She loved the unborn child with a fierce protectiveness which took her by surprise. Here was a baby about to be born – an innocent, vulnerable child – and undoubtedly a huge responsibility. Could Beth change? Could her selfish nature be softened and moulded by caring for someone else?

Beth had no doubt Amy had been a better person than she – was that because Amy thought of others more than of herself? And even Callum had confessed to his crime in order to protect Amy's good name when he could so easily have kept quiet.

Perhaps Beth could change. Becoming a mother may well be her second chance at life, an opportunity to build something worthwhile. And while she was wishing and dreaming, maybe even Callum could find it in his heart to forgive her. She would wait for him and hope there was a chance they could build a happy life together – as Amy had wished for them.

THE END

AUTHOR'S NOTES

Thank you for reading The Dead Husband. For some unknown reason, my husband was unsure about the title, but it fits the narrative for this third novel featuring Samantha Freeman and her colleague, Jenny Newcombe.

I've enjoyed presenting the duo with some slippery characters to deal with. Perhaps like me, you felt Sam's frustrations when dealing with the stroppy teenage Ethan during his *no-comment* interview – and felt her pain at the end when Ravi was cruelly taken from her. Maybe I should apologise for this twist in the plot, but life isn't always happy ever after, even for the heroines of the books we read.

The characters of Amy and Beth illustrate the bond of family, in this instance, siblings close in age who have shared a difficult childhood. Beth's loyalty to her sister falters under the pressure of her selfish desires, and the breakdown of relationships becomes apparent as the plot progresses. I hope you enjoyed the story and didn't guess the twists too early.

To keep in touch with future publications, follow me on Twitter @GillianJackson7 or Facebook, Gillian Jackson Fiction Author.

ALSO BY GILLIAN JACKSON

The Pharmacist

The Victim

The Deception

Abduction

Snatched

The Accident

The Shape of Truth

The Charcoal House

A NOTE FROM THE PUBLISHER

Thank you for reading this book. If you enjoyed it please do consider leaving a review on Amazon to help others find it too.

We hate typos. All of our books have been rigorously edited and proofread, but sometimes mistakes do slip through. If you have spotted a typo, please do let us know and we can get it amended within hours.

info@bloodhoundbooks.com

Printed in Great Britain
by Amazon

39326662R00179